BOSNIAN INFERNO

SAS
OPERATION

Bosnian Inferno

DAVID MONNERY

HARPER

Harper
An imprint of HarperCollins*Publishers*
1 London Bridge Street,
London SE1 9GF
www.harpercollins.co.uk

This paperback edition 2016
1

First published by 22 Books/Bloomsbury Publishing plc 1994

A catalogue record for this book
is available from the British Library

ISBN: 978 0 00 815521 6

Set   ress

to assure consumers that they come from forests that are managed
to meet the social, economic and ecological needs
of present and future generations.

Find out more about HarperCollins and the environment at
www.harpercollins.co.uk/green

Prelude

Zavik, 17 July 1992

The knock on the door was loud enough to wake the dead, and John Reeve had little doubt what it meant. 'I have to go now,' he told his son, putting the book to one side. The boy must have read the seriousness of the situation on his father's face because he didn't object. Reeve kissed him lightly on the forehead and hurried down the new wooden staircase he'd just finished installing in his parents-in-law's house.

Ekrem Abdic had already opened the door to admit the others. There were four of them: Tijanic, Bobetko, Cehajic and Filipovic. One Serb, one Croat and two Muslims. Reeve knew which was which, but only because he had talked to them, visited their homes. If he had met them as strangers on the street, wearing the same jeans and T-shirts they were wearing now, he would have had no idea. The dark Tijanic looked more like a stereotypical Muslim than the blond Filipovic, whose father taught children the Koran at the town's mosque.

'They're here,' Tijanic said without preamble.

As if to verify the statement, a gunshot sounded in the distance, and then another.

1

'How many of them are there?' Reeve asked, reclaiming the Kalashnikov from where it had been hanging on the wall, out of reach of the children.

'I counted twenty-seven, so far. One transit van and three cars, all jammed full.'

'Let's go,' Reeve said. He stopped in the doorway. 'No partisan heroics,' he told his seventy-year-old father-in-law. 'If it looks like we've failed, just take the kids and head for Zilovice.'

The old man nodded. 'Good luck,' he said.

The four men emerged into the early dusk, the town of Zavik spread beneath them. The sun had fallen behind the far wall of the valley, but the light it had left behind cast a meagre glow across the steep, terracotta-tiled roofs. The thought of the kids and their grandparents struggling up the mountain behind the town produced a sinking feeling in Reeve's stomach.

At least it was summer. A light breeze was blowing down the valley but the day's heat still clung to the narrow streets. In the distance they could hear a man shouting through a megaphone.

'They are all in the town square,' Cehajic told Reeve.

'How many townspeople have gone over to them?'

'The five who disappeared this morning, but no more that we know of.'

They were only about a hundred yards from the square now, and Reeve led them down the darker side of the street in single file. The voice grew louder, more hectoring. The leader of the intruders was demanding that all weapons and cars be brought to the square immediately, and that anyone found defying this order would have their house burnt to the ground.

Reeve smiled grimly at the reference to weapons. As far as he knew there had been only about seven working guns in the town before the Serbs arrived, and his group was carrying five of them. Two others were in the hands of Muslim ex-partisans like his father-in-law, and they intended defending their own homes and families to the death.

The five men reached the rear of the building earmarked for their observation post, and filed in across the yard and up the rickety steps at the back. The old couple who lived there waved them through to the front room, where latticed windows overlooked the town square. Once this room would have housed a harem, and its windows had been designed so that the women could look out without being seen. As such, they served Reeve's current purpose admirably.

Several hundred people were gathered in the square, most of them looking up at the man with the megaphone, who was standing on the roof of the transit van. He wore a broad-brimmed hat, sunglasses and camouflage fatigues. A long, straggly beard hung down his chest.

On the ground in front of him two bodies lay side by side. Reeve recognized one as the town's mayor, a Muslim named Sulejman. The other looked like his brother.

Across to one side of the square, in front of the Catholic church, the irregulars' cars were parked in a line. All were Lada Nivas, and one had the word 'massacre' spray-painted along its side. Some of the invaders were leaning up against these cars, while others stood between them and the transit van, staring contemptuously at the crowd. Most were dressed like their apparent leader, though a couple had nylon stockings pulled bank-robber-style across their heads, and several were sporting Chetnik 'Freedom or Death' T-shirts, the words interwoven through skull and cross-bones.

Their leader had finished addressing the crowd, and was now talking to one of his cronies. Both men glanced across at the two corpses on the ground and then called over one of the men wearing a nylon mask. 'It's Cosic,' Tijanic said, recognizing the local man by his walk.

The man listened to the irregulars' leader and then pointed to one of the streets leading off the square.

'He's telling them where Sulejman lived,' Reeve said. He turned to Filipovic. 'You keep watch. One of us will be back as soon as we can.'

The other four hurried back through the house, down the steps and into the empty street. Sulejman's house was halfway up the hill to the ruined castle, and they reached it in minutes.

The big house was deserted – either Sulejman had had the sense to move his family away, or they had witnessed his death in the square. Reeve and his men walked in through the unlocked front door and took up positions behind the colonnaded partition between hallway and living-room.

The Serbs arrived about five minutes later. There were three of them, and they sounded in a good mood, laughing and singing as they kicked their way in through the door. Several were now carrying open bottles, and not much caring how much they slopped on the floor.

'I expect the women are hiding upstairs,' one man said.

'Come on down, darlings!' another shouted out.

Reeve and the others stepped out together, firing the Kalashnikovs from the hip, and the three Serbs did a frantic dance of death as their bottles smashed on the wooden floor.

Tijanic walked forward and extracted the weapons from their grasp. 'I'll get these to Zukic and his boys,' he said.

'Three down,' Reeve said. 'Twenty-four to go.'

1

'Daddy, help me!' Marie insisted.

Her plea brought Jamie Docherty's attention back to the matter in hand. His six-year-old daughter was busy trying to wrap up the present she had chosen for her younger brother, and in danger of completely immobilizing herself in holly-patterned sticky tape.

'OK,' he said, smiling at her and beginning the task of disentanglement. His mind had been on his wife, who at that moment was upstairs going through the same process with four-year-old Ricardo. Christmas was never a good time for Isabel, or at least not for the past eighteen years. She had spent the 1975 festive season incarcerated in the cells and torture chambers of the Naval Mechanical School outside Buenos Aires, and though the physical scars had almost faded, the mental ones still came back to haunt her.

His mind went back to their first meeting, in the hotel lobby in Rio Gallegos. It had been at the height of the Falklands War, on the evening of the day the troops went ashore at San Carlos. He had been leading an SAS intelligence-gathering patrol on Argentinian soil, and she had been a British agent, drawn to betray her country by hatred of the junta which had killed and tortured her friends, and driven her into exile. Together they had fought and driven and walked their way across the mountains to Chile.

More than ten years had passed since that day, and they had been married for almost as long. At first Docherty had thought that their mutual love had exorcized her memories, as it had exorcized his pain at the sudden loss of his first wife, but gradually it had become clear to him that, much as she loved him and the children, something inside her had been damaged beyond repair. Most of the time she could turn it off, but she would never be free of the memories, or of what she had learned of what human beings could do to one another.

Docherty had talked to his old friend Liam McCall about it; he had even, unknown to Isabel, had several conversations with the SAS's resident counsellor. Both the retired priest and his secular colleague had told him that talking about it might help, but that he had to accept that some wounds never healed.

He had tried talking to her. After all, he had told himself, he had seen enough of death and cruelty in his army career: from Oman to Guatemala to the Falls Road. That wasn't the same, she'd said. Nature was full of death and what looked like cruelty. What she had seen was something altogether more human – the face of evil. And he had not, and she hoped he never would.

Somehow this had created a distance between them. Not a rift – there was no conflict involved – but a distance. He felt that he had failed her in some way. That was ridiculous, and he knew it. But still he felt it.

'Daddy!' Marie cried out in exasperation. 'Pay attention!'

Docherty grinned at her. 'Sorry,' he said. 'I was thinking about Mummy,' he explained.

His daughter considered this, her blue eyes looking as extraordinary as ever against the rich skin tone she'd inherited from her mother. 'You can think about her when I've gone to bed,' Marie decided.

'Right,' Docherty agreed, and for the next ten minutes he gave her his full attention, completing the wrapping of Ricardo's present and conferring parental approval on Marie's suggested alterations to his positioning of the silver balls and tinsel on the tree. And then it was bedtime, and his turn to read to Ricardo. When he had finished he stood for a moment in the doorway to Marie's room, listening to Isabel reading, the bedside lamp making a corona around his wife's dark head as she bent over the book.

He walked downstairs, blessing his luck for finding her. Few men, he reckoned, found one such woman in their lives, and he had found two. True, with both there had been a price. Chrissie had been killed in a road accident only months after their marriage, sending him into a downward spiral of drunkenness and self-pity which had almost cost him his career and self-respect. Like Margaret Thatcher, he had been saved by the Falklands War, and in the middle of that conflict fate had led him to Isabel, who came complete with a hurt he longed in vain to heal. But he wasn't complaining – now, at the grand old age of forty-two, Jamie Docherty would not have swapped places with any man.

He went through to the kitchen, opened a can of beer and poured it into the half-pint mug he had liberated from an officers' mess in Dhofar nearly twenty years before.

'How about one for me?' Isabel asked him from the doorway, a smile on her face.

He smiled back and reached for another can.

She sat down on the other side of the kitchen table, and they shared the silence for a few moments. Her smile had gone, he noticed.

'What is worrying you?' she asked suddenly.

You, he thought. 'Nothing really,' he said, 'maybe the future. I've never been retired before. It's a strange feeling.' He grinned suddenly. 'Let's face it, we haven't even decided which continent we're going to live in.'

'There's no hurry,' she said. 'Let's get Christmas out of the way first.' She put down her half-empty glass. 'You still want fish and chips?' she asked.

'Yeah, I'll go and get them.'

'You stay with the children. I feel like some fresh air.'

And some time on your own, Docherty thought. 'You sure?' he asked.

'*Sí, noes problema.*'

Docherty continued sipping his beer, wondering how many other households there were in Glasgow where all four occupants often moved back and forth between English and Spanish without even noticing they had done so. He had become fluent in the latter during the half year's compassionate leave he had spent travelling in Mexico after Chrissie's death. Isabel had acquired her bilingual skills before meeting him, during the seven years of her enforced exile in England.

Still, their linguistic habits were hardly the strangest thing about their relationship. When they had met he had been a ten-year veteran of the SAS and she one of the few surviving members of an Argentinian urban guerrilla group. If the *Sun* had got hold of the story their marriage would have made the front page – something along the lines of 'SAS Hero Weds Argie Red'.

In the public mind, and particularly on the liberal left, the Regiment was assumed to be a highly trained bunch of right-wing stormtroopers. There was some truth in this impression, particularly since the large influx during the eighties of gung-ho paras – but only some. Men like Docherty, who came from families imbued with the old labour traditions, were also well represented among the older hands, and among the new intake of younger men the SAS emphasis on intelligence and self-reliance tended to militate against the rightist bias implicit in any military organization.

On returning from the Falklands, conscious of Isabel's opinions, Docherty had thought long and hard about whether to continue in the Army. Up to that time, he decided, none of the tasks allotted him by successive British governments had seriously troubled his conscience. When one arrived that did, then that would be the time to hand in his cards.

So, for most of the past ten years he and Isabel had lived just outside Hereford. Her cover during the mission in Argentina had been as a travel-guide writer, and a couple of enquiries were enough to confirm that the market in such books was expanding at enormous speed. She never finished the one she was supposedly researching in southern Argentina, but an offer to become one third of a team covering Chile was happily accepted, and this led to two other books on Central American countries. It meant her being away for weeks at a time, but Docherty was also often abroad for extended periods, particularly after his attachment to the SAS Training Wing. Whenever possible they joined each other, and Docherty was able to continue and deepen the love affair with Latin America which he had begun in Mexico.

Then Marie had arrived, and Ricardo two years later. Isabel had been forced to take a more editorial role, which, while more rewarding financially, often seemed considerably less fulfilling. Now with Ricardo approaching school age, and Docherty one week into retirement from the Army, they had big decisions to take. What was he going to do for a living?

Did they want to live in Scotland or somewhere in Latin America? As Isabel had said, there was no urgency. She had recently inherited – somewhat to her surprise – a few thousand pounds from her mother, and the house they were now staying in had been virtually a gift from Liam McCall. The priest had inherited a cottage on Harris in the Outer Hebrides, decided to retire there, and offered the Dochertys an indefinite free loan of his Glasgow house.

No urgency, perhaps, but much as Docherty loved having more time with Isabel and the children, he wasn't used to doing nothing. The military life was full of dead periods, but there was always the chance that the next day you would be swept across the world to face a challenge that stretched mind, body and soul to the limit. Docherty knew he had to find himself a new challenge, somehow, somewhere.

He got up to collect plates, salt, ketchup and vinegar. Just in time, for the ever-wonderful smell of fish and chips wafted in through the door ahead of his wife.

'Cod for you, haddock for me,' she said, placing the two bundles on the empty plates. 'And I bought a bottle of wine,' she added, pulling it out of the coat pocket. 'I thought . . .'

The telephone started ringing in the living-room.

'Who can that be?' she asked, walking towards it.

Docherty had unwrapped one bundle when she returned. 'It's your old CO,' she said, like any English military wife. 'Barney Davies. And he sounds like he's calling from a pub.'

'Maybe they've realized my pension should have been twice as much,' Docherty joked, wondering what in God's name Davies wanted with him.

He soon found out.

'Docherty? I'm sorry to call you at this hour, but I'd appreciate a meeting,' Davies said.

10

Docherty raised his eyebrows. It did sound like a pub in the background. He tried to remember which of Hereford's hostelries Barney Davies favoured. 'OK. What about? Can it wait till after Christmas?'

'Tonight would be better.'

'Where are you?' Docherty asked.

'In the bar at Central Station.'

The CO was in Glasgow. Had maybe even come to Glasgow just to see him. What the fuck was this about?

'I'm sorry about the short notice, but . . .'

'No problem. In an hour, say, at nine.'

'Wonderful. Can you suggest somewhere better than this?'

'Aye, the Slug & Sporran in Brennan Street. It's about a ten-minute walk, or you can take a cab . . .'

'I'll walk.'

'OK. Just go straight down the road opposite the station entrance, then left into Sauchiehall Street and Brennan Street's about three hundred yards down on the right. The pub's about halfway down, opposite a pool hall.'

'Roger.'

The phone clicked dead. Docherty stood there for a minute, a sinking heart and a rising sense of excitement competing for his soul, and then went back to his fish and chips. He removed the plate which Isabel had used to keep them warm. 'He wants to see me,' he said, in as offhand a voice as he could muster. 'Tonight.'

She looked up, her eyes anxious. '*Por qué?*' she asked.

'He didn't say.'

Lieutenant-Colonel Barney Davies, Commanding Officer 22 SAS Regiment, found the Slug & Sporran without much difficulty, and could immediately see why Docherty had

11

recommended it. Unlike most British pubs it was neither a yuppified monstrosity nor a noisy pigsty. The wooden beams on the ceiling were real, and the polished wooden booths looked old enough to remember another century. There were no amusement machines in sight, no jukebox music loud enough to drown any conversation – just the more comforting sound of darts burying themselves in a dartboard. The TV set was turned off.

Davies bought himself a double malt, surveyed the available seating, and laid claim to the empty booth which seemed to offer the most privacy. At the nearest table a group of young-sters sporting punk hairstyles were arguing about someone he'd never heard of – someone called 'Fooco'. Listening to them, Davies found it impossible to decide whether the man was a footballer, a philosopher or a film director. They looked so young, he thought.

It was ten to nine. Davies started trying to work out what he was going to say to Docherty, but soon gave up the attempt. It would be better not to sound rehearsed, to just be natural. This was not a job he wanted to offer anybody, least of all someone like Docherty, who had children to think about and a wife to leave behind.

There was no choice though. He had to ask him. Maybe Docherty would have the sense to refuse.

But he doubted it. He himself wouldn't have had the sense, back when he still had a wife and children who lived with him.

'Hello, boss,' Docherty said, appearing at his shoulder and slipping back into the habit of using the usual SAS term for a superior officer. 'Want another?'

'No, but this is my round,' Davies said, getting up. 'What would you like?'

'A pint of Guinness would probably hit the spot,' Docherty said. He sat down and let his eyes wander round the half-empty pub, feeling more expectant than he wanted to be. Why had he suggested this pub, he asked himself. That was the TV on which he'd watched the Task Force sail out of Portsmouth Harbour. That was the bar at which he'd picked up his first tart after getting back from Mexico. The place always boded ill. The booth in the corner was where he and Liam had comprehensively drowned their sorrows the day Dalglish left for Liverpool.

Davies was returning with the black nectar. Docherty had always respected the man as a soldier and, what was rarer, felt drawn to him as a man. There was a sadness about Davies which made him appealingly human.

'So what's brought you all the way to Glasgow?' Docherty asked.

Davies grimaced. 'Duty, I'm afraid.' He took a sip of the malt. 'I don't suppose there's any point in beating about the bush. When did you last hear from John Reeve?'

'Almost a year ago, I think. He sent us a Christmas card from Zimbabwe – that must have been about a month after he got there – and then a short letter, but nothing since. Neither of us is much good at writing letters, but usually Nena and Isabel manage to write . . . What's John . . .'

'You were best man at their wedding, weren't you?'

'And he was at mine. What's this about?'

'John Reeve's not been in Zimbabwe for eight months now – he's been in Bosnia.'

Docherty placed his pint down carefully and waited for Davies to continue.

'This is what we think happened,' the CO began. 'Reeve and his wife seem to have hit a bad patch while he was working in Zimbabwe. Or maybe it was just a break-up waiting to happen,' he added, with all the feeling of someone who had shared the experience. 'Whatever. She left him there and headed back to where she came from, which, as you know, was Yugoslavia. How did they meet – do you know?'

'In Germany,' Docherty said. 'Nena was a guest-worker in Osnabrück, where Reeve was stationed. She was working as a nurse while she trained to be a doctor.' He could see her in his mind's eye, a tall blonde with high Slavic cheekbones and cornflower-blue eyes. Her family was nominally Muslim, but as for many Bosnians it was more a matter of culture than religion. She had never professed any faith in Docherty's hearing.

He felt saddened by the news that they had split up. 'Did she take the children with her?' he asked.

'Yes. To the small town where she grew up. Place called Zavik. It's up in the mountains a long way from anywhere.'

'Her parents still lived there, last I knew.'

'Ah. Well all this was just before the shit hit the fan in Bosnia, and you can imagine what Reeve must have thought. I don't know what Zimbabwean TV's like, but I imagine those pictures were pretty hard to escape last spring wherever you were in the world. Maybe not. For all we know he was already on his way. He seems to have arrived early in April, but this is where our information peters out. We think Nena Reeve used the opportunity of his visit to Zavik to make one of her own to Sarajevo, either because he could babysit the children or just as a way of avoiding him – who knows? Either way she chose the wrong time. All hell broke loose in Sarajevo and the Serbs started lobbing artillery shells at anything that moved and their snipers started picking off children playing football in the street. And she either couldn't get out or didn't want to . . .'

'Doctors must be pretty thin on the ground in Sarajevo,' Docherty thought out loud.

Davies grunted his agreement. 'As far as we know, she's still there. But Reeve – well, this is mostly guesswork. We got a letter from him early in June, explaining why he'd not returned to Zimbabwe, and that as long as he feared for the safety of his children he'd stay in Zavik . . .'

'I never heard anything about it,' Docherty said.

'No one did,' Davies said. 'An SAS soldier on the active list stuck in the middle of Bosnia wasn't something we wanted to advertise. For any number of reasons, his own safety included. Anyway, it seems that the town wasn't as safe as Reeve's wife had thought, and sometime in July it found itself with some unwelcome visitors – a large group of Serbian irregulars. We've no idea what happened, but we do know that the Serbs were sent packing . . .'

'You think Reeve helped organize a defence?'

Davies shrugged. 'It would hardly be out of character, would it? But we don't know. All we have since then is six months of silence, followed by two months of rumours.'

'Rumours of what?'

'Atrocities of one kind and another.'

'Reeve? I don't believe it.'

'Neither do I, but . . . We're guessing that Reeve – or someone else with the same sort of skills – managed to turn Zavik into a town that was too well defended to be worth attacking. Which would work fine until the winter came, when the town would start running short of food and fuel and God knows what else, and either have to freeze and starve or take the offensive and go after what it needed. And that's what seems to have happened. They've been absolutely even-handed: they've stolen from everyone – Muslims, Serbs and Croats. And since none of these groups, with the partial exception of the Muslims, likes admitting that somewhere there's a town in which all three groups are fighting alongside each other against the tribal armies, you can guess who they're all choosing to concentrate their anger against.'

'Us?'

'In a nutshell. According to the Serbs and the Croats there's this renegade Englishman holed up in central Bosnia like Marlon Brando in *Apocalypse Now*, launching raids against anyone and everyone, delighting in slaughter and madness, and probably waiting to mutter "the horror, the horror" to the man who arrives intent on terminating him with extreme prejudice.'

'I take it our political masters are embarrassed,' Docherty said drily.

'Not only that – they're angry. They like touting the Regiment as an example of British excellence, and since the cold war ended they've begun to home in on the idea of selling our troops as mercenaries to the UN. All for a good cause, of course, and what the hell else do we have to sell any more? The Army top brass are all for it – it's their only real argument for keeping the sort of resource allocations they're used to. Finding out that one of their élite soldiers is running riot in the middle of the media's War of the Moment is not their idea of good advertising.'

Docherty smiled grimly. 'Surprise, surprise,' he said, and emptied his glass. He could see now where this conversation was leading. 'Same again?' he asked.

'Thanks.'

Docherty gave his order to the barman and stood there thinking about John Reeve. They'd known each other almost twenty years, since they'd been thrown into the deep end together in Oman. Reeve had been pretty wild back then, and he hadn't noticeably calmed down with age, but Docherty had thought that if anyone could turn down the fire without extinguishing it altogether then Nena was the one.

What would Isabel say about his going to Bosnia? he asked himself. She'd probably shoot him herself.

Back at the booth he asked Davies the obvious question: 'What do you want me to do?'

'I have no right to ask you to do anything,' Davies answered. 'You're no longer a member of the Regiment, and you've already done more than your bit.'

'Aye,' Docherty agreed, 'but what do you want me to do?'

'Someone has to get into Zavik and talk Reeve into getting out. I don't imagine either is going to be easy, but he's more likely to listen to you than anyone else.'

'Maybe.' Reeve had never been very good at listening to anyone, at least until Nena came along. 'How would I get to Zavik?' he asked. 'And where is it, come to that?'

'About fifty miles west of Sarajevo. But we haven't even thought about access yet. We can start thinking about the hows if and when you decide . . .'

'If you should choose to accept this mission . . .' Docherty quoted ironically.

'. . . the tape will self-destruct in ten seconds,' Davies completed for him. Clearly both men had wasted their youth watching crap like *Mission Impossible*.

'I'll need to talk with my wife,' Docherty said. 'What sort of time-frame are we talking about?' It occurred to him, absurdly, that he was willing to go and risk his life in Bosnia, but only if he could first enjoy this Christmas with his family.

'It's not a day-on-day situation,' Davies said. 'Not as far as we know, anyway. But we want to send a team out early next week.'

17

'The condemned men ate a hearty Christmas dinner,' Docherty murmured.

'I hope not,' Davies said. 'This is not a suicide mission. If it looks like you can't get to Zavik, you can't. I'm not sacrificing good men just to put a smile on the faces of the Army's accountants.'

'Who dares wins,' Docherty said with a smile.

'That's probably what they told Icarus,' Davies observed.

'Don't you want me to go?' Docherty asked, only half-seriously.

'To be completely honest,' Davies said, 'I don't know. Have you been following what's happening in Bosnia?'

'Not as much as I should have. My wife probably knows more about it than I do.'

'It's a nightmare,' Davies said, 'and I'm not using the word loosely. All the intelligence we're getting tells us that humans are doing things to each other in Bosnia that haven't been seen in Europe since the religious wars of the seventeenth century, with the possible exception of the Russian Front in the last war. We're talking about mass shootings, whole villages herded into churches and burnt alive, rape on a scale so widespread that it must be a coordinated policy, torture and mutilation for no other reason than pleasure, war without any moral or human restraint . . .'

'A heart of darkness,' Docherty murmured, and felt a shiver run down his spine, sitting there in his favourite pub, in the city of his birth.

After giving Davies a lift to his hotel Docherty drove slowly home, thinking about what the CO had told him. Part of him wanted to go, part of him wasn't so sure. Did he feel the tug of loyalty, or was his brain just using that as a cover for the tug of adventure? And in any case, didn't his wife and children have first claim on his loyalty now? He wasn't even in the Army any more.

She was watching *Newsnight* on TV, already in her dressing-gown, a glass of wine in her hand. The anxiety seemed to have left her eyes, but there was a hint of coldness there instead, as if she was already protecting herself against his desertion.

Ironically, the item she was watching concerned the war in Bosnia, and the refugee problem which had developed as a result. An immaculately groomed Conservative minister was explaining how, alas, Britain had no more room for these tragic victims. After all, the UK had already taken more than Liechtenstein. Docherty wished he could use the *Enterprise's* transporter system to beam the bastard into the middle of Tuzla, or Srebenica, or wherever it was this week that he had the best chance of being shredded by reality.

He poured himself what remained of the wine, and found Isabel's dark eyes boring into him. 'Well?' she asked. 'What did he want?'

'He wants me to go and collect John Reeve from there,' he said, gesturing at the screen.

'But they're in Zimbabwe . . .'

'Not any more.' He told her the story that Davies had told him.

When he was finished she examined the bottom of her glass for a few seconds, then lifted her eyes to his. 'They just want you to go and talk to him?'

'They want to know what's really happening.'

'What do they expect you to say to him?'

'They don't know. That will depend on whatever it is he's doing out there.'

She thought about that for a moment. 'But he's your

friend,' she said, 'your comrade. Don't you trust him? Don't you believe that, whatever he's doing, he has a good reason for doing it.'

It was Docherty's turn to consider. 'No,' he said eventually. 'I didn't become his friend because I thought he had flawless judgement. If I agree with whatever it is he's doing, I shall say so. To him and Barney Davies. And if I don't, the same applies.'

'Are they sending you in alone?'

'I don't know. And that's *if* I agree to go.'

'You mean, once I give you my blessing.'

'No, no, I don't. That's not what I mean at all. I'm out of the Army, out of the Regiment. I can choose.'

There was both amusement and sadness in her smile. 'They've still got you for this one,' she said. 'Duty and loyalty to a friend would have been enough in any case, but they've even given you a mystery to solve.'

He smiled ruefully back at her.

She got up and came to sit beside him on the sofa. He put an arm round her shoulder and pulled her in. 'If it wasn't for the *niños* I'd come with you,' she said. 'You'll probably need someone good to watch your back.'

'I'll find someone,' he said, kissing her on the forehead. For a minute or more they sat there in silence.

'How dangerous will it be?' she asked at last.

He shrugged. 'I'm not sure there's any way of knowing before we get there. There are UN troops there now, but I don't know where in relation to where Reeve is. The fact that it's winter will help – there won't be as many amateur psychopaths running around if the snow's six feet deep. But a war zone is a war zone. It won't be a picnic.'

'Who dares had better damn well come home,' she said.

'I will,' he said softly.

20

2

Nena Reeve pressed the spoon down on the tea-bag, trying to drain from it what little strength remained without bursting it. She wondered what they were drinking in Zavik. Probably melted snow.

Her holdall was packed and ready to go, sitting on the narrow bed. The room, one of many which had been abandoned in the old nurses' dormitory, was about six feet by eight, with one small window. It was hardly a generous space for living, but since Nena usually arrived back from the hospital with nothing more than sleep in mind, this didn't greatly concern her.

Through the window she had a view across the roofs below and the slopes rising up on the other side of the Miljacka valley. In the square to the right there had once been a mosque surrounded by acacias, its slim minaret reaching hopefully towards heaven, but citizens hungry for fuel had taken the trees and a Serbian shell had cut the graceful tower in half.

There was a rap on the door, and Nena walked across to let in her friend Hajrija Mejra.

'Ready?' Hajrija asked, flopping down on the bed. She was wearing a thick, somewhat worn coat over camouflage fatigue trousers, army boots and a green woollen scarf. Her long, black hair was bundled up beneath a black woolly cap, but strands were escaping on all sides. Hajrija's face, which Nena had always thought so beautiful, looked as gaunt as her own these days: the dark eyes were sunken, the high cheekbones sharp enough to cast deep shadows.

Well, Hajrija was still in her twenties. There was nothing wrong with either of them that less stress and more food wouldn't put right. The miracle wasn't how ill they looked – it was how the city's 300,000 people were still coping at all.

She put on her own coat, hoping that two sweaters, thermal long johns and jeans would be warm enough, and picked up the bag. 'I'm ready,' she said reluctantly.

Hajrija pulled herself upright, took a deep breath and stood up. 'I don't suppose there's any point in trying to persuade you not to go?'

'None,' Nena said, holding the door open for her friend.

'Tell me again what this Englishman said to you,' Hajrija said as they descended the first flight of stairs. The lift had been out of operation for months. 'He came to the hospital, right?'

'Yes. He didn't say much . . .'

'Did he tell you his name?'

'Yes. Thornton, I think. He said he came from the British Consulate . . .'

'I didn't know there was a British Consulate.'

'There isn't – I checked.'

'So where did he come from?'

'Who knows? He didn't tell me anything, he just asked questions about John and what I knew about what was happening in Zavik. I said, "Nothing. What *is* happening in Zavik?" He said that's what *he* wanted to know. It was like a conversation in one of those Hungarian movies. You know, two peasants swapping cryptic comments in the middle of an endless cornfield . . .'

'Only you weren't in a cornfield.'

'No, I was trying to deal with about a dozen bullet and shrapnel wounds.'

They reached the bottom of the stairs and cautiously approached the doors. It had only been light for about half an hour, and the Serb snipers in the high-rise buildings across the river were probably deep in drunken sleep, but there was no point in taking chances. The fifty yards of open ground between the dormitory doors and the shelter of the old medieval walls was the most dangerous stretch of their journey. Over the last six months more than a dozen people had been shot attempting it, three fatally.

'Ready?' Hajrija asked.

'I guess.'

The two women flung themselves through the door and ran as fast as they could, zigzagging across the open space. Burdened down by the holdall, Nena was soon behind, and she could feel her stomach clenching with the tension, her body braced for the bullet. Thirty metres more, twenty metres, ten . . .

She sank into the old Ottoman stone, gasping for breath.

'You're out of shape,' Hajrija said, only half-joking.

'Whole bloody world's out of shape,' Nena said. 'Let's get going.'

They walked along the narrow street, confident that they were hidden from snipers' eyes. There was no one about, and the silence seemed eerily complete. Usually by this time the first shells of the daily bombardment had landed.

It was amazing how they had all got used to the bombardment, Nena thought. Was it a tribute to human resilience, or just a stubborn refusal to face up to reality? Probably a bit of both. She remembered the queue in front of the Orthodox Cathedral when the first food supplies had come in by air. A sniper had cut down one of the people in the line, but only a few people had run for cover. There were probably a thousand people in the queue, and like participants in a dangerous sport each was prepared to accept the odds against being the next victim. Such a deadening of the nerve-ends brought a chill to her spine, but she understood it well enough. How many times had she made that sprint from the dormitory doors? A hundred? Two hundred?

'Even if you're right,' Hajrija said, 'even if Reeve has got himself involved somehow, I don't see how you can help by rushing out there. You do know how unsafe it is, don't you? There's no guarantee you'll even get there . . .'

Nena stopped in mid-stride. 'Please, Rija,' she said, 'don't make it any more difficult. I'm already scared enough, not to mention full of guilt for leaving the hospital in the lurch. But if Reeve is playing the local warlord while he's supposed to be looking after the children, then . . .' She shook her head violently. 'I have to find out.'

'Then let me come with you. At least you'll have some protection.'

'No, your place is here.'

'But . . .'

'No argument.'

Sometimes Nena still found it hard to believe that her friend, who six months before had been a journalism student paying her way through college as a part-time nurse, was now a valued member of an élite anti-sniper unit. Someone who had killed several men, and yet still seemed the same person she had always been. Sometimes Nena worried that there was no way

Hajrija had not been changed by the experiences, and that it would be healthier if these changes showed on the surface, but at others she simply put it down to the madness that was all around them both. Maybe the fact that they were *all* going through this utter craziness would be their salvation.

Maybe they had all gone to hell, but no one had bothered to make it official.

'I'll be all right,' she said.

Hajrija looked at her with exasperated eyes.

'Well, if I'm not, I certainly don't want to know I've dragged you down with me.'

'I know.'

They continued on down the Marsala Tita, sprinting across two dangerously open intersections. There were more people on the street now, all of them keeping as close to the build-ings as possible, all with skin stretched tight across the bones of their scarf-enfolded faces.

It was almost eight when they reached the Holiday Inn, wending their way swiftly through the Muslim gun emplace-ments in and around the old forecourt. The hotel itself looked like Beirut on a bad day, its walls pock-marked with bullet holes and cratered by mortar shells. Most of its windows had long since been broken, but it was still accommodating guests, albeit a restricted clientele of foreign journalists and ominous-looking 'military delegations'.

'He's not here yet,' Hajrija said, looking round the lobby.

Nena followed her friend's gaze, and noticed an AK47 resting symbolically on the receptionist's desk.

'Here he is,' Hajrija said, and Nena turned to see a hand-some young American walking towards them. Dwight Bailey was a journalist, and several weeks earlier he had followed the well-beaten path to Hajrija's unit in search of a story. She was not the only woman involved in such activities, but she was probably, Nena guessed, one of the more photogenic. Bailey had not been the first to request follow-up interviews in a more intimate atmosphere. Like his bed at the Holiday Inn, for example. So far, or at least as far as Nena knew, Hajrija had resisted any temptation.

Bailey offered the two women a boyish smile full of perfect American teeth, and asked Hajrija about the other members of her unit. He seemed genuinely interested in how they were, Nena thought. If age made all journalists cynical, he was still young.

And somewhat hyperactive. 'Dmitri's late,' he announced, hopping from one foot to the other. 'He and Viktor are our bodyguards,' he told Nena. 'Russian journalists. Good guys. The Serbs don't mess with the Russians if they can help it,' he explained. 'The Russians are about the only friends they have left.'

He said this with absolute seriousness, as if he could hardly believe it.

'Hey, here they are,' he called out as the two Russians came into view on the stairs. Both men had classically flat Russian faces beneath the fur hats; both were either bear-shaped or wearing enough undergarments to survive a cold day in Siberia. In fact the only obvious way of distinguishing one from the other was by their eyebrows: Viktor's were fair and almost invisible, Dmitri's bushy and black enough for him to enter a Brezhnev-lookalike contest. Both seemed highly affable, as if they'd drunk half a pint of vodka for breakfast.

The two women embraced each other. 'Be careful,' Hajrija insisted. 'And don't take any risks. And come back as soon as you can.' She turned to the American. 'And you take care of my friend,' she ordered him.

He tipped his head and bowed.

The four travellers threaded their way out through the hotel's kitchens to where a black Toyota was parked out of sight of snipers. The two Russians climbed into the front, and Nena and Bailey into the back.

Two distant explosions, one following closely on the other, signalled the beginning of the daily bombardment. The shells had fallen at least two kilometres away, Nena judged, but that didn't mean the next ones wouldn't fall on the Toyota's roof.

Viktor started up the car and pulled it out of the car park, accelerating all the while. The most dangerous stretch of road ran between the Holiday Inn and the airport, and they were doing more than sixty miles per hour by the time the car hit open ground. Viktor had obviously passed this way more than once, for as he zigzagged wildly to and fro, past the burnt-out hulks of previous failed attempts, he was casually lighting up an evil-smelling cigarette from the dashboard lighter.

Nena resisted the temptation to squeeze herself down into the space behind the driver's seat, and was rewarded with a glimpse of an old woman searching for dandelion leaves in the partially snow-covered verge, oblivious to their car as it hurtled past.

Thirty seconds later and they were through 'Murder Mile', and slowing for the first in a series of checkpoints. This one was manned by Bosnian police, who waved them through without even bothering to examine the three men's journalistic accreditation. Half a mile further, they were waved down by a Serb unit on the outskirts of Ilidza, a Serb-held suburb. The men here wore uniforms identifying them as members of the Yugoslav National Army. They were courteous almost to a fault.

'Hard to believe they come from Mordor,' Bailey said with a grin.

It was, Nena thought. Sometimes it was just too easy to think all Serbs were monsters, to forget that there were still 80,000 of them in Sarajevo, undergoing much the same hardships and traumas as everyone else. And then it became hard to understand how the men on the hills above Sarajevo could deliberately target their big guns on the hospitals below, and how the snipers in the burnt-out tower blocks could deliberately blow away children barely old enough to start school.

They passed safely through another Serb checkpoint and, as the two Russians pumped Bailey about their chances of emigration to the USA, the road ran up out of the valley, the railway track climbing to its left, the rushing river falling back towards the city on its right. Stretches of dark conifers alternated with broad swathes of snow-blanketed moorland as they crested a pass and followed the sweeping curves of the road down into Sanjic. Here a minaret still rose above the roofs of the small town nestling in its valley, and as they drove through its streets Nena could see that the Christian churches had not paid the price for the mosque's survival. Sanjic had somehow escaped the war, at least for the moment. She hoped Zavik had fared as well.

'This must have been what all of Bosnia was like before the war,' Bailey said beside her. There was a genuine sadness in his voice which made her wonder if she had underestimated him.

'How long have you been here?' she asked.

'I came in early November,' he said.

'Who do you work for?'

'No one specific. I'm a freelance.'

She looked out of the window. 'If you get the chance,' she said, 'and if this war ever ends, you should come in the spring, when the trees are in blossom. It can look like an enchanted land at that time of year.'

'I'd love to,' he said. 'I . . . I thought I knew quite a lot of the world before I came here,' he said. 'I've been all over Europe, all over the States of course, to Australia and Singapore . . . But I feel like I've never been anywhere like this. And I don't mean the war,' he said hurriedly, 'though maybe that's what makes everything more vivid. I don't know . . .'

She smiled at him, and felt almost like patting his hand.

The road was climbing again now, a range of snow-covered mountains looming on their left. She remembered the trip across the mountains to Umtali while they were in Africa. The children had been bored in the back seat and she'd been short-tempered with them. Reeve, though, had for once been an exemplary father, painstakingly prising them out of their sulk. But he'd always been a good father, much to her surprise. She'd expected a great husband and a poor father, and ended up with the opposite.

No, that was harsh.

She wondered again what she would find in Zavik, always assuming she got there. The three journalists were only taking her as far as Bugojno, and from there she would probably still have a problem making it up into the mountains. The roads might be open, might be closed – at this time of the year the chances were about fifty-fifty.

The car began slowing down and she looked up to see a block on the road ahead. A tractor and a car had been positioned nose to nose at an angle, and beside them four men were standing waiting. Two of them were wearing broad-brimmed hats. 'Chetniks,' one of the Russians said, and she could see the straggling beards sported by three of the four. The other man, it soon became clear, wasn't old enough to grow one.

From the first moment Nena had a bad feeling about the situation. The Russians' *bonhomie* was ignored, their papers checked with a mixture of insolence and sarcasm by the tall Serb who seemed to be in charge. 'Don't you think Yeltsin is a useless wanker?' he asked Viktor, who agreed vociferously with him, and said that in his opinion Russia could declare itself in favour of a Greater Serbia. The Chetnik just laughed at him, and moved on to Bailey. 'You like Guns 'N' Roses?' he asked him in English.

'Who?' Bailey asked.

'Rock 'n' roll,' the Chetnik said. 'American.'

'Sorry,' Bailey said.

'It's OK,' the Chetnik said magnanimously, and looked at Nena. His pupils seemed dilated, probably by drugs of some kind or another. 'Leave the woman behind,' he told the Russians in Serbo-Croat.

The Russians started arguing – not, Nena thought, with any great conviction.

'What's going on?' Bailey wanted to know.

She told him.

'But they can't do that!' he exclaimed, and before Nena could stop him he was opening the door and climbing out on to the road. 'Look . . .' he started to say, and the Chetnik's machine pistol cracked. The American slid back into Nena's view, a gaping hole where an eye had been.

The Russians in the front seat seemed suddenly frozen into statues.

'We just want the woman,' the Chetnik was telling them.

Viktor turned round to face her, his eyes wide with fear. 'I think . . .'

She shifted across the back seat and climbed out of the same door the American had used. She started bending down to examine him, but was yanked away by one of the Chetniks. The leader grabbed the dead man by the feet and unceremoniously dragged him away through the light snow and slush to the roadside verge. There he gave the body one sharp kick. 'Guns 'N' Roses,' he muttered to himself.

The Russians had turned the Toyota around as ordered, and were anxiously awaiting permission to leave. Both were making certain they avoided any eye contact with her.

'Get the fuck out of here,' the leader said contemptuously, and the car accelerated away, bullets flying above it from the guns of the grinning Chetniks.

She stood there, waiting for them to do whatever they were going to do.

The CO's office looked much as Docherty remembered it: the inevitable mug of tea perched on a pile of papers, the maps and framed photographs on the wall, the glimpse through the window of bare trees lining the parade ground, and beyond them the faint silhouette of the distant Black Mountains. The only obvious change concerned the photograph on Barney Davies's desk: his children were now a year older, and his wife was nowhere to be seen.

'Bring in a cup of tea,' the CO was saying into the intercom. 'And a rock cake?' he asked Docherty.

'Why not,' Docherty said. He might as well get used to living dangerously again. There were some at the SAS's Stirling Lines barracks who claimed that the Regiment had lost more men to the Mess's rock cakes than to international terrorism. It was a vicious lie, of course – the rock cakes were disabling rather than lethal.

'Is there any news of Reeve?' Docherty asked.

'None, but his wife's still in Sarajevo, working at the hospital as far as we know.'

'Where's the information coming from?'

'MI6 has a man in the city. Don't ask me why. The Foreign Office has got him digging around for us.'

Docherty's tea arrived, together with an ominous-looking rock cake. 'I'm hoping to take her with me,' he told Davies. 'Even if they've separated I still think he's more likely to listen to her than anyone else.'

'Well, you can ask her when you get there . . .'

'Sarajevo?' Docherty asked, his mouth half full of what tasted like an actual rock. Sweet perhaps, but hard and gritty all the same.

'It's not been a very good year for them,' Davies said, observing the expression on Docherty's face, and causing the Scot to wonder whether the CO had racks of the damn things in his cellar, each bearing their vintage.

'Sarajevo looks like the best place to begin,' Davies continued. 'Nena Reeve is there, and your MI6 contact. His name's Thornton, by the way. There must be people from Zavik who can fill you in on the town and its surroundings. Plus, there's the UN command and a lot of journalists. You should be able to pick up a good idea of what the best access route is, and what to expect on the way. Always assuming we can get you into the damn city, of course.'

'I thought the airport was closed.'

'Opened again a couple of days ago for relief flights, but there's no certainty it will still be open tomorrow. If it's not the Serbs lobbing shells from the hilltops it's the Muslims and Serbs exchanging fire across the damn runway, and even if they're all on their best behaviour it's probably only because there's a blizzard.'

'Lots of package tours, are there?' Docherty asked.

'The more I know about this war the less I'm looking forward to seeing any of my men involved in it,' Davies said.

Docherty took a gulp of tea, which at least scoured his mouth of cake. 'How many men am I taking in?' he asked.

'It's up to you, within reason. But I'd stick with a four-man patrol . . .'

'So would I. Are Razor Wilkinson and Ben Nevis available?' Darren Wilkinson and Stewart Nevis were two of the three men who had been landed on the Argentinian mainland with him during the Falklands – the third, Nick Wacknadze, had left the SAS – and Docherty had found both to be near-perfect comrades-in-arms.

'Nevis is in plaster, I'm afraid. He and his wife went skiing over Christmas – French Alps, I think – and he broke a leg. Sergeant Wilkinson is around, though. And I think he'll probably jump at the chance to get away from mothering the new boys up on the Beacons.'

'Good. I've missed his appalling cockney sense of humour.'

'Any other ideas?'

Docherty thought for a moment. 'I'm out of touch, boss . . .'

'Do you remember the Colombian business?' Davies asked.

'Who could forget it?'

Back in 1989 an SAS instructor on loan to the Colombian Army Anti-Narcotics Unit had been kidnapped, along with a prominent local politician, by one of the cocaine cartels. A four-man team had been inserted under cover to provide reconnaissance, and then an entire squadron parachuted in to assist with the rescue. One of the helicopters sent in to extract everyone was destroyed by sabotage and the original four-man patrol, plus the instructor, had been forced to flee Colombia on foot. In the process two of them had been killed, but the patrol's crossing of a 10,000-foot mountain range, pursued all the way by agents of the cartel, had acquired almost legendary status in Special Forces circles.

'Wynwood's in Hong Kong,' Davies said, 'but how about Corporals Martinson and Robson? They've proved they can walk across mountains, and it seems Yugoslavia – or whatever we have to call it these days – is full of them. And' – the CO's face suffused with sudden enthusiasm – 'I have a feeling Martinson has another useful qualification.' He reached for the intercom. 'Get me Corporal Martinson's service record,' he told the orderly.

Docherty sipped his tea, allowing Davies his moment of drama.

The file arrived, Davies skimmed through it, and stabbed a finger at the last page. 'Serbo-Croat,' he said triumphantly.

'What?' Docherty exclaimed. He could hardly believe there was a Serbo-Croat speaker in the Regiment.

'You know what it's like,' Davies said. 'The chances for action are few and far between these days, so the moment some part of the world looks like going bad the keen ones pick that language to learn, just in case. If nothing happens, any new language is still a plus on their record, and if by chance we get involved, they're first in the queue.'

'Looks like Martinson's won the jackpot this time,' Docherty said, reaching for the file to examine the photograph. 'He even looks like a Slav,' he added.

'He's a medic, like Wilkinson, but that might well come in useful where you're going. And he's a twitcher, too. A bird-watcher,' Davies explained, seeing the expression on Docherty's face. 'Bosnia's probably knee-deep in rare species.'

'I'll keep my eyes open,' Docherty said drily. He had never been able to understand the fascination some people had with birds. 'What about Robson?'

'He's an explosives man, and a crack shot with a sniper rifle. Which leaves you without a signals specialist, but I imagine you can fill in there yourself.'

'Those PRC 319s work themselves,' Docherty replied, 'and anyway, who will we have to send signals to?'

'Well, you might need to make contact with one of the British units who are serving with the UN.'

'But they wouldn't be able to get involved with this mission?'

'No, and in any case you won't be in uniform. This mission is about as official as Kim Philby's.'

'So when it comes down to it we're just a bunch of Brits dropping in to help out a mate.'

Davies opened his mouth to object, and closed it again. 'I suppose you are,' he agreed.

A little more than twenty miles to the south, Chris Martinson was moving stealthily, trying not to step on any of the twigs spread across the forest floor. He halted for a moment, ears straining, and right on cue heard the 'yah-yah-yah' laughing sound. It was nearer now, but he still couldn't see the bird. And then, suddenly, it seemed to be flying straight towards him down an avenue between the bare trees, its red crown, black face and green-gold back looking almost tropical in the winter forest. It seemed to see him at the last moment, and veered away to the left, into a stand of conifers.

The green woodpecker wasn't a rare bird, but it was one of Martinson's favourites, and, since a day trip from Hereford to the Forest of Dean never seemed quite complete if he didn't see one, there was a smile on his face as he continued his walk.

Another quarter of a mile brought him to the crown of a small hill giving a view out across the top of the trees towards the Severn Estuary. Some kind soul had arranged for a wrought-iron seat to be placed there, and Chris gratefully sat himself down, putting his binoculars to one side and unwrapping the packed lunch he had brought with him. As he bit into the first tuna roll a flock of white-faced geese flew overhead towards the estuary.

It had been a good idea to come out for the day, Chris decided. The older he got the more claustrophobic the barracks seemed to get. He supposed it was time he got a place of his own, but somehow he had always resisted the idea. Flats were hard to find and you had all the hassle of dealing with a landlord, and as for buying somewhere . . . well, it would only be a millstone round his neck when he eventually left the Regiment and did some serious travelling.

He had turned thirty that year, and the time for decision couldn't be that far off. And, he had to admit, he was getting bored with the same old routines – routines that only seemed to be interrupted these days by a few hairy weeks in sun-soaked Armagh or exotic Crossmaglen. Even the birds in Northern Ireland seemed depressed by the weather.

He ran a hand through his spiky hair. His life was in a rut, he thought. Not an unpleasant one – in fact quite a comfortable one – but a rut nevertheless. He hadn't really made any close friends in the Regiment since Eddie Wilshaw, and the man from Hackney had died in Colombia three years before. And he hadn't had anything approaching a relationship with a woman for almost as long. The last one he'd gone out with had told him he seemed to be living on a separate planet from the rest of humanity.

He smiled good-naturedly at the memory. She was probably right, and it was no doubt time he started reaching out to people a bit more, but . . .

A robin landed in a tree across the clearing and began making its 'tick' calling sound. Chris sat there watching it, feeling full of nature's wonder, thinking that life on your own planet had its compensations.

3

Docherty could hear the familiar London accent before he was halfway down the corridor.

'. . . and in hot climates there's one last resort when it comes to infected wounds. Any ideas?'

'A day on the beach, boss?' a northern voice asked.

'Several rum and cokes?'

'I can see you've all read the book. The answer is maggots. Since they only eat dead tissue they act as cleaning agents in any open wound . . .'

'But boss, if I've just been cut open by some guerrilla psycho with a machete I'm probably going to be a long way from the local fishing tackle shop . . .'

'No problem, Ripley. Once the wound gets infected you can just sit yourself down somewhere and ooze pus. The maggots will come to you. Especially you. Right. Yesterday you were all given five minutes to write down the basic rules of dealing with dog bites, snake bites and bee stings. Most of you managed to survive all three. Trooper Dawson, however,' – a collective groan was audible through the room's open skylight – 'used the opportunity to attempt suicide. He didn't report the dog bite, so he may have rabies by now. It's true that in this country he'd need to be very unlucky, but the Regiment does occasionally venture abroad. And it doesn't really matter in any case because the snake got him. He not only wasted time trying to suck out the venom, but managed to lose an arm or a leg by applying a tourniquet instead of a simple bandage. Of course he probably didn't notice the limb dropping off because of the pain from the bee sting, which he'd made worse by squeezing the poison sac.'

In his mind's eye Docherty could see the expression on Razor's face.

'Well done, Dawson,' Razor concluded. 'Your only worry now is whether your mates will bother to bury you. Any questions from those of you still in the land of the almost-living?'

'What do you do about a lovebite from a beautiful enemy agent?' a Welsh voice asked.

'In your case, Edwards, dream of getting one. Class dismissed. And read the fucking book.'

The Continuation Training class filed out, looking as young and fit as Docherty remembered being twenty years before. When the last man had emerged he could see Darren Wilkinson bent over a ring binder of notes on the instructor's desk. Razor looked, like Docherty himself, as wiry as ever, but there was a seriousness of expression on the face which Docherty didn't remember seeing very often in the past. Maybe life in the Training Wing was calming him down.

Razor looked up suddenly, conscious of someone's eyes on him, and his face slowly split open in the familiar grin. 'Boss. What are you doing here? If you've not retired I want my twenty pee back.'

'Which twenty pee might that be?'

'The one I gave to your passing-out collection.'

39

Docherty sat down in the front row and eyed him toler-
antly. 'I'm recruiting,' he said.

'What for?'

'A journey into hell by all accounts.'

'Forget it. I'm not going to watch Arsenal for anybody.'

'How about Red Star Sarajevo?'

Razor lifted himself on to the edge of the desk. 'Tell me
about it,' he said.

'Do you know John Reeve?' Docherty asked.

'To say hello to. Not well. I never did an op with him.'

'I did,' Docherty said. 'Several of them. We may not have
actually saved each other's lives in Oman, but we probably
saved each other from dying of boredom. We became good
mates, and though we never fought together again, we stayed
that way, you know the way some friends are – you only
need to see them once a year, or even every five years, and
it's still always like you've never been apart.'

He paused, obviously remembering something. 'Reeve was
one of the people who helped me through my first wife's
death. In fact if he hadn't persuaded me to get compassionate
leave rather than simply go AWOL I'd have been out of this
Regiment long ago . . . Anyway, I was best man at his
wedding, and he was at mine. And we both married
foreigners, which sort of further cemented the friendship.
You know my wife – you were there when we met . . .'

'Almost. I was there when you had your first argument.
About which way we should be running, I think.'

'Aye, well, we've had a few since, but . . .' Docherty smiled
inwardly. 'Reeve married a Yugoslav, a Bosnian Muslim as it
turns out, though no one seemed too bothered by such things
back in 1984. He and Nena had two children, a girl first and
then a boy, just like me and Isabel. Nena seemed happy enough

living in England, and then about eighteen months ago Reeve got an advisory secondment to the Zimbabwean Army. I haven't seen him since, and I hadn't heard anything since last Christmas, which should have worried me, but, you know how it is . . . Then last week, two days before Christmas, the CO comes to visit me in Glasgow.'

'Barney Davies? He just turned up?'

'Aye, he did.'

'With news of Reeve?'

'Aye.'

Docherty told Razor the story as Davies had told it to him, ending with the CO's request for him to lead in a four-man team.

'And it looks like you said yes.'

'Aye, eventually. Christ knows why.'

'Have they reinstated you?'

'Temporarily. But since the team won't be wearing uniform, and will have no access whatsoever to any military back-up it doesn't seem particularly relevant.'

Razor stared at him. 'Let me get this straight,' he said eventually. 'They want us to fight our way across a war zone so we can have a friendly chat with your friend Reeve, either slap his wrist or not when we hear his side of the story, and then fight our way back across the same war zone. And we start off by visiting the one city in the world which no one can get into or out of.'

Docherty grinned at him. 'You're in, then?'

'Of course I'm fucking in. You think I like teaching first aid to ex-paras for a living?'

'I now pronounce you man and wife,' the vicar said, and perhaps it was the familiarity of the words which jolted

Damien Robson out of his reverie. The Dame, as he was known to all his regimental comrades, cast a guilty glance around him, but no one seemed to have noticed his mental absence from the proceedings.

'You may kiss the bride,' the vicar added with a smile, and the Dame's sister, Evie, duly uplifted her face to meet the lips of her new husband. She then turned round to find the Dame, and gave him an affectionate kiss on the cheek. 'Thank you for giving me away,' she said, her eyes shining.

'My pleasure,' he told her. She seemed as happy as he'd ever seen her, he thought, and hoped to God it would last. David Cross wasn't the man he would have chosen for her, but he didn't actually have anything specific against him. Yet.

The newly-weds were led off to sign the register, and the Dame walked out of the church with the best man to check that the photographer was ready. He was.

'We haven't seen you lately,' a voice said in his ear.

He turned to find the vicar looking at him with that expression of pained concern which the Dame had always associated with people who were paid to care. 'No, 'fraid not,' he replied. 'The call of duty,' he explained with a smile.

The vicar examined the uniform which Evie had insisted her brother wear, his eyes coming to rest on the beige beret and its winged-dagger badge. 'Well, I hope we see you again soon,' he said.

The Dame nodded, and watched the man walk over to talk with his and Evie's sister, Rosemary. A couple of years before, after the Colombian operation, he had started attending church regularly, this one here in Sunderland when he was at home, and another on the outskirts of Hereford during tours of duty. He could have used the Regimental chapel, but, without being quite sure why, had chosen to keep his devotions a secret from his comrades. It wasn't that he feared they'd take the piss – though they undoubtedly would – it was just that he felt none of it had anything to do with anyone else.

He soon realized that this feeling encompassed vicars and other practising Christians, and in effect the Church itself. He stopped attending services, and started looking for other ways of expressing a yearning inside him which he could hardly begin to explain to himself, let alone to others. He wasn't even sure it had anything to do with God – at least as other people seemed to understand the concept. The best he could manage by way of explanation was a feeling of being simultaneously drawn to something bigger than himself, something spiritual he supposed, and increasingly detached from the people around him.

The latter feeling was much in evidence at the wedding reception. It was good to see so many old friends: lads he'd been to school with, played football with, but none of them seemed to have much to say to him, and he couldn't find much to say to them. A few old memories, a couple of jokes about Sunderland – town and football team – and that was about it. Most of them seemed bored with their jobs and, if they were married, bored with that too. They seemed more interested in one another's wives than their own. The Dame hoped his sister . . . well, if David Cross cheated on her then the bastard would have him to deal with.

The time eventually arrived for the honeymooners' departure, their hired car trailing its retinue of rattling tin cans. Soon after that, feeling increasingly oppressed by the reception's accelerating descent into a drunken wife-swap, the Dame started off across the town, intent on enjoying the solitude of a twilight walk along the seafront.

It was a beautiful day still: cold but crystal-clear, gulls circling in the deepening blue sky, above the blue-grey waters of the North Sea. He walked for a couple of miles, up on to the cliffs outside the town, not really thinking about anything, letting the wind sweep the turmoil of other people from his mind.

He got back home to find his mother and Rosemary asleep in front of the TV, the living-room still littered with the debris of Christmas. On the table by the telephone there was a message for him to ring Hereford.

She sat with her knees pulled up to her chest, her head bowed down, on the stinking mattress in the slowly lightening room. The first night was over, she thought, but the first of how many?

The left side of her face still ached from where he had hit her, and the pain between her legs showed no signs of easing. She longed to be able to wash herself, and knew the longing was as much psychological as it was physical. Either way, she doubted if they would allow it.

This time yesterday, she thought, I was waiting for Hajrija in the nurses' dormitory.

The previous morning, after the two Russians had been sent running back towards Sarajevo with their tails between their legs, the four Chetniks had simply abandoned their road-block, as if it had accomplished its purpose. They had casually left the young American's body by the side of the road, bundled her into the back seat of their Fiat Uno, and driven on down the valley to the next village. Here she could see no signs of the local population, either alive or dead, and only one black-ened hulk of a barn bore testimony to recent conflict. As they pulled up in the centre of the village another group of Chetnik irregulars, a dozen or so strong, was preparing to leave in a convoy of cars.

The leader of her group exchanged a few pleasantries with the leader of the outgoing troops, and she was led into a nearby house, which, though stripped of all personal or religious items, had obviously once belonged to a Muslim family. Since their departure it had apparently served as a billet for pigs. The Chetniks' idea of eating seemed to be to throw food at one another in the vain hope some of it went in through the mouth. Their idea of bathing was non-existent. The house stank.

What remained of the furniture was waiting to be burnt on the fire. And there was a large bloodstain on the rug in the main room which didn't seem that old.

Nena was led through to a small room at the back, which was empty save for a soiled mattress and empty bucket. The only light filtered round the edges of the shutters on the single window.

'I need to wash,' she told her escort. They were the first words she had spoken since her abduction.

'Later,' he said. 'There's no need now,' he added, and closed the door.

She had spent the rest of the day trying not to panic, trying to prepare herself for what she knew was coming. She wanted to survive, she kept telling herself, like a litany. If they were going to kill her anyway then there was nothing she could do about it, but she mustn't give them an excuse to kill her in a fit of anger. She should keep her mouth shut, say as little as possible. Perhaps tell them she was a doctor – they might decide she could be of use to them.

The afternoon passed by, and the light faded outside. No one brought her food or water, but even above the sound of the wind she could hear people in the house and even smell something cooking. Eventually she heard the clink of bottles, and guessed that they had begun drinking. It was about an hour later that the first man appeared in the doorway.

In the dim light she could see he had a gun in one hand. 'Take off the trousers,' he said abruptly. She swallowed once and did as he said.

'And the knickers.'

She pulled them off.

'Now lie down, darling,' he ordered.

She did so, and he was looming above her, dropping his jungle fatigues and long johns down to his knees, and thrusting his swollen penis between her legs.

'Wider,' he said, taking his finger off the gun's safety-catch only inches from her ear.

He pushed himself inside her, and started pumping. He made no attempt to feel her breasts, let alone kiss her, and out of nowhere she found herself remembering her father's dog, and its habit of trying to fuck the large cushion which someone had made for it to lie on. Now she was the cushion and this Serb was the dog. As smelly, as inhuman, as any dog.

He came with a furious rush, and almost leapt off her, as if she was suddenly contagious.

The second man was much the same, except for the fact that he didn't utter a single word between entering the room and leaving it. Then there was a respite of ten minutes or so, before the group's leader came in. He stripped from the waist down, grabbed a handful of her hair and lifted up her face to meet his own, as if determined to impress on her exactly who it was she was submitting to.

She let out an involuntary sob, and that seemed to satisfy him. He pushed inside her quickly, but then took his time, savouring the moment with slow, methodical strokes, stopping himself several times as he approached a climax, before finally letting himself slip over the edge.

The young one was last, and the other three brought him in like a bull being brought to a heifer. He couldn't have been more than fourteen and he looked almost as nervous as he did excited. 'Come on,' the others said, 'show her what you've got.' He unveiled his penis almost shyly. It was already erect, quivering with anticipation.

'I think he's ready,' the leader joked, and the other two grabbed hold of Nena and pushed her back across the mattress, legs hanging out across the floor. Then they pulled them wide. 'That's where you aim for, Sergei,' one of them said, running a finger down her bloodied vulva. 'We've got her nice and lubricated for you.'

He came when he was only halfway inside her, to the drunken jeers of his companions.

After that they retired to the room next door, leaving her lying, rolled up in a ball. She tried to ignore the pain, wondering how they could let her live after what they had done. Did they think the war would last for ever, that law and decency would never return, that they were immune to any retribution?

They probably did. She hoped they did, because what other reason could they have for leaving her alive to tell the story?

And if they did make that mistake . . . She lay there trying to fix all the details in her mind: the place, the faces, the tattoos, the names they had called each other, the individual smells . . .

She could hear them talking in the next room, and laughing too. She started to cry, silently at first, then in great, wracking sobs which seemed to go on and on and on.

Exhaustion must have driven her to sleep for a few moments, because she suddenly woke to find the group's leader standing over her once more.

'You're in luck,' he told her. 'The rest of the lads haven't come back, so you've had an easy night. But I thought I'd come for dessert.'

He pulled down his trousers and stood there, his cock hanging in front of her face. She could smell it, smell herself on it. 'Make it grow,' he said with a leer, and she took hold of it, trying to imagine she was back in the hospital, examining someone. And in his case, hoping to find something seriously wrong.

It swelled in her hand.

'Now suck,' he said, looking down at her.

She didn't say no, but there must have been something in her eyes, because he abruptly changed his mind, pushing her back across the mattress, roughly pulling off her jeans, and rolling her over. 'You'd bite it off, wouldn't you?' he hissed into her ear, and thrust himself into her anus. She cried out involuntarily, which seemed only to increase his ardour. After a minute of energetic pumping he pulled himself out rolled her back over, wedged her legs open with his own, and rammed himself into her vagina, this time coming almost instantly.

He exhaled noisily and lifted himself up, looking down at her. 'You enjoy it really, don't you. All you Muslim whores enjoy it.'

She said nothing, but she couldn't control the look in her eyes, and he hit her once, as hard as she had ever imagined being hit, across the side of the face.

Perhaps she had blacked out for a few seconds, because her next conscious thought was of the door closing behind him. And then she had lain awake for what seemed like hours, feeling that a stain had been etched into her soul, and that nothing would ever be the same again. And when the morning light had appeared around the edge of the shutter it had seemed the greyest of lights.

Now she sat there, hugging herself around the knees, waiting to find out which fate awaited her – death or more nights like the last.

They were awake in the room next door, and this morning she could hear them talking, as the wind outside had died down.

'I like blondes,' one man was saying. 'Fucking a blonde is . . . it's sort of cleaner, know what I mean? Dark women feel dirtier somehow . . .'

'Why can't we keep her?' a younger voice asked.

'Listen to the kid. Thinks he's a stud already.'

'But why can't we keep her?' an older voice asked. 'They expect us to look after the area, freeze our balls off on that road. We only get down to Stovic about once a month.'

There were a few moments of silence, moments in which Nena tried not to wonder what the alternative was to being kept.

'We're not keeping her,' the group leader said. 'Keep a woman here permanently and we have to feed her, watch her, keep her clean . . .'

'What for?'

'Because they don't feel as nice if they've been rolling around in their own shit,' the leader said.

'She could do the cooking,' someone objected.

'Yeah? The moment you let her out of that room she needs a guard, right? Which means one of us will have to stay here. It's not worth it. She's not that great a fuck, anyway. All bones. She's old enough to be Koca's grandmother. She's going to Vogosca.'

Those last four words caused Nena to almost gasp with relief. Vogosca was a small, predominantly Serb town about four miles north of Sarajevo, and though she didn't know what awaited her there it had to be better than dying in this mountain village whose name she didn't even know.

Hold on, she told herself, hold on. She put her coat on and waited.

One of the men came to get her an hour or so later – the one who had not said a word as he raped her. 'You have to get washed,' he said, and he prodded her out through the house's back door. The clouds were almost touching the ground, the mountains completely obscured from view, but the snow still seemed dazzling to her eyes. 'You can clean yourself with that,' he said, pointing at the nearest snowdrift.

She looked at it. 'What kind of men are you?' she asked before she could stop herself.

He wasn't offended by the question. 'We are Serbs,' he replied. 'Your men are taking our women just the same way.'

She walked across to the snowdrift, took down the bloody jeans and squatted in such a way that she could wash between her legs. The snow made the abrasions sting, but somehow that seemed almost a blessing.

After she had finished he took her round the outside of the house to where the Fiat was parked and told her to get inside. She sat alone in the car for about ten minutes, and then he returned, climbed in and started the car.

'Where are we going?' she asked.

'Not far,' he said. Once they were outside the village he lit a cigarette, and, after a moment's hesitation, offered her one.

'I don't smoke,' she said. 'I'm a doctor,' she added, without thinking.

'Yeah?' he said, interested. 'I've got a pain in my chest right here,' he said, tapping it with the hand that held the cigarette and giving her an enquiring glance.

'That could be a lot of things,' she said. Hopefully lung cancer, she thought.

'You think it could be serious?' he asked anxiously.

'It could. Why not just stop smoking,' she said coldly.

'After the war's over,' he said. 'It's too fucking nerve-racking without cigarettes.'

After the war's over you'll be on trial for rape and murder, she thought.

Another ten minutes and they had reached a larger village. In its centre both Serb irregulars and uniformed Yugoslav Army troops were in evidence. A tank sat to one side, its gun barrel depressed towards the slushy ground, and on the other side of the road two empty armoured personnel carriers were tilted against the verge. Beyond the tank a civilian bus was parked. The indicator board still announced Travnik as its destination, but the driver was wearing military uniform, and the passengers were exclusively female.

Nena's abductor pulled her out of the car and pushed her on to the bus.

'Only one this week?' the driver asked sarcastically.

Nena was surveying her fellow-passengers. There were about a dozen of them, and they all seemed to be Muslims, ranging in age from the mid-forties to just past puberty. Every one of them appeared to be in a state of semi-shock, as if the worst had already happened but they didn't yet know what it was.

'Where are you from?' Nena asked the woman nearest the front.

'No talking,' the driver screamed at her.

The two women's eyes met in shared resignation, and Nena sat down across the aisle from her.

At least three hours went by before a couple of uniformed soldiers came on board, and the journey began. Nena was growing increasingly conscious of how thirsty she was – one handful of snow in twenty-four hours was nowhere near enough to satisfy anyone. Hunger was less of a problem. She realized that living in Sarajevo for the last few months, she had grown accustomed to life on an empty stomach.

The afternoon dragged on, the bus coughing its way up hills and rattling its way down them. It was growing dark as they finally entered Vogosca. Nena had driven through the small town many times, but couldn't remember ever stopping. The bus drew up outside the Partisan Sports Hall, and the twelve women and girls were ordered off. A Serb irregular sporting the badge of the White Eagles gestured them in through the front doors, and once inside another man pointed them through a further pair of twin doors.

It was dark inside the room, but as Nena's eyes grew accustomed to the gloom it became apparent that they were in a gymnasium; one, moreover, that was already home to other women. All around the walls they sat or lay, thirty or forty of them, and as yet not one of them had uttered a word.

'What is this?' Nena asked, her voice echoing in the cavernous space. As if in response someone started to cry.

'It's the shop window of a brothel,' a dry voice said.

4

Chris Martinson pulled the jeep into the car park of Hereford Station and looked at his watch. The Dame's connection from Worcester was not due for another five minutes, which probably meant a twenty-minute wait. A ferocious rain was beating a tattoo on the jeep's convertible roof, and almost visibly deepening the puddles in the car park, but at least it was relatively warm for the time of year. Chris decided to stay where he was until the train came into view under the bridge.

Sergeant Docherty had called him with the request to pick the Dame up at the station, and though Chris had not had much to do with Docherty during his eight years in the SAS – the older man had left B Squadron for the Training Wing before Chris won his badge – he had managed to piece together an impression of him from what others had said. It would have been hard not to, for Docherty was something of a legend – the man who had almost succumbed to personal tragedy, and then come home the hard way from Argentina during the Falklands War, walking out across the Andes with a new wife.

Chris had a good idea how hard that must have been, having been involved in something similar himself in Colombia. Only he had neglected to bring a wife.

Docherty was not just known for his toughness though. He was supposed to be something close to the old SAS ideal, a thinking soldier. There were many in the Regiment who lamented the shift in selection policy over the last decade, which seemed to put a lower premium on thought and a higher one on physical and emotional strength. Others, of course, said it was just a sign of the times. The Dochertys of this world, like the George Bests, were becoming extinct. Their breeding grounds had been overrun by progress.

It suddenly dawned on Chris why Docherty had sent him to collect the Dame. The Scot had thought it would be a good idea for the two of them to talk before being confronted with whatever it was they were about to be confronted with. To psych each other up. Chris smiled to himself. A thinking soldier indeed.

A two-tone horn announced the arrival of the train, seconds before the diesel's yellow nose appeared beneath the bridge. Chris jumped down from the jeep and made a run for the ticket hall, his boots sending water flying up from the puddles.

The Dame was one of the last to reach the barrier, his dark face set, as usual, in an almost otherworldly seriousness, as if he was deeply involved in pondering some abstruse philosophical puzzle.

The face broke into a smile when he saw Chris.

'Your humble chauffeur awaits,' the latter said.

'I suppose the birds aren't flying today,' the Dame said, eyeing the torrential rain from the station entrance. 'How many miles away have you parked?'

Chris pointed out the jeep. 'Do you think you can manage twenty yards?'

The two men dashed madly through the half-flooded car park and scrambled into the jeep.

'What's this all about?' the Dame half-shouted above the din of rain on the roof.

'No idea,' Chris said, starting up the engine. 'But we're about to find out – the briefing's due to begin in about twenty-five minutes.'

'You don't even know where we're going?'

'Nope. They're playing it really close to the chest. All I know is that it's a four-man op.'

'Who are the other two?'

'Sergeant Docherty and . . .'

'I thought he'd retired.'

'He had. He's been reinstated, presumably just for this one show.'

'Christ, he must be about forty-five by now. It can't be anything too strenuous.'

Chris laughed. 'I shouldn't say anything like that when he's around. He didn't look too decrepit the last time I saw him.'

'Maybe. Who's Number Four?'

'Sergeant Wilkinson. Training Wing.'

'I know him. At least, I've played football with him. He must be about thirty-five . . .'

'Hey, I've turned thirty, you know. Someone obviously decided they needed experience for this one, and you were just included to provide some mindless energy.'

'Probably,' the Dame said equably. 'Wilkinson always reminds me a bit of Eddie. London to the bone. A joker. He's even a Tottenham supporter.'

'Yeah, well,' Chris said, and both men were silent for a few moments, thinking of their old comrade, who had died in the village by the jungle river in Colombia. Probably with some witty rejoinder frozen on his lips.

'How was your Christmas?' the Dame asked eventually.

'Fine,' Chris said, though he'd spent most evenings desperately bored. 'Yours?'

'It was great. My sister got married yesterday, and I had to give her away. It was great,' he said again, as if he was trying to convince himself.

Chris looked at his watch as he turned the jeep in through the gates of the Stirling Lines barracks. 'Time for a brew,' he said.

The water-buffalo's head which reigned over 'the Kremlin's' briefing room – a memento of the Regiment's Malayan days – seemed to be leaning slightly to one side, as if it was trying to hear some distant mating call. Forget it, Docherty thought, you don't have a body any more.

He knew the feeling, after the previous night's evening in the pub with old friends. The good news was that he and Isabel couldn't be drinking as much as they thought they were – not if his head felt like this after only half a dozen pints and chasers.

'Bad news,' Barney Davies said, as he came in through the door. 'Nena Reeve seems to have gone missing. She's not been to work at the hospital for the last couple of days. Of course, things being the way they are in Sarajevo, she may just be at home with the flu and unable to phone in. Or she may have been wounded by a sniper, or be looking after a friend who was. They're trying to find out.'

'MI6?'

'Presumably. Did Robson get here all right?'

'Yes, boss,' a voice with a Wearside accent said from behind him. The Dame and Chris filed in, swiftly followed by Razor Wilkinson.

Docherty got to his feet, shook hands with the new arrivals, and then took up a position half-sitting on the table at the front, while the other four arranged themselves in a semicircle of upright chairs.

He began by introducing everyone. 'You two have been recommended to me by the CO,' he told Chris and the Dame. 'Though you may wish he hadn't by the time we're finished. We're going to Bosnia, gentlemen,' he added, almost as an afterthought.

He went through the whole story from the beginning, all the while keeping a careful watch on the two new men's faces. The mere mention of Bosnia seemed to have brought a gleam into the eyes of the lad from Sunderland, and as Docherty talked he could almost feel the Dame's intense eagerness to get started.

The Essex lad was a different type altogether: very cool and collected, very self-contained, almost as if he was in some sort of reverie. There were a couple of moments when Docherty wasn't even sure he was listening, but once he'd finished his outline it was Chris who came up with the first question, and one that went straight to the heart of the matter.

'What are we going in as, boss?' he asked.

'That's a good question,' Barney Davies said. 'You'll be flying into Split on the coast of Croatia, and while you're there waiting for transport to Sarajevo – which may be a few hours, may be a few days – your cover will be as supervisory staff attached to the Sarajevo civilian supply line. Once you're in Sarajevo . . . well, not to put too fine a point on it, you'll just be one more bunch of irregulars in a situation which is not too far from anarchy.'

'But we have troops there, right?' the Dame asked. 'The Cheshires and the Royal Irish.'

'One battalion from each,' Davies confirmed, 'and a squadron of Lancers, but they're under UN control, and that means they can only fire off weapons in self-defence. Their own, not yours. You should get some useful intelligence from our people out there, but don't expect anything more. The whole point of this op, at least as far as our political masters are concerned, is to restore our reputation as peace-keepers, with the least possible publicity . . .'

'You make it sound like the Regiment has a different priority, boss,' Razor said, surprising Docherty.

'I think it might be fairer to say we have an additional priority,' Davies said. 'Looking after our own. John Reeve has been an outstanding soldier for the Regiment, and he deserves whatever help we can give him.'

There was a rap on the door, and an adjutant poked his head around it. 'The man from the Foreign Office is here, boss,' he told Davies.

'Bring him through,' the CO ordered. 'He's going to brief you on the local background,' he told the four men.

A suited young man, carrying a briefcase in one hand and what appeared to be a large wad of maps in the other, walked confidently into the room. He had longish, curly hair, circular, black-framed spectacles, and the overall look of an anorexic Malcolm Rifkind.

'This is Mr Castle, from the Foreign Office's Balkan Section,' Davies said formally, as he walked across to make sure the door was firmly closed. Docherty suddenly realized how unusual it was for the CO to introduce a briefing. He wondered how many other members of the Regiment knew of this mission. If any.

'He is going to give you a basic introduction to what the newspapers now like to call "the former Yugoslavia", the CO went on. 'I know you all read the *Sun* voraciously,' he added with a broad smile, 'so most of what he has to say may be only too familiar, but just in case you've missed the odd page of detailed analysis . . . Mr Castle.'

The man from the Foreign Office was still struggling to fix his unwieldy pile of maps to the Kremlin's antique easel. Chris gave him a hand.

'Good morning,' Castle said finally, in a voice that was mercifully dissimilar to Malcolm Rifkind's. 'Despite your CO's testimonial to your reading habits, I'm going to assume you know nothing.'

'Good assumption,' Razor agreed.

Castle grinned. 'Right. Well, Yugoslavia, roughly translated, means Land of the Southern Slavs, and these Slavs originally came south to populate the area more than a thousand years ago. The peoples we now call the Croats, Serbs, Slovenes, Montenegrins, Bosnian Muslims are all descendants of these Slavs. They are not separate races, any more than Yorkshiremen are a separate race from Brummies, no matter what Geoff Boycott might tell you. If you visited an imaginary nudist colony in Bosnia you wouldn't be able to tell a Bosnian Muslim from a Slovene, or a Serb from a Croat.'

He paused for breath, and smiled at them. 'What these peoples don't have in common is history. I'm simplifying a lot, but for most of the last five hundred years, up to the beginning of this century, the area has been divided into three, with each third dominated by a different culture. The Austrians and sometimes the Italians were dominant in Slovenia, Croatia and along the coast, imposing a West European, Catholic culture. In the mountains of Bosnia and Hercegovina – here,' he said, pointing at the map, 'there was a continuous Turkish occupation for several centuries, and many of the Slavs were converted to Islam. In the east, in Serbia and to a lesser extent in Montenegro, the Eastern

Orthodox Church, with its mostly Russian cultural outlook, managed to survive the more sporadic periods of Turkish domination. In fact, fighting the Turks was probably what gave the Serbs their exaggerated sense of identity.

'So, by the time we reach the twentieth century we have a reasonably homogenous racial group divided into three cultural camps. Rather like what Northern Ireland might be like if a large group of Arabs had been settled there in the seventeenth century, at the same time as the Protestants.'

'Christ almighty,' Razor muttered.

'A fair comment,' Castle agreed. He seemed to be enjoying himself. 'The problem with people who only have cultures to identify themselves is that the cultures tend to get rabid. Since much of the last millennium in the Balkans has been a matter of Muslim versus Christian there's plenty of fertile ground for raking up old Muslim–Croat and Muslim–Serb quarrels. And in both world wars the Russians fought the Austrians, which meant Serbs against Croats. In World War Two this relationship reached a real nadir – the Croats were allowed their own little state by the Nazis, managed to find home-grown Nazis to run it – Ustashi they were called – and took the chance to butcher a large number of Serbs. No one knows how many, but hundreds of thousands.

'But I'm getting a bit ahead of the story. Yugoslavia was formed after World War One, partly as a recognition that these peoples did have a lot in common, and partly as a way of containing their differences for everyone else's sake. After all, the war had been triggered by a Bosnian Serb assassinating an Austrian archduke in the mainly Muslim city of Sarajevo.'

Castle checked to see if they were awake, found no one had glazed eyes yet, and turned back to the map. 'There are a few other minor divisions I should mention. The Albanians

– who are a different racial group – have large minorities in the Serbian region of Kosovo and in Macedonia. Macedonians are not a separate ethnic group, and their territory has been variously claimed by Bulgaria – which claims that Macedonians are just confused Bulgars – and Greece, which claims etc., etc.' He grinned owlishly at them.

'It's a right fucking mess, then,' Razor observed.

'But all their own,' Chris murmured.

'At the end of the last war a temporary solution appeared – communism. It was the communists, under Tito, who led the guerrilla war against the Germans, and after the war they took over the government. The ethnic tensions were basically put on ice. Each major group was given its own state in what was nominally a federal system, but Tito and the Party took all the important decisions. The hope was that the new secular religion of communism would see the withering away of the old national-religious identities – everyone would have a house and a car and a TV and be like every other consumer.

'But when Tito died in 1980 there was no one of the same stature to hold it all together. The system just about stumbled along through the eighties, with the Party bosses holding it all together between them, but when communism collapsed everywhere else in eastern Europe, the rug got pulled out from under their feet.

'What was left was an economy not doing that badly, at least by other communist standards, but a country with nothing to bind it together, and of course all the accumulated grievances came pouring out. Under Tito the richer areas like Slovenia and Croatia had been forced to subsidize the poorer ones, but they hadn't been given much of anything in return. The Serbs, who dominated the Party and the federal institutions – and particularly the national army – had no interest in changing things, and the power to stop those who had. Not surprisingly the Slovenes and Croats decided to opt out.

'Slovenia presented no great problems, except that it set a precedent – if Slovenia could go, then why not Croatia? The trouble was that Croatia had a large Serb minority, and the Croat leaders made no effort whatsoever to reassure it.

'By this time everyone was acting very badly, like a bunch of mad prima donnas. The Croats decided to secede from Yugoslavia, and their Serb minority areas decided to secede from Croatia. That was a year and a half ago, the summer of 1991, and both secessions have stuck, so to speak. Croatia has been recognized as an independent state, but since the cease-fire at the beginning of this year the Serb areas are nominally "UN-protected" – in other words under Serb military control. There's no foreseeable hope of Croatia taking them back.

'Which brings us to Bosnia – your destination. The most enthusiastic Yugoslavs always thought of this as the heart of the federation. It was the most ethnically mixed area, the one where mutual tolerance, and even mutual enjoyment, of the separate cultural traditions seemed most deep-rooted. It's mostly mountainous country, full of deep valleys and high passes, with towns clustered in the hollows. I travelled there several years ago, and found it beautiful. Most people do.' He grimaced. 'But an awful lot has been destroyed in the last six months.

'Anyway, once Croatia and Slovenia opted out, the Bosnian Government had an impossible choice to make – either accept a subsidiary position in a Serb-dominated mini-Yugoslavia or try opting out themselves, with the Yugoslav Army already encamped in their country and the Serb minority committed to opposing Bosnian independence by force of arms. They chose the latter, no doubt hoping that the international community would come to their aid. No such luck.

'I should say one more thing about Bosnia-Hercegovina. Each of the three peoples – Croats, Serbs, Muslims – have areas in which they are the majority, but there is intermingling everywhere. There was no way, a year ago, that you could have divided Bosnia tidily along ethnic grounds. Small villages were split two ways, sometimes even three ways – let alone regions.

'But of course the moment the international community started talking partition – quite mistakenly in my view – the rush was on. If a particular town had forty per cent Serbs, forty per cent Croats and twenty per cent Muslims, then the Serbs' chance of including it in a Greater Serbia would be much improved if the other sixty per cent could be persuaded to move on. And if two towns like that were separated by an area eighty per cent Muslim or Croat, then strategic necessity dictated that they be moved on too. This pattern is being repeated everywhere. Since no one's too sure of what is theirs, they're grabbing it anyway.'

'Is this what they call ethnic cleansing?' the Dame asked.

'Yes. Wonderful phrase, isn't it? The lucky ones are being simply moved on, but it looks like an enormous number of men have been killed, and an equally vast number of women have been raped, with the dual aim of humiliating them and making them pregnant. In both cases the Serbs seem the guiltiest party, by quite a considerable degree.'

'Isn't that like comparing Genghis Khan to Attila the Hun?' Barney Davies asked.

'No,' Castle answered immediately. 'At least, there doesn't seem to be that sort of equivalence. Why should there be? The Serbs in World War Two came nowhere near to matching the record of the Croat Ustashi for atrocities. And in this war, though individual groups of Croat and Muslim soldiers have undoubtedly been guilty of rape, the widespread reports of mass rape in Serb-dominated areas suggest that there is a systematic policy being coordinated from the top.'

'Jesus,' Chris muttered.

'At the moment,' Castle continued, turning round to flip over another map, 'this is the overall military situation on the ground. The Croats and Muslims have this' – he traced an area with an index finger – 'and the Serbs this. But of course the Muslim-Croat alliance is stronger in some areas than others . . .'

'Where's Zavik?' Docherty asked. He had looked it up in an atlas, but he wanted to see where it was in terms of the military situation.

'Here,' Castle said, pointing to a spot about twelve miles behind Serb lines.

'What sort of military units are we dealing with here?' Docherty asked. 'Regular Army divisions?'

'A good question. Everything from regular units down to gangs of bandits, with all the various possibilities in between. The official Bosnian Army is mostly Muslim but also includes Serbs and Croats. There are also various exclusively Muslim militias, and even volunteer units made up from Islamic veterans of Beirut, Iran, Afghanistan, etc.'

'Wonderful,' Chris murmured sarcastically.

'The Croatian Army has regular units in Bosnia, the Bosnian Croats have their own army, and there are also private militias. The worst of them are basically reborn Ustashi – they dress like designer stormtroopers and behave even worse. It's basically the same story on the Serbian side, with the old Federal Army now basically the Serbian Army, a Serbian Army of

Bosnia, the Serbian Police of Bosnia, and any number of militias. The most famous are the Arkanovci, who are led by a man who calls himself Arkan and is wanted in about five European countries for armed robbery. Then there's the White Eagles and the Chetniks. Croats and Muslims, by the way, call all Serb irregulars Chetniks, after the nationalist guerrillas from World War Two, and they do tend to look alike – the fashion here is broad-brimmed hats and long beards, so they look like psychotic Australian Rasputins. By the same token, all Croat militiamen are called Ustashi, after the World War Two fascists.'

'What are these bands of merry men armed with?' Razor asked. Even he seemed subdued by Castle's account, Docherty thought.

'And how many men are we talking about?' Chris wanted to know.

'Serbs – about 70,000 fighters; 50,000 Croats; maybe 40,000 Muslims. They all have APCs for moving men around, and the usual automatic weapons. The Serbs have some Soviet tanks, and as much heavy artillery as they need, up to 155mm. Plus, probably twenty combat aircraft – Super Galebs and Oraos. Between thirty and forty helicopters – Gazelles, for the most part. The Croats and the Muslims have no planes, no tanks and, in the Muslims' case, not much artillery to speak of.'

'No wonder they need their fedayeen,' Docherty observed.

'Well, they can't get any weapons from outside because of the arms embargo,' Castle said. 'Any other questions?'

'Will it all have a happy ending?' Razor asked.

'I doubt it,' Castle said simply.

When he had gone, one question was uppermost in the Dame's mind. 'What weaponry are we taking in?' he wanted to know.

'Whatever we can carry without looking too much like an Action Team,' Docherty said. 'Certainly MP5s and High Powers. Any particular requests?'

'An Accuracy International,' the Dame said.

'Good idea,' Docherty agreed, remembering the Dame's reported prowess with a sniper rifle.

'How about a Chieftain tank?' Razor asked.

'If you can carry it, you can bring it,' Docherty shot back.

5

The plane touched down at Split airport soon after ten a.m. on Thursday 30 December 1992, and the bright sunshine and English summer temperature which greeted them at the open door was a welcome change from the freezing drizzle they had left behind in Oxfordshire.

In years gone by, Docherty reminded himself, thousands of Brits had arrived here on package tours for a week of Mediterranean winter warmth, armed with trashy novels and suntan lotion rather than Heckler & Koch MP5 sub-machine-guns.

A quarter of a mile or so across the tarmac a long line of Hercules C-130 transport planes were parked wing-tip to wing-tip, each bearing the UN logo. Behind them the Dalmatian mountains rose up from the coastal plain into a clear blue sky.

A tall, clean-shaven RAF officer sporting a pale-blue UN beret was waiting for them at the bottom of the mobile stairway. 'Flight-Lieutenant Frobisher,' he introduced himself, offering his hand to each of the foursome in turn. 'Which are the bags containing the winter clothing and the you-know-what?'

'Those two,' Docherty said, indicating the two large canvas holdalls Chris and the Dame were carrying. They'd been warned before leaving to pack the Arctic clothing and the weaponry separately from the rest of the equipment.

'I'll take care of them,' Frobisher said, and carried the bags across to where another RAF officer was talking to the pilot, dumped them at his feet, and exchanged a few words. Then he rejoined the SAS men, and gestured them towards a white jeep parked a few yards away.

Docherty clambered into the front seat, while the other three squeezed themselves into the back.

'The stuff will be kept here for you until you leave,' Frobisher explained. 'On one of those,' he added, indicating the distant line of transport planes, 'but when that will be depends very much on weather conditions. Oh, it's lovely down here,' he agreed, seeing their surprised faces, 'but up in the mountains it's a different kettle of fish altogether. Go thirty miles east of here and the temperature will drop about twenty degrees – Celsius, that is. Sarajevo's in the middle of a blizzard right now, with ground visibility down to about six inches. So don't expect an imminent departure. But don't not expect one either. If a window opens up we want you ready to go.'

'So we're not staying out here?' Docherty asked.

'There isn't anywhere, unless you fancy kipping down for a week in a C-130. In any case, the Croats watch what's happening at this airport like hawks, and the town's only twelve miles away. We thought you'd be a bit less noticeable there, so we booked you into one of the hotels. As you can imagine there's quite a lot of vacancies this year.' He looked at Docherty, as if expecting formal approval of the arrangements.

'Sounds good,' the Scot said.

'Is there room service?' Razor asked.

'I don't know,' Frobisher said doubtfully, as if uncertain whether the question was serious. It seemed unlikely that he'd ever had dealings with the SAS before.

Docherty had been expecting at least some formalities to mark their official arrival in a foreign country, but Frobisher simply drove the jeep around the end of the forlorn-looking terminal building, through an open gate and out on to a wide highway that ran along parallel to the coast, at times almost directly above the breaking waves. In the distance silhouetted islands loomed abruptly out of the shining Adriatic, giving Docherty the impression of a warmer west coast of Scotland. On the other side of the highway sunlit slopes tumbled down almost to the verge. An almost idyllic setting, it was hardly what they had been expecting.

'It doesn't look like the war's reached here,' Chris observed.

'Not really,' Frobisher agreed. 'There's no argument about whose territory this is. Still, having said that, Split is home to some of the nastier Croat groups, and there has been trouble. There was a lot of intimidation against the minorities in the town a year or so back, people being fired from their jobs, scared out of their houses, a lot of beatings, a few deaths. Most of the Serbs and Muslims upped and left, though God knows where they went. The place doesn't have a nice feeling to it – at least I don't think so. Looks nice, though,' he added, then, pointing forward and to the right, said: 'That's it over there, on the peninsula.'

It did look nice, too nice for beatings and deaths. A lighthouse sat on the end of the headland, and behind it the ground rose in a high, wooded hill, which seemed to stand guard over the town nestling beneath it.

'One of the Roman Emperors built his retirement palace here,' Frobisher said.

'Tottenham played Hadjuk Split in the UEFA Cup once,' Razor added.

'Well, that's the last two thousand years taken care of, then,' Chris said.

Ten minutes later they were entering the outskirts of the town, climbing up and across the peninsula's spine, and motoring down towards the sea on its southern side. Their hotel, which bore the unpronounceable name of the Prenociste Slavija, was on one of the narrow side-streets inside the walls of the old Roman palace. Its interior was less impressive than its location, but all of them had stayed in worse.

'The rooms are booked for a week,' Frobisher told them. 'There's no chance you'll be going in today, but if tomorrow looks like a possibility I'll come by tonight and tell you. The telephones are not what you'd call reliable,' he added cryptically. 'Anything else? Ah yes,' he answered himself, pulling something from his pocket. 'This is a map of the town in case you need it. The hotel is here' – he pointed to the spot – 'and there's a decent enough restaurant here, just inside the East Gate. You've got money, I take it.'

'Aye. Dinars and dollars.'

'I should forget the dinars. Anything else?'

'How can we get hold of you?' Docherty asked.

'Just take a taxi out to the airport. The UN Operations HQ is on the second floor of the terminal building.'

When Frobisher had gone, Docherty turned to find the other three looking at him expectantly.

'Food, boss?' Razor asked.

'Sounds good. And then I think we'll go for a run, get used to the altitude.'

The others groaned in unison.

An hour and a half later, as the four men toiled their way up towards the summit of Marjan Hill for the third time, the Dame was beginning to revise his opinions about Docherty's readiness for retirement. A few yards behind him Chris was wondering whether Docherty had planned this demonstration with just such an aim in mind. Was the Patrol Commander intent on dispelling any doubts the younger men might have about his fitness? If so, he had succeeded.

Bringing up the rear, Razor was breathing heavily but still smiling to himself. Running up and down a hill in the sunshine sure beat teaching Continuation Training classes, he decided.

'That'll do,' Docherty told them at the summit. 'I don't want to wear you out before we get there.' He looked at his watch. 'OK, it's just gone four. We'll eat at seven. So you've got three hours to lie in the bath, write a classical symphony or take a look around. And we'll meet up in the same restaurant.'

The others nodded.

'I'll write the symphony,' Razor said. 'Wilkinson's Fourth.'

'Let's pray it's Unfinished,' Chris muttered.

Docherty eyed them fondly. There was nothing quite like bullshit for cementing the relationships in a four-man patrol.

Docherty took a quick shower, dressed and went out on his own. For half an hour or so he wandered through the narrow streets of the old town, inspecting the buildings with a slightly jaundiced eye. As a lover of Islamic and Spanish architecture – the legacy of time spent on active service in Oman and off duty in Mexico – he found Graeco-Roman styles too brutal and the later Renaissance architecture too florid by half. He was looking forward to seeing the minarets of Sarajevo, always assuming there were any left.

He knew that most people would think it wrong to lament the loss of an architectural heritage when so many people of all ages were being killed every day, but, as his friend Liam McCall had pointed out, there was no God-given limit on how many different things a man could lament at the same time.

And the Serbs weren't destroying those buildings by accident. Representing a thousand years of a culture's history, they were the visual embodiment of the lives of countless generations of Bosnian Muslims. Destroy them, and the books and the pictures they contained, and it was like erasing a people's memory.

He sighed. Maybe he was getting too old for this game after all.

He emerged on to Titova Obala, the seafront promenade. A couple of hundred yards to his left he could see Razor and Chris walking in the opposite direction, and smiled hopefully to himself. A friendship between those two could only strengthen the chemistry of the patrol, which Docherty already considered as good as any he'd known.

He crossed the wide street and turned right along the sea wall, looking out across the myriad boats lying at anchor across the harbour. Many seemed neglected, even dilapidated, and there was a sad air about the whole scene, as there was about the town as a whole. It was a Sleeping Beauty town, he decided, waiting for peace to kiss it awake.

A tousle-haired man in a thick woollen sweater was leaning against the harbour wall, staring out to where the sun was rapidly sinking behind an arm of the harbour. To Docherty's surprise he had a copy of that day's *Daily Mirror* sticking out of the back pocket of his jeans. It had to have arrived on the same plane as they had.

'Good evening,' he said, wondering whether he'd get an English response.

'My God, the Scots have arrived,' the man said with a smile and a Midlands accent. He was younger than Docherty, probably in his mid-thirties.

'We understand what it's like being an oppressed minority,' Docherty said, 'so they called us in to sort things out. My name's Jamie, by the way.'

'Jim,' the man said, offering his hand. 'And what are you really doing here?'

'Admin work for the UN,' Docherty lied. 'How about you?'

'I'm on the lorries. The supply run to Sarajevo,' he explained. 'Got back this morning, and I'll probably be going back Saturday.'

'What's the situation like there?' Docherty asked.

'Bloody terrible. Imagine how bad it could get, and then imagine it being ten times worse – that's Sarajevo. The people there – the ordinary people – are bloody amazing, but . . . there seem to be more dyed-in-the-wool bastards per square foot in this country than you'd find anywhere outside a Conservative Party conference. I hope you're not a Tory, mate.'

Docherty grinned. 'No. How about the journey – no trouble on the road from irregulars? Or regulars, come to that?'

Jim shrugged. 'We have UN troops riding shotgun, for what it's worth. There's a lot of hassle, you know, having to get free passage agreed each time, and being stopped every few miles to have our papers looked at and the loads checked . . .' He shrugged again. 'But by God it's worth it when you see the faces at the other end.'

Docherty found himself envying the man. 'It must be,' he said.

'You know,' Jim said, turning to face him, 'I spent most of the last ten years delivering fitted bathrooms to people who didn't really need them. Can you imagine what that's like – spending your life doing something completely unnecessary? And then I saw this job advertised, and I just had to take it. My wife thought I was nuts, at least in the beginning, and maybe I am, but for the first time in my life I'm delivering something that people really need, and Christ it feels good.'

Walking back towards the hotel Docherty wondered, not for the first time, how the same species could accommodate the utter meanness which targeted minarets and the generosity of spirit which made a man like Jim risk everything because helping people felt so good. He would have liked to talk to Liam McCall about it – they could have shared each other's incomprehension.

The restaurant was not so empty as it had been at lunchtime: three other tables were already occupied, and two more had 'reserved' signs on them. A family of four was seated at one of the occupied tables, but the others contained only men, and young men at that. None of them was wearing uniform, and it might have been Docherty's imagination, but there seemed a hint of latent aggression in the air. It smelt of what Isabel liked to call a 'testosterone overload situation'.

Once again Chris translated the menu for them. He and Docherty settled for *brodet* – mixed fish stewed with rice – while the Dame opted for a seafood platter and Razor for an anchovy pizza. Four small glasses of plum brandy served as aperitifs, and they ordered a large carafe of Riesling to complement the meal. 'Here's to the taxpayer, who's paying for it all,' Razor said, raising his glass.

'In Sarajevo they're eating dandelion leaves,' Chris said soberly.

'Christ, I hate greens,' Razor complained, just as the door opened to admit another group of four men. The words 'designer stormtroopers' went through all four SAS minds at the same moment. Each of the newcomers had hair cut close-to-stubble short and clean-shaven faces. Each was wearing a jet-black uniform, black boots and black leather mittens with silver studs. Two of them were sporting Ray-Ban Aviator shades, and one had a black sweatband around his head, presumably to keep his non-existent hair out of his eyes.

Docherty's first impulse was to laugh out loud, but he restrained himself. For five reasons. One was their need to remain as anonymous as possible, the other four rested in low-slung holsters on each man's thigh – black, Czech-made Scorpion machine pistols.

'Jesus,' Razor muttered under his breath.

'More like Hell's Angels,' Docherty murmured. He remembered gangs of leather-clad rockers in the sixties who had walked into Glasgow cafés and pubs with exactly the same cold-hearted swagger. They had only been carrying bicycle chains and knives, and they had scared the shit out of him. Not so much because they were stronger, or because there were more of them, but because their only means of communication with each other was through finding strangers to victimize.

The new arrivals took a table about fifteen feet away from the SAS men.

'Keep the talk down and avoid eye contact,' Docherty softly told the others. 'We'll just enjoy our meal and get the hell out of here.'

The food arrived sooner than expected, as if the waiter was also keen to see them on their way as quickly as possible. As far as Docherty could remember, he was the only man who had heard them speaking English, and another waiter was dealing with the black-clad irregulars. Maybe there wouldn't be a problem.

Or maybe there would.

'You can tell how a man is by his friends,' a voice said loudly in English.

'A friend of Serbs is a pig,' one of his companions agreed. Docherty could feel the eyes boring into the side of his head, and fought the temptation to turn towards them.

'It is like they say – there are two peoples in Europe who do not like to wash – the Serbs and the English,' the first voice continued conversationally. Someone else laughed, and the other two followed his cue, like an echo. Presumably they didn't know enough English to join in the baiting.

It was all so ludicrously childish, Docherty thought, like a thousand scenes in a thousand bad Westerns. Sure, there were bullies everywhere in real life, but they usually had a better script than this. He placed a forkful of fish in his mouth; it tasted sourer than it should have.

He looked round at the others. Razor was smiling to himself, revelling in the luxury of having his back to the taunters. Chris was managing to look indifferent, but the Dame's mouth was set in a grim and angry line.

'We took an English nurse in Knin,' the voice said. 'She said she was a virgin.' He laughed. 'Not now. Now she has a hundred men to remember.'

Docherty took a deep breath. He was confident they could cope with any amount of bullshit, but could the shitheads in black cope with being ignored much longer? And if they couldn't then what form would the escalation take? And how the hell could they defuse the situation?

'*De dónde viene este vino?*' Razor asked suddenly, picking up the bottle and examining it with great interest. It had occurred to him that all four of them were both semi-fluent in Spanish and relatively dark-complexioned.

'Dalmatia,' Chris said. '*Es bueno, sí?*

'*Sí*,' Razor agreed.

Docherty smiled inwardly and said he had always liked Yugoslavian wines.

The four SAS men launched into an enthusiastic discussion, in Spanish, of the relative merits of different wines. All of them were speaking the Latin-American variant, but Docherty doubted whether the Croats would know the difference. They had reverted to their own language, he realized with relief.

'They're talking about their plans for tomorrow,' Chris explained in Spanish, as if reading Docherty's mind.

'I hope they include a run-in with the fashion police,' Razor said.

They walked back to their hotel along the darkened street feeling good.

'Jesus, I'm ready for a bed,' Docherty said, as they walked in through the front door, only to find Flight-Lieutenant Frobisher rising out of the single, threadbare armchair to greet them.

'The weathermen say there may be a window around dawn tomorrow,' he said, 'so you'd better wait out at the airport.'

Ten minutes later they were back in Frobisher's jeep, motoring out through the empty streets of the port and on to the coast highway. The day's clear sky had given way to heavy, rolling clouds, with a hint of rain in the air. Their beds for the night turned out to be sackfuls of rice in the belly of a Hercules C-130.

6

Dawn was still half an hour away when the transport plane rattled off the runway and into the dark sky. Docherty stared at the solid wall of the fuselage and remembered the view they had enjoyed coming in to Split the previous morning, the islands scattered across the deep-blue sea.

The RAF pilots had both seemed cheerful enough, and the younger of the two had even relished telling them they were in for a 'Khe Sanh' landing at Sarajevo. Docherty had not spoiled the other three's flight by passing on everything he had heard about such landings from Americans who'd served in Vietnam. Just so long as they were all well strapped in when the time came . . .

They were in their full Arctic gear now: thermal vests and long johns, quilted under-trousers and jackets, thick woollen socks, gloves and high-neck combat boots, the latter a great improvement on their Falklands-era predecessors. As the quartermaster had told them: 'You might get shot dead but you won't get trench foot.'

Gore-tex jackets normally completed the outfit, but for this trip they were also wearing flak-jackets. Both Serbs and Muslims had reportedly acquired the nasty habit of using Sarajevo's runway for target practice.

Docherty leaned his head back against the plane's metal skin and closed his eyes, his mind reaching forward towards their arrival in the Bosnian capital. What would it be like? Would they find Nena Reeve? And if they did, would she agree to come with them?

He wondered again if this chosen course of action hadn't been a mistake. A C-130 like this one could have dropped the four of them within easy reach of Zavik. Granted, they would never have got clearance for a flight out of Split, but these planes had a range of close on 3000 miles. The whole mission could have been mounted from the UK.

Too much chance of political hassle, perhaps. And there was always a lot to be said for a thorough acclimatization. The town of Zavik, the immediate vicinity, the military situation in the area – all were complete unknowns. The chances of dropping a team into the heart of a battle zone might not be high, but it hardly seemed a risk worth taking.

Against that, they now had to countenance a landing in Sarajevo and an overland odyssey to Zavik. If the latest reports were correct then most of the journey would be through Muslim-held territory, but even with snow on the ground the military situation seemed alarmingly fluid. If all four of them came through this without a serious scratch, Docherty thought to himself, then he'd retire once more a happy man.

He glanced round at the other three. Chris was sitting opposite him, squinting in the dim light at the book he was studying – *Birds of Southern Europe*. His face even seemed relaxed when he was concentrating, which boded well. Already, after knowing the man less than forty-eight hours, Docherty had almost complete confidence in him.

The Dame was another matter. He had stopped reading his novel – some thriller about submarines – and was staring blankly into space. His expression was usually as serene as Chris's, but the similarity, Docherty thought, was at least partly superficial. Both men seemed supremely self-sufficient – most SAS men were – but Docherty sensed that for Chris there was little or no struggle involved in the process. The Wearsider, by contrast, had mastered the art of retreating into himself, and of functioning effectively in the world outside, but the self he retreated into seemed a troubled one.

Which might bode ill for the patrol as a whole, or might have no effect whatsoever on the way the Dame handled himself. But it was something worth watching out for, that was certain. Like any decent football team, an SAS patrol had to grow into more than the sum of its parts. And it was up to the PC, the Patrol Commander, to make sure it did. He need not have been trained as a clinical psychiatrist, but he did need some idea of how to read other men.

'How much longer, boss?' Razor asked.

Docherty looked at his watch. 'Pilot said fifty-odd minutes, and we've been airborne forty-one. They'll tell us when they come to make sure we're strapped in.'

'It's that bad, is it, this Khe Sanh business?'

'No worse than taking off in the Space Shuttle, so I'm told.'

'Christ. Still, whatever it is, it'll beat being dropped in the fucking sea.'

Docherty smiled, remembering the look of blissful relief on Razor's face when, ten years before, the boat had picked him out of the Atlantic swell. On that mission the Londoner had spent much of his time thinking up 'mixed proverbs'; 'time waits for an old fool' had been Docherty's personal favourite. Razor still seemed full of jokes, but there was something else there now, something more sombre under-neath. Maybe he was just growing up, in the best sense of the phrase. He'd certainly lost none of his sharpness – the switch into Spanish in the restaurant had been brilliant . . .

'Time to make your wills, gentlemen,' the pilot said, appearing between the rows of crated foodstuffs. 'Are you all strapped in like good lads? We don't want you flying around inside the plane getting blood on everything. Good.' He turned to go. 'We'll be on the ground in about five minutes,' he said over his shoulder, 'one way or another.'

'I love the fucking RAF,' Razor growled.

'Don't be surprised if the bottom of your stomach starts pressing up against the top of your head,' Docherty told them, and the words were hardly out of his mouth before they came true. With a gut-wrenching suddenness the plane seemed to stop flying and start falling, as if a wing had snapped off or all four engines had chosen the same moment to die. Within seconds the SAS men could feel the pull of gravity weaken, and what Docherty could only describe as a breathlessness inside his head. So this is what space travel is like, he thought, and then, just as his body was adapting to its presence within a plummeting shell, the plane seemed to rear up like a bucking bronco, dropping his stomach down to his feet. For what seemed like a very long couple of seconds he felt on the verge of blacking out.

The brakes slammed on, and with a great jolt the wheels hit the runway. A few moments later they were taxiing along at a speed which would have had them arrested for speeding on the M40, the Hercules seemingly on the verge of shaking itself into a heap of scrap metal.

From outside the plane there was the sound of a loud blast in the distance. And then another, much closer.

They looked at each other.

'Welcome to Bosnia,' Razor said.

For another two or three minutes they sat in the belly of the taxiing plane, the sounds of shell fire audible above the noise of their passage. They had no way of seeing out, no real idea of how close the shells were landing, and there was nothing they could have done about it anyway.

'Everyone OK?' Docherty asked. He felt like he'd been picked up by a giant and given a thorough shaking.

They all said they were.

The Hercules rumbled to a standstill, and the pilot's head popped up between the line of crates. 'Journey's end,' he announced, in what for him seemed an almost funereal tone. 'I don't suppose you lads feel like helping us unload this beauty,' he said, setting in motion the slow descent of the tail ramp.

'Sorry, prior commitments,' Docherty said drily, as he watched the wall of an airport building coming into view. The ground had only a light covering of snow, but shovelled mounds of the stuff offered evidence of previous falls. The air seemed as damp as it did cold.

'That's the international arrivals door,' the RAF man said sardonically, pointing out a single red door marked 'No Exit' in English.

'Thanks for the ride,' Docherty said, and led the other three down the ramp. Once clear of the plane he could see, across the tarmac, the control tower with all of its windows boarded up. On both sides of the airfield slopes seemed to climb steeply away from the valley, their heights lost in cloud. It might have been one of the South Wales valleys on a bad day, if not for the occasional thump of artillery fire.

They were halfway to the building when two UN soldiers emerged from it, demanding in rapid-fire French to see their identification. Docherty produced the UN accreditations. The two soldiers inspected each SAS man's face with a thoroughness which any beautician would have envied, and then allowed them to pass.

Inside the building they found a vast expanse of floor littered with broken glass and spent cartridge cases, and another UN soldier hurrying across the debris to meet them, plastic bag in hand, as if he was on his way home from the shops. 'Sergeant Docherty?' he asked tersely, while he was still some ten yards away.

Docherty nodded. The officer was a Brit, a major in the Cheshires. He was wearing a flak-jacket under his greatcoat.

'Good. My name's Brindley.' He looked round the vast building. 'I'm just here to escort you to your hotel. Strictly against UN rules, but what the hell. Here' – he delved into the plastic bag and pulled out four pale-blue berets – 'just for the trip. We'll have to pass through a few checkpoints, and it's always better if they think they know who you are.' He looked round at them. 'OK. Let's go. The earlier in the day you make this ride the better it usually is. Most of the snipers seem to sleep until mid-morning.'

Chris and the Dame raised their eyebrows at each other.

In what had once been an elegant semicircular forecourt yet another jeep was waiting for them. This one was armoured, more like the vehicles they'd all used at various times in Northern Ireland. The level of respect accorded the UN was apparent in the line of bullet scars which stretched across the two large letters on the jeep's flank.

'Tighten your safety belts,' Brindley advised. 'And let me do the talking at the checkpoints.'

They started off at a steady twenty-five miles per hour, with Major Brindley carefully negotiating the threefold problem of treacherous winter conditions, potholes and shell craters. Visibility seemed to be getting worse rather than better as the morning advanced, which Docherty supposed was good news. Nevertheless he felt an absurd pang of regret at being denied a better view of the countryside surrounding the city.

They reached the first checkpoint within five minutes. It was manned by several Serbs in uniform, one of whom seemed on friendly terms with Brindley.

'Yugoslav National Army uniforms,' the major explained as they drove on. 'They're the most disciplined of the Serb forces. By a long way,' he added as an afterthought.

The next checkpoint was also manned by Serbs, but here only one was in uniform, and though he was clearly in charge, and coldly courteous in his examination of their credentials, the SAS men were more struck by the demeanour of the irregulars behind him. On their faces an overweening contempt was not masked by any obvious sign of intelligence. This, Docherty thought, was the rural version of the black-uniformed thugs they had seen in the Split restaurant.

'See that?' Brindley gestured with his head.

The SAS men craned their necks. 'Welcome to Hell' the sign by the side of the road read in bloody red letters.

'"Murder Mile" begins around that corner,' Brindley went on conversationally, pointing ahead. 'Though I doubt if we'll have any trouble this morning.'

He accelerated the jeep, as if uncertain of his own prophetic powers, and they were soon barrelling down a stretch of straight road between two expanses of open ground, the jeep lurching from side to side as Brindley wove his way round the shell craters. They could see nothing through the mist to either left or right, but somewhere out there someone was tracking the noise of their passage, because a bullet suddenly pinged viciously off the outside of the jeep just above Razor's window.

'Fuck a pig!' he exclaimed. 'How the fuck can they see us in this?'

No one answered him, but Brindley trod down again, causing the jeep to lurch even more wildly. A dark shape loomed out of the mist – the burnt-out hulk of a car which hadn't made it – and Brindley sent the jeep careering past it. For a moment the wheels seemed to lose their grip on the packed snow, but somehow they righted themselves, just as another bullet bounced off the back of the vehicle.

'Almost there,' Brindley said, and within seconds they were entering the relative safety of a street lined with industrial premises. The collective sigh of relief was still clouding the air when the jeep pulled into the forecourt of an apparently wrecked hotel. The sign still claimed it was the Holiday Inn, but there were gun emplacements in the garden and the face of the building had clearly been ravaged by shell fire. At least half the windows had been boarded over, and half the remainder offered mosaics of broken glass.

'You'll be staying here,' Brindley said. 'It looks better inside,' he added, noticing their horrified expressions.

'It could hardly look worse,' Chris said.

'Who stays here?' Docherty wanted to know.

Brindley eased the jeep round the building and into what seemed a reasonably sheltered parking space. 'Only about a quarter of the rooms are full,' he went on, switching off the engine. 'With journalists mostly, though you'll see the odd group of Croatians doing a passable imitation of Nazis. They tend to drink too much and start waving their guns around.'

'We met some of them in Split,' Docherty said.

'Just ignore them,' Brindley advised. 'You'll also notice lots of men huddling in corners, pretending they're bona fide Balkans conspirators. They look more like fictional agents than real ones, and for all I know they're residents of a local mental hospital that the Bosnian Government has sent back into the community. I always get the feeling that they've all read a chapter of *The Mask of Dimitrios* in their rooms before coming down to the bar to try out the gestures.'

Docherty grinned. He was beginning to like Brindley.

'And they'll have a field day trying to work out who you lot are,' the major added. 'Four tough-looking Brit bastards with bergens full of God knows what. Maybe you'd better keep the berets for a while. I don't suppose the UN will miss them.'

They entered the hotel by a back entrance, and walked down a short corridor to the reception area. There were indeed several seedy-looking men in trilbies with the collars of their coats turned up. History repeats itself once as tragedy, and then again as farce, Docherty remembered. Who had said that?

Brindley was dealing with the receptionist, a young man with an impudent smile and what looked like the barrel of an AK47 protruding out from under his counter. 'Don't stand in front of any open windows,' the youth said, with all the animation of an air hostess demonstrating safety regulations, 'we have lost several guests that way already.'

'Room service with a bullet,' Razor murmured.

'Fourth floor,' Brindley told them. 'It could be worse.' He led the way to the bottom of the stairs. 'The bar and restaurant are on the mezzanine and first floors, gentlemen.'

'What's the food like?' Chris asked.

'Not bad, considering half the city are surviving on a diet of dandelion soup and dog biscuits.'

They started up the stairs.

'Someone found a spent bullet in their pizza the other day,' Brindley added conversationally.

'I didn't really think it was possible to feel homesick for Walthamstow,' Razor muttered.

Eight flights of stairs latter they found themselves outside rooms 417 and 418. Both had curtains drawn across boarded-up windows and single bare light-bulbs for illumination.

'I'm glad we're not staying in a dump,' Razor said, testing out one of the beds. 'Not bad,' he admitted.

Docherty was examining the view though a narrow slit between board and window frame. The mist seemed to be lifting gradually, revealing snow-covered slopes on the other side of the valley.

'I'd better fill you in on the local geography,' Brindley said, as he unfolded a large-scale map of the Sarajevo area and spread it across the floor. The four SAS men gathered around it.

'The city is more or less surrounded,' Brindley began. 'Basically, the Serbs hold the high ground, which includes not only these mountains but the upper reaches of the valleys to the north, east and south. The lower valley to the west is still contested territory; you could say the Serbs have a cork in the bottle, but it's not a very tight-fitting affair.'

'As the bishop said to the actress,' Razor murmured.

Brindley eyed him with what might have been affection. 'There are a few complications in the general picture,' he went on.

'Dobrinja, which we skirted round after leaving the airport, is a Serb enclave in Muslim territory, a siege within the siege. There are a couple of others like it, and since the roads wind in and out of the two sides' territories you can find yourself being stopped at checkpoints every mile or so. Which is more than a pain in the rear, incidentally – it drastically increases your chances of meeting some trigger-happy irregular who's full of the wrong sort of pills.'

'Where do they get them?' Docherty asked.

'God knows. But we know some of the militia leaders were heavies in the Belgrade underworld not so long ago, and there's no reason why they shouldn't have kept up their contacts with their old buddies. This isn't such a big country, you know – it just seems like one. We're not much more than a hundred miles from Belgrade as the crow flies.'

By 'this country', Docherty realized, Brindley meant Yugoslavia. 'What about here in the city?' he asked. 'Are there any safe areas?'

'Everything's in range of the Serb artillery, if that's what you mean. The shelling is sporadic these days – the visibility's often poor – but if you're above ground there's always the chance. Snipers are more of a problem. Most of the high-rises have been deserted by the people who lived in them, and the snipers have taken up residence instead. They shoot at anything that moves, small children included.' He looked up, a mixture of disbelief and tired outrage in his eyes. 'It's hard to credit. Still, at least you can take precautions against them. Once you're outside you'll soon get a good idea of which places are safe and which aren't. Nothing overlooks the narrow streets of the old town, for example, but any wide street intersection is probably in someone's sights. But don't just take your cue from the locals – some of them have become incredibly blasé. You get the feeling that they've been playing Russian roulette so long that they've almost begun to enjoy it.' He shook his head, as if he was trying to shake such lunacy out. 'So, where you see a local run, you run, but when you see one walking along with a big smile on his face, take a look around anyway. He may be sniper-happy.'

'Christ, what a place,' Razor exclaimed softly.

'These days it's about as far from Christ as you can get,' Brindley replied. 'But I don't want to give you the wrong impression. Some kind of normal life still goes on here, despite everything. The shelling stops for fifteen minutes, and it's like a rainstorm has stopped anywhere else – people come out. You see women walking past all smartly dressed with their handbags, people in cafés arguing about politics, people looking round the shops – those that have anything to sell. The last supermarket I went in had only razors and champagne.'

'Nice combination,' Chris said grimly.

'What about after dark?' Razor asked. 'I take it the night-life is a bit on the thin side?'

'You could say that. There's a curfew from ten p.m. to six a.m., and the whole city's basically blacked out. But nowhere's safe any time after dark. There's no civilian reason for anyone to be on the street, so anyone out there is considered fair game.'

'Kind of puts Belfast in perspective, doesn't it?' Chris said.

Brindley grunted. 'By the way,' he added, pointing at the map, 'this is where the British UN staff HQ is. If you need anything in the way of equipment there's no harm in asking.' He looked round. 'Anything else you can think of?'

'I don't think so,' Docherty said. 'The first thing we have to do is find a woman. A particular woman,' he added, in response to Brindley's raised eyebrow. He explained about Nena Reeve. 'But the FO already have someone working on that for us.'

'OK,' Brindley said, getting up.

'We appreciate the help,' Docherty told him.

'You're welcome. I wish we could do more, but soldiering for the UN – well, it's all in a great cause but it's like soldiering with both hands tied behind your back.' He smiled ruefully. 'Any idea how long you'll be staying?'

'None.'

'There is one piece of good news, gentlemen,' Brindley said. 'The bar here hasn't run dry once.' He reached for the door, just as someone rapped on it.

Brindley again raised his eyebrows at Docherty, who shrugged.

'Thornton,' a voice said through the door.

'The FO man,' Docherty said. He opened the door to reveal a man of medium height with short, curly hair and the sort of dissolute face favoured by producers of epic serials when casting young wastrels and cads.

'God, that's a lot of stairs to climb,' he said, coming in and flopping himself down on the edge of a bed.

'Good luck, lads,' Brindley told the SAS men, and shut the door behind him.

Thornton seemed to be recovering his breath; enough at least to fish in his pocket for a cigarette. He lit up with a Zippo lighter and blew smoke at the ceiling. Docherty, who had grown to dislike the man intensely in something under a minute, restrained himself from tearing the cigarette out of his mouth. After all, with the amount of cold draught that was blowing in around the boarded-up window, they were more likely to die of hypothermia than passive smoking.

'Welcome to Sarajevo,' the MI6 man said. 'Have you got a drink up here by any chance? No? Pity. How was the flight in? A bit on the bumpy side?'

'Have you got some information for us?' Docherty asked him.

'No, not really. But I do have the names of several people in the city who know Zavik well. They should be able to fill you in . . .'

'What about Nena Reeve?'

Thornton took a drag on his cigarette and looked round for an ashtray. Razor reached for the one on the bedside table and handed it to him.

'Thanks,' he said, nearly missing it with his ash. 'The woman has vanished into thin air. I went up to the hospital and talked to her boss and some of her colleagues, but none of them have a clue. I looked round her room – on the quiet, of course – but there's nothing there to suggest where she's gone. Oh, and I checked out the morgue, just in case. No joy.'

Docherty looked at him thoughtfully. 'How do you rate our chances of getting to Zavik?' he asked.

Thornton shrugged. 'I've got no information on the situation there . . .'

'I'm more interested in how we get ourselves out of Sarajevo.'

'Yes, I'm working on that. One of the Muslim militia leaders might be prepared to help out, if we can strike a decent deal. They'll probably want a few SMGs, something like that. I was supposed to see him this morning, but my translator didn't show up . . .'

'You don't speak Serbo-Croat?' Docherty interrupted, trying to keep the disbelief out of his voice.

If Thornton noticed, he didn't seem perturbed. 'No need in the old days – all the people who mattered spoke English. But don't worry, I'll get hold of him tomorrow.'

'Good,' Docherty said. 'Is there any news of Reeve himself.'

'Nothing lately. You know the stories, I suppose. The Croats say the Serbs burned all their people alive in Zavik, in their church of course. The Serbs say they know for certain he had a party of their irregulars shot in cold blood, and that his men have raped and killed their way through several villages in Serb-held territory. The Muslims claim he razed the mosque in Zavik and forced their children to eat pork. It's all the usual stories rolled into one.'

'Have there been no refugees from Zavik?'

'None that we've found, either at the coast or in Zagreb. Whatever's happening up there, it looks like the locals either can't or won't leave.'

'That's it?'

'That's it. There's no telephone link, of course, and the place is off the beaten track, way up in the mountains. Since it's inside territory the Serbs say they control, they presumably have it surrounded, or at least cut off. But no one knows for certain. There are rumours that the missing American – you hear about him? – ah, well, he disappeared about a week ago somewhere out there, and the story was that he was trying to get to Zavik.'

'What was his name?'

'Bailey, I think. The other Americans here can tell you about him.'

Thornton reached for another cigarette, and found his packet was empty. 'I'll get hold of Muftic tomorrow,' he said, getting up to leave and scratching his neck. 'I'll be in the bar downstairs tonight.'

'How about eight o'clock?' Docherty asked.

'Sure, I'll be there all evening.'

'I bet you will,' Docherty muttered as the MI6 man's footsteps receded down the hallway.

'What a wanker,' the Dame murmured.

'The Cheshires can't help, and this tosspot won't,' Razor said. 'I think we're on our own for this one, boss.'

Docherty smiled. 'Looks like it. But here's the good news. If he only talked to the members of the hospital staff who can speak fluent English then there's a good chance Chris can pick up something he didn't.'

It was approaching noon when Docherty and Chris left the hotel. Grey clouds still hung above the city, but they were higher now, and the crests of the hills on either side of the valley were visible. No shells had fallen on the city for a couple of hours.

The hospital where Nena Reeve had worked was in the old town, a mile or so along the valley to the east. Docherty and Chris made their way up the gently sloping Marsala Tita, keeping as close to the walls as possible, hurrying from doorway to doorway on what looked vulnerable stretches, and sprinting like mad across the wide intersections.

Docherty was taken back to his Glasgow childhood, of going shopping with his mother, and the two of them alternating walking and running between pairs of lampposts. Doing something similar on the streets of Sarajevo, at the grand old age of forty-two, it all felt a bit unreal, right up to the moment the sniper's bullet whistled past his head and dug a large chunk out of the kerb across the street.

He scuttled on across the intersection and looked up to find an old woman grinning toothlessly at him from a half-boarded window. She said something in Serbo-Croat which Chris translated as 'that was a close one'. Docherty wondered if the intersection she lived by had replaced TV as her prime source of entertainment.

The two men continued on their erratically paced way, leaving Docherty's feelings of unreality at the crossroads, and both felt a deep sense of relief as they entered the old town, with its narrow, sheltered streets.

Using Brindley's map, they found the hospital with no difficulty. Its walls and windows had fared even worse than the Holiday Inn's, and the main entrance was as littered with broken glass as the airport building's. Uniformed Bosnian Government soldiers were much in evidence, though exactly what they thought they were guarding seemed hard to fathom.

Most of them simply stood there stony-faced as a steady stream of weeping visitors passed in and out.

The UN accreditations got Docherty and Chris inside, and the latter's linguistic skills won them directions to the chief administrator's office. She sat behind a desk overflowing with paper, eyes red-rimmed in a gaunt face. They should see Dr Raznatovic, she said; he had been Dr Reeve's boss.

A young orderly – he couldn't have been more than fifteen – escorted them through the maze, past patients lying in corridors, some of them with what looked simple fractures, some with gaping wounds and pain-racked faces, others with the serene expression of the dead. One corridor was slippery with blood, as if someone had been dragged along it.

Dr Raznatovic was between operations, and clearly torn between impatience at having to answer Docherty's questions and a wish to be helpful for Nena Reeve's sake. He spoke perfect English, so it seemed unlikely that they would learn any more from him than Thornton had.

'I don't know her well,' he said, banging a tap in the hope of inducing it to deliver some water. 'But she's a good doctor, and she stayed when many left. I talked to her sometimes when we worked together, but that was all. Sarajevo is not the sort of place you go out for a drink after work,' he added with a half-smile.

Docherty asked if Raznatovic knew of any closer friends that Nena had had in the hospital. He didn't, but suggested they try a sister on one of the wards, Sister Rodzic.

The young orderly, who had listened to their questions with profound fascination in his dark eyes, escorted them on another trip through the corridors. They found Sister Rodzic almost asleep on her feet, and only too pleased to be given the excuse for a few moments in a chair.

She didn't speak English, which was a good sign. Still, it didn't seem as if she could tell them anything useful either, until, as the two men got up to go, she suddenly remembered something. 'There's a nurse in the emergency department,' she said. 'Dzeilana Begovic. I think Nena used to play squash with her sometimes. There are courts in the basement.'

The orderly took them back down, leading them through a children's ward where row upon row of pitifully thin children watched them pass with doleful eyes.

They found Dzeilana Begovic literally up to her elbows in blood. She was having slightly more luck than Raznatovic with a tap, coaxing a thin trickle of water from the pipes. 'Yes, I know Nena Reeve,' she agreed, 'but I have no time to talk.'

'It's important,' Chris said, realizing how thin the words must sound to someone engaged in work like hers.

She frowned, leaning forward on her arms against the wash-basin. 'OK,' she said after several seconds, and looked at her watch. 'I'm off in an hour. I will meet you in the Princip Café as soon as I can. It's on Boscarsija,' she added, and was gone.

'Where now?' the orderly asked in Serbo-Croat.

'The mortuary, I suppose,' Docherty said reluctantly. He had seen his share of war casualties, of blood and pain, but he still felt almost stunned by what he had seen in this hospital.

'This way,' the orderly announced, after Chris had translated their destination. He led them up two flights of stairs, along a long corridor and across a bridge between two buildings which had lost all of its windows.

They could smell the mortuary before they reached it, and the pungent whiff of plum brandy on the attendant's breath was something of a relief. 'We get twenty a day dead on arrival,' the attendant told them proudly, 'and the ground's too damn hard to bury them, even if you can find someone mad enough to show himself in the cemetery. The Serb snipers like shooting at funeral parties,' he explained.

'We just want to check that a friend of ours isn't here,' Chris said.

'Be my guests.'

'Stay here,' Docherty told Chris. There was no need for both of them to do it.

He walked slowly down the aisles, between the ranks of corpses. In some of the wounds there was movement, and Docherty remembered Razor's lesson about maggots – they only ate dead flesh. Well, that was the only kind of flesh on offer here. If they sealed the doors would the maggots consume it all?

He walked back down the other aisle. Nena Reeve was not there. He supposed it was something to be grateful for, that someone else's friend had died instead of his. He wondered how people would ever recover from this, and for a second he glimpsed an understanding of the scars on his own wife's soul.

'Thank you,' he told the attendant.

The orderly walked them down to the main entrance, and Docherty tried to give him a five-dollar bill, but the youth refused it. Glancing back over his shoulder as they went out through the main doors, Docherty could see the boy staring after them, a look of awe on his face, as if he'd just been privileged to meet visitors from another planet.

Outside on Saraci Street they inhaled the cold mountain air with unusual relish. As Docherty consulted their map there was a sudden loud explosion, followed almost immediately by another. Smoke billowed into the air a couple of streets away to the west.

'This way,' Docherty said, and the two men began to run. At first they thought the streets had magically emptied, but they soon realized their mistake. Every doorway held a group of people, sheltering from the man-made storm. The two SAS men found a niche for themselves, alongside two youngish women.

Minutes went by, and there were no more explosions. 'Just trying to keep us guessing,' Chris heard one of the women say. 'Bastards,' the other said quietly.

People started drifting away from their places of shelter, some shrugging their anxiety away, others casting nervous glances upwards, as if they thought the sight of an incoming shell would give them time to take evasive action. Docherty and Chris continued on past several badly damaged Islamic buildings and found Boscarsija Street.

The Princip Café was halfway down on the left, a European-style coffee house half full of students reading newspapers and smoking cigarettes. The walls were plastered with sepia photographs of days gone by, with pride of place given to a large portrait of Gavrilo Princip, the Bosnian Serb who had assassinated Archduke Franz Ferdinand in June 1914, and set in motion the events that led to World War One.

Docherty wondered where the assassination had actually taken place, and decided he would try to visit the location before they left. It seemed a thoroughly appropriate piece of tourism, he thought. He and Chris ordered two coffees, and found themselves sipping at a bitter, nutty-favoured brew which tasted strangely likeable. Inside the café men and women sat talking and laughing with each other, and at first the handguns laid casually down beside the coffee cups seemed ludicrously out of place. But gradually Docherty became more aware of the restless eyes, the twisting hands and fingers, the hasty drags on cigarettes. Then it was the laughter which seemed unreal, more like a nervous howl than a recognition of humour.

They had been waiting almost two hours when Dzeilana Begovic appeared, looking drawn with fatigue.

'What do you want to know?' she asked, after more coffees had been ordered.

'You know Nena's missing?' Chris asked in Serbo-Croat.

'Yes. But I don't know where she's gone.'

'Do you know any of her friends outside the hospital.'

'Only Hajrija.'

'Who is Hajrija? What is her other name?'

'Her best friend – haven't you spoken to her? Her last name? Let me think. It begins with M. Mejic? No, Mejra, that's it . . .'

Chris told Docherty what he'd learned.

'Ask her where this woman works,' Docherty said.

'She used to be a student at the journalism school,' was Dzeilana's reply. 'But she's in the Army now. One of the anti-sniper units. I saw her in Emergency a few weeks ago, with one of their men who'd been shot.'

'How could we find her?'

'I don't know.'

'You have no idea where she lives?'

Dzeilana searched her memory. 'No,' she said eventually.

'Does Nena have any other good friends at the hospital?' Chris asked.

'I don't think so . . .'

Chris questioned her for another five minutes, but she had no other real leads to give them.

'Hajrija Mejra,' Docherty murmured after she had left, having refused their offer of an escort with a look which clearly said: this is my town, and I know how to deal with it a damn sight better than you do. Still, she had smiled at them through the window as she walked past.

'How do we go about finding an anti-sniper unit?' Chris asked. 'Brindley or Thornton?'

Docherty grimaced. 'Thornton, I'm afraid.'

The MI6 man seemed pleased with himself when Docherty found him in the bar at seven that evening. 'Here's all the journalistic accreditations you'll need,' he said, passing a wad of papers across the table. 'UN, Bosnian Government, Croatian, local Serb. The last one doesn't travel well – it's only good for the immediate area. And I've done a deal with Muftic. Half a dozen MP5s for your team's safe passage through to open country. Delivery on completion. He just wants twenty-four hours' notice.'

'That's great,' Docherty said, his attention momentarily distracted by the fact that a man in tails had just sat down at the piano and begun playing a Chopin waltz. 'I need to get in contact with some people,' he told Thornton. 'Do you know anything about Bosnian Army anti-sniper units?'

'Of course. The *crème de la crème*. The beautiful Strivela . . .' He smiled at the thought. 'The name means "Arrow",' he explained. 'She's become a legend in her own time. Gorgeous textile-design student sees four-year-old child shot down, pleads to be allowed to join the anti-sniper unit, at first gets scorned by the men, then wins them over by her bravery, sharpshooting ability, etc., etc. It would make a great movie. Probably will when this is all over.'

'Is there only one unit?' Docherty asked patiently.

'Two or three, I think.'

'How can I reach them?'

Thornton took a sip of his whisky, trying to decide, Docherty thought, whether to ask the reason for the request. The fear of inviting more work overcame the curiosity.

'One of them's based in the Starigrad Hotel, about a quarter of a mile north of here, near the railway station. The other ones, I don't know, but they'll know at the Starigrad.'

'Thanks,' Docherty said, getting up.

'Dawn would be a good time to pay them a visit,' Thornton suggested.

Docherty walked across to the bar and inspected what was on offer. He chose a bottle of Glenfiddich, paid for it in dollars, and took it back upstairs. All three men were in his and Razor's room.

'You clowns may have forgotten it,' he said, reaching for the grimy glasses above the wash-basin, 'but this is New Year's Eve.' He poured two generous shots into the glasses, and then two more into the ones Chris fetched from the other room. 'Here's to us,' Docherty said, 'and everyone we love back home.'

A thousand miles away, in their Glasgow home, Isabel was sitting on the couch, reliving in her mind's eye a scene from the morning on which he had left. She had come to their bedroom door and seen Marie seated at the dressing-table, her father kneeling on the floor behind her, lovingly running the comb through her dark hair. He had become such a gentle man, and though she knew the gentleness must always have been there inside him, she knew that she and the children had helped to bring it out. Now a part of her was afraid that in some impossible-to-know way it would make him more vulnerable. 'Please send him home to me,' she whispered, pulling her knees up under her chin and clasping herself tightly.

7

Docherty and Chris left the hotel at the first hint of light, leaving behind a mutinous Razor and the Dame. The PC could understand how frustrating it must be sitting in the hotel while he and Chris had all the 'fun', but he could see no justification for risking an extra two lives just to alleviate boredom. 'The moment something comes up which requires your talents, it's all yours,' Docherty told Razor.

'But who's going to charm the lovely Hajrija?' Razor wanted to know. 'You two?' he added disbelievingly.

Docherty grinned to himself as he followed Chris up the side of the wide boulevard. As on the previous morning the clouds were riding low in the valley, and despite the growing glimmer of dawn, visibility was still poor enough to deter any but the most determined sniper.

Halfway up the road a trio of burnt-out Japanese cars reminded him of what a dangerous walk this would be in sunlight. And then, as if to scoff at his presuming to know anything, a brightly lit bus sailed serenely past, crowded with people on their way to work.

'This place is like *Alice in Wonderland*,' Chris said.

'You can say that again.'

They crossed a meeting of five roads and found themselves in the more densely built-up area around the railway station. 'There it is, boss,' Chris said, pointing across the street to where an unlit sign bearing the legend Starigrad Hotel hung from a dingy three-storey building.

'Freeze,' a voice grated behind them. 'Hands on your heads.'

Chris rapidly translated the commands for Docherty. 'We're English,' he shouted. 'We're looking for someone.'

At least two pairs of footsteps came up behind them.

'Who?' another voice asked.

'Her name is Hajrija Mejra,' Chris said.

'Why do you want her?'

'We are looking for a friend of hers, and we think she might be able to help us.'

There was a silence lasting several moments.

'How did you know to look here?' the first voice asked.

'A journalist told us this was where one of the units was based,' Chris replied, deciding that something close to honesty was probably the best policy in this situation.

'Are you journalists?'

'No. We are with the UN.'

'You have papers?' the voice asked, its tone changing from hostility to mere caution.

'Yes.'

'Let me see them,' the man said, walking round to face them. He had long, brown hair surrounding a lean, bewhiskered face, and carried a machine pistol in his left hand. He looked, Docherty thought, like an extra in a spaghetti western.

He examined their papers with interest and then led them into the hotel. The drabness of the outside was mirrored within, where more pale, bearded men sat cleaning rifles on a black plastic sofa. They ignored the new arrivals.

102

The SAS men's interrogator had disappeared, hopefully to find Hajrija Mejra.

A minute passed, and another. He reappeared, leading a tall, slim young woman in camouflage fatigues. She walked gracefully, head held high, her face dominated by dark Latin eyes. Between twenty-five and thirty, Docherty guessed. A woman surrounded by men.

'I'm Hajrija Mejra,' she said without preamble, in English. 'Who are you?'

'My name is Jamie Docherty,' he said. 'This is Chris Martinson.'

'What do you want?' she asked simply.

'I was the best man at John and Nena's wedding,' Docherty said, as if that explained everything. 'I'm looking for Nena.'

Her face broke into a smile, which quickly became a frown. She looked around. 'There is nowhere to talk here,' she said. 'Come, follow me.'

She led them across the lobby, up a single flight of stairs, and into what had probably been a dining-room. Now it contained six mattresses and small piles of personal belongings. A man lay on one of the mattresses, listening to a Walkman. He grinned up at them. 'Beastie Boys,' he said.

A door on the far side led through to a smaller room, which showed signs of having once been an office. A small brown couch stood under the single, shuttered window, across from a desk, upright chair and wall of empty shelves.

'Please, sit down,' Hajrija said, offering them the couch and taking the chair.

Docherty sat down, but Chris decided to stand, rather than squeeze in next to him.

'Now,' Hajrija said. 'I will tell you. You know about the Russians?'

'What Russians?'

'The two journalists.'

'All we know is that she's missing,' Docherty explained. 'We don't know whether she's still in Sarajevo, or if not, where she's gone, or when . . .'

'She is not in Sarajevo. She leave here four days now. With the two Russians and my American journalist friend, Dwight Bailey . . .'

'Where were they going?'

'Nena and Dwight go to Zavik. She hear stories . . . you must know them, yes?'

Docherty nodded.

'She worries about her children. And John, but she never says that. Dwight hopes to get the big story about the Englishman fighting in our war.'

'And he never came back.'

'No, but the Russians, they come back. I go to see them at the Holiday Inn and ask them what happens. They say that they leave Nena and Dwight in Bugojno and not see them again, but they do not speak the truth.'

'How do you know that?'

'I know. They hide the truth. I know. I go to see the American journalist friends of Dwight and they agree. Something is smelly, they say. But they say there is nothing to do.'

Docherty considered what she had told them. Maybe she was wrong, and Nena was already in Zavik. If she was right, Nena could be anywhere, always assuming she was still alive.

'Why are you looking for Nena?' Hajrija asked.

'We are from the same regiment as John Reeve . . .'

'Ha! The famous SAS.'

Docherty smiled. 'Aye. Our political bosses are getting worried about what Reeve is doing in Zavik, for all sorts of reasons. We've been sent to find out what is happening there, and if it turns out that Reeve has lost his senses, I'm supposed to talk him back into them. Or something like that. It seemed a reasonable enough notion when it was first put to me.'

He shrugged. 'We came to Sarajevo partly to talk to people who know something about Zavik, and partly because we hoped Nena was here. I thought she'd be the best person to ask about Reeve's state of mind, and, if she was willing to come with us, the best person to make him see sense.'

Hajrija nodded. 'She understands him, I think. Though she is still very angry with him at the moment. Or she thinks she is angry – it is hard to know.' She smiled to herself. 'But I can tell you about Zavik – I am born there, and grow up there. Nena is my friend since I am a small girl. Our fathers are comrades in the partisans.'

'What we need is a good map of the town, and the area around it. Could you draw one?' Docherty asked.

'Of course. You go soon?'

'I don't know. Do you know where these Russians are staying?'

'At the Holiday Inn.'

'Probably down the corridor from us,' Chris said.

'Maybe we should pay them a visit,' Docherty decided. 'Do they speak English?' he asked Hajrija.

'Some, I think.'

'What are their names?'

'I only know Viktor and Dmitri. But I come with you, yes?' she said, her mouth setting in an obstinate line.

She had probably had a hard time getting accepted as a woman fighter, Docherty thought, but she needn't expect any opposition from him. He had married one. 'If you want,' he said simply.

'I go to speak with my commander,' she said. 'You wait here.'

105

She was only gone a few moments, and returned dressed for the outside world in a long, fur-lined anorak that had seen better days, though it looked warm enough.

The two SAS men were not looking forward to the walk back down the street, but they needn't have worried. Hajrija led them by a slightly longer, more circuitous route which only involved negotiating two open spaces. They sprinted across both without drawing fire.

At the Holiday Inn she tackled the receptionist with the insolent grin, and came away with the Russians' room number. 'He no see them this morning,' she said. 'They are sleeping still, I think. Russians all lazy,' she added conclusively.

'Let's pick up Razor and the Dame first,' Docherty said, as they headed for the stairs. 'With any luck sheer weight of numbers will scare the truth out of them.'

'This "Razor" and "Dame",' she asked, 'they are people?'

'As far as we know,' Chris said.

'They are nicknames,' Docherty said, 'names that friends use.'

'Silly names?'

'You could say that.'

Razor had, appropriately enough, just finished shaving. The Dame was, as usual, deeply engrossed in a trashy novel. Both men looked relieved to be offered a reason to leave their rooms.

'Just follow my lead,' Docherty said, as they climbed yet another flight of steps. The Russians were on the sixth floor, in a room at the back of the hotel.

Docherty knocked on their door and waited, ignoring the questioning voice inside the room. When the door inched open he shoved it backwards, pushing the man who had opened it back into the room. 'Viktor?' he asked.

The other Russian looked up from the edge of the bed, where he was sitting surrounded by what looked like bottles of pills, and said something sharply in his native language. 'Who are you?' he added, switching to English, as the other four crowded in, herding his colleague towards the bed. Razor closed the door and leant on it, feeling like someone out of *The Godfather*.

Then the darker of the Russians recognized Hajrija. 'You again,' he said. 'We have told you everything.'

'You lied to her,' Docherty said. 'We know that you lied,' he bluffed, 'and now we want the truth.' He casually reached under the hem of the Gore-tex jacket and pulled the Browning High Power handgun out from its cross-draw holster.

The eyes of the two Russians on the bed opened wider.

'Who are you?' the darker one asked again.

Docherty ignored the question. 'We want to know where you left the woman and the American,' he said. 'Tell us the truth and you won't get hurt. Keep lying and . . .' He shrugged.

'You cannot do this in the Holiday Inn,' the fairer Russian half-shouted, as if outraged by the damage such activities might do to the hotel chain's international reputation.

'This is Sarajevo,' Docherty said, 'and we can do just about anything we want.'

'We left them in Bugojno,' the dark one said, and they both stared defiantly back at him.

Hajrija had been right, Docherty thought: they were lying. He wondered how far he was prepared to go to force the truth out of them, and realized he didn't know. This war was already tugging at his notion of who he was.

He mentally shook his head, and tried another tack. If they were lying, why were they lying? To cover up misdeeds? He doubted it. To cover up shame? More likely.

'We are only interested in finding the woman,' he said. 'Anything you tell us will remain a secret between us. I promise you that. And I also promise you that if you do not tell us, one of you – you, I think,' he said, looking at the fair one, 'will be thrown out of that window there. And then your friend here will tell us to avoid the same thing happening to him.'

'You will not do this,' the dark one said.

'Lads,' Docherty said, gesturing Chris and the Dame forward, and catching the anxious look on Razor's face as he did so.

The two SAS men grabbed the Russian and pulled him to his feet.

Docherty watched with a stony face. Talk, he silently pleaded with the Russian, please talk. Don't call my bluff.

They started dragging him towards the window.

'OK, OK, I tell you,' the potential victim spluttered. 'They just say leave the woman behind . . .'

Chris and the Dame threw him back on the bed, turning away to conceal their sighs of relief.

'The whole story,' Docherty ordered.

The fair one shot a reproachful glance at his colleague and started recounting what had happened.

'Do you know where he means?' Docherty asked Hajrija when the Russian's account reached the roadblock.

'Yes,' she said, not taking her angry eyes off the two Russians, 'it is thirty kilometres in the west.'

Razor was watching her, and noticed the single tear that rolled down her cheek when she heard of the American's death, a tear that she didn't bother to wipe away, or even seem to notice. Her face remained unchanged, as if the part of her which grieved had no connection with the rest of who she was.

He was struck by how lovely she was, and wondered at how he could feel something like desire at such a moment.

He remembered something his mother had said to him years before, that at heart he was a carer, and how bizarre it was that he'd opted for a life in the military, who only came into contact with needy people at the end of a gun.

The Russian finished his story, and then looked up with the unspoken question in his eyes: which of you would have preferred to die than run away?

Docherty had no answer for him. He put away the Browning and started for the door.

Hajrija had. 'You are cowards,' she said. 'Not for running away, but for lying to me about my friend.' Then she turned and strode from the room.

They reconvened in Docherty and Razor's room.

'Where is she likely to be now?' Docherty asked Hajrija.

The woman took a deep breath. 'There are three, how do you say, possibilities? One, she is dead. Two, the pigs keep her where she is taken. Three, they move her to one of the brothels in the area.' She ran a hand through her hair, anguish on her face.

'These brothels,' Docherty asked gently, 'are there many? Do you know where they are?'

'We know some. There is one in Visograd near border with Serbia, and one in Vogosca, which is only a few kilometres away on other side of mountain. And there are many others. The Serbs think they can make every Muslim woman pregnant with a Serb baby . . .' She shook her head, as if she was trying to shake out the thought of her friend in the beasts' hands.

'Is there any way we can find out if she has been taken to one of these?' Docherty asked, wondering how far he could take such a search. Finding Nena, which had been a means to an end, was becoming an end in itself. And so it should, he told himself, for a friend. But the other three men in the room had never even met her. Could he risk their lives for something that was only marginally relevant to their mission?

'I can try,' Hajrija said. 'There are always new people coming to the city, and someone can know something. But what good will it do? You cannot go and talk to her.'

'If she's only a few miles away we can try,' Razor said.

'We are the famous SAS,' Docherty told her with a wry smile.

An hour later Hajrija, Razor and the Dame were surveying the interior of what had once been the city's skating rink. Docherty had reluctantly accepted the need for the other two men to have their turn in the outside world. And if they needed a translator, they had Hajrija.

They didn't need one to describe this, Razor thought, as he studied the scene in front of him. Where there once would have been throngs of skaters gliding across the ice, and room for thousands more in the surrounding seats, there was now a refugee camp. Across the thawed rink, scattered across the seats and aisles, small groups of people were huddled list-lessly together. The only heat came from a multitude of small butane stoves, and on most of these a saucepan containing water and a few desolate bits of greenery was quietly sim-mering. Most of the adults seemed to be staring into space, and only the younger children seemed unresigned to the passing hours.

'Most of them come from the city,' Hajrija explained. 'The big buildings, yes, and some have shells destroy their homes. We look for people from outside.'

They started working their way methodically through the hall, asking the groups where they came from. A few refused to say, but most seemed happy to tell them – what difference does it make now, their faces seemed to say. There was no one from Zavik, and none of those who had recently arrived from Serb-held territory recognized the photograph of Nena Reeve which Docherty had brought from home.

Until, that is, Hajrija stooped to ask two women who were sitting with their backs to the rink wall, heads bowed as if they were deep in thought. At the sound of Hajrija's voice both raised weary faces. Then, catching sight of Razor and the Dame behind her, they seemed to shrink back into the wall.

'We'll wait for you over there,' Razor said, nodding towards an area of empty seats. He and the Dame went and sat down, both feeling sombre.

'It's like something out of the Bible,' the Dame said.

'Yeah,' Razor agreed. He studied the back of Hajrija's head, which bobbed up and down as she talked to the two women.

The Dame was remembering his sister's wedding reception, and all the food they'd had to throw away. And all the petty problems everyone seemed so full of.

'What do you think of her?' Razor asked.

The Dame followed his gaze, and a slight smile crossed his face. 'Not my type,' he said.

'Not mine either,' Razor said. Or not usually, he thought.

Hajrija's shoulders suddenly slumped, as if she had just had bad news. Where Nena Reeve was concerned, Razor wasn't sure whether no news was good news. They would soon know.

But it was another ten minutes before Hajrija got to her feet, slowly walked across and sat down next to him. She had been crying, Razor instantly realized. 'Are you OK?' he asked, putting a hand on her shoulder.

'No,' she said and, half-falling forward, began sobbing into his chest.

A minute or so later, and almost as abruptly, she raised her head and ran a hand defiantly through her hair. 'I am sorry,' she said.

'Don't be,' Razor said.

She closed her eyes, took a deep breath. 'I have the news,' she said, opening them again. 'Nena is at Vogosca. The women here, they come from there, and they are leaving when Nena comes.'

'When was that?' Razor asked.

'They think three days, but they are not certain.'

'Why did the Serbs let them go?'

Hajrija made a noise which was part sob, part laugh. 'Because they are pregnant six months. You understand? Too late for abortion.'

Back at the Holiday Inn, Docherty listened to what the women had told Hajrija. There were about forty women at Vogosca, most of them between fourteen and twenty-five, though there were a few older women, even a couple in their forties. They were kept at the Partisan Sports Hall, but each night different groups – which always included the youngest and prettiest – were taken to the Sonja Motel, about half a mile away, for the pleasure of the local Serb forces. The women Hajrija talked to had no idea how many guards there were around either the Sports Hall or the motel, but the town was full of Serb soldiers, uniformed and irregulars.

'How long would it take to walk there?' Docherty asked her. 'Avoiding contact with the enemy,' he added.

She thought about it. If they could get through the Serb lines without being seen – a big if, considering they had little knowledge of where the Serb positions were – she reckoned they could reach the town in between four and five hours.

But, she went on, thinking out loud, unless they managed to extract Nena from her imprisonment without raising the alarm, the Serbs would be waiting for them on their way back.

'We wouldn't be coming back,' Docherty said. 'We'd be heading straight for Zavik.'

'But how can we leave all the other women behind?' Hajrija asked.

It was an impossible question. 'I don't know,' Docherty said. 'I don't know if we should be thinking about Vogosca at all.' He looked at the others, then turned back to Hajrija. 'You said "we" just now. Would you come with us as a guide?'

'Of course – she is my best friend. And I will ask others to come – good men. How many is the right number for this? Six? Ten? Twenty?'

'Hold on,' Docherty said, raising a hand. 'She's my friend too, but these three reprobates here have never set eyes on Nena Reeve. I want to know if they think I'm going over the top to suggest this little detour. The moment we start fighting alongside any of the local forces we're going way beyond our instructions. In fact, we'll be halfway to doing what we've been sent out here to persuade John Reeve to stop doing. Not to mention risking our necks in a country we hardly know at all.'

'Seems to me, boss,' Razor said, 'that we have to get to Zavik. Which means we have to get out of this city. No one told us which route we had to take. And I'd rather trust my luck with Hajrija's mob than go along with some deal that MI6 creep has done with someone we've never even met. And if we get to do good works on the way, then that seems like a bonus.'

'You old softie. Chris?'

'Seconded.'

'Dame?'

'Count me in.'

'OK.'

Docherty turned to Hajrija. 'I think around ten would be a good number, so if you can find four or five good men – men who can move quietly and won't start blazing away at rabbits – that would be ideal.'

She grinned at him. 'Would you like to give them audition?' she asked.

'No . . .'

'They may give you one,' she said, on her way to the door. 'I come back this evening,' she added over her shoulder.

8

They had waited, the ten of them, in the fourth-floor room of an abandoned building, taking turns at training the nightscope on the upper floors of the ten-storey high-rises half a mile away. There were six towers in the distant cluster, and from this vantage-point they looked like an array of giant skittles leaning forward, with the three at the rear looking out over the shoulders of the two in the middle, and this pair standing over the lone tower at the front.

There were occasional glimmers of light in the bottom two or three storeys of each building, but none above that. A mixture of stubborn long-term residents, refugees and people with nowhere else to go might risk life close to the ground, but throughout the city the top floors of such buildings were the exclusive preserve of snipers. Hopefully the man or woman they were looking for was still holed up in one of these six buildings, biding his or her time.

This sniper's latest victim had been a fourteen-year-old girl. She had been on her way home with the family bread when the dum-dum bullet had almost blown her in half, the fourth child victim in as many days in the same neighbourhood. Hajrija's unit was out to get him, and it had seemed

115

like an ideal time to see what these Englishmen, the 'foreign super-soldiers', were made of.

The five male members of the unit had all seemed friendly enough, if somewhat sceptical of their guests' alleged prowess. They were all in their twenties or thirties and, like most groups of Bosnians, looked remarkably heterogeneous. Two looked liked stereotypical Muslim guerrillas – Kaltak and the leader, Hadzic, were dark-haired, moustached and with stubbly chins – while Abdulahu was strikingly blond, and might have been taken for a Scandinavian. Began and Lujinovic were both brown-haired and blue-eyed. What all five had in common were an unkempt look, eyes red-rimmed from exhaustion, and the air of having been through the fire of combat and out the other side.

They had been passing round the nightscope for four hours now, and it seemed to Razor, whose shift it was, that the sniper was probably either asleep or gone. He started slowly scanning the top floor of the target building once more, searching for the movement he didn't really expect to find.

A small flare erupted in the corner of the nightscope, and vanished almost as quickly. Razor swung it back to where he thought it had been.

There was nothing. Had he imagined it?

No, there was another flare, fainter, much fainter than the last. The man's dragging on a cigarette, Razor realized. The first, brighter flare had been from a match or a lighter.

'Hajrija,' he said softly, liking the sound of the name. He passed her the nightscope, saying: 'Fourth building from the left, second floor down, second window from the left.'

She trained the scope. 'I cannot see . . . oh yes, there's the bastard.' She flashed Razor a smile in the dark, and got up to tell the others.

Two minutes later they were assembled and ready to go. Hadzic led the way, followed by Docherty. The SAS men were all carrying the silenced Heckler & Koch MP5 sub-machine-guns, as well as Browning High Power 9mm semi-automatic handguns. Each Bosnian carried a Kalashnikov and a Czech machine pistol, and Abdulahu had a Dragunov sniper rifle strapped across his back. All four SAS men were wearing American-designed passive night goggles, or PNGs, while Hadzic sported a cruder Soviet-made counterpart.

They marched down the stairs in single file, the sound of their steps echoing in the empty building. As they emerged into the night a series of tracer bullets arced red across the sky in front of them, bright as flares through the PNGs.

There was snow in the air now, falling desultorily for the moment, but the flakes did not melt on impact. The Bosnian commander led them off at a brisk pace, down a long, sloping street towards the audible waters of the River Miljacka. About fifty yards short of the bank they turned right through an area of abandoned factories, traversing several yards and clambering through old holes in two high wire fences. This was a route the unit had often used before, Docherty realized. Which made him feel nervous.

They emerged on to a small road of houses, several of which had been destroyed by shells. None looked occupied. A scrawny cat suddenly darted across the street, its eyes bright-green orbs in the PNGs, before disappearing into the space between two high-rises. The nearest of the towers was now not much more than three hundred yards distant, looming above the expanse of open ground which sloped upwards from the end of the street. This looked to Docherty as if it had once been used for allotments, but now only weeds and pieces of broken cane poked through the thin coating of snow.

'That is Serb territory,' Hadzic told Docherty, pointing forward. 'I used to live over there,' he added bitterly, 'with my fellow-Serbs.'

Docherty showed his surprise.

'Oh, I am a Serb,' the man said, 'though sometimes I am ashamed to be so.' He waved his hands outward, as if to dismiss the subject. 'And over there is a Serb cemetery,' he said, 'the only way in which is not guarded or mined. The dead make poor sentries,' he added, 'even in Sarajevo.'

They started across the open ground, the snow falling more heavily now. Soon there would be enough to leave noticeable footprints for any Serb patrol, which didn't bode well for their return journey. The cemetery was set on a shallower slope, and surrounded by a low wall. They clambered across it, and advanced in single file up a path between the rows of headstones. A sudden flurry of tracer fire turned everyone's head, and Docherty thought he caught a streak of red reflected in the distant river below.

They reached the far side of the cemetery, where a higher wall offered a good observation point. Beyond the wall there was a wide and empty road, and beyond that the nearest of the high-rises reared up from a concrete sea.

'We can use the front building as cover,' Hadzic said, 'but after that we're in the open.'

'Do they have nightscopes?' Docherty asked.

Hadzic shrugged in the gloom. 'Some of them do. But this bastard has only killed people in daylight.' He turned to make sure everyone was ready, and led them across the dark and empty road to the shelter of the first tower. There they waited another five minutes, scanning the neighbourhood for movement through the PNGs until they were satisfied that they had not been spotted.

Hugging the wall of the building, they moved round to its rear, where a line of rubbish containers offered convenient cover. The doorway of the target high-rise was now only an eighty-yard run away. Unfortunately, as Docherty discovered when he trained his nightscope on the doorway, two men were sitting just inside the glass doors, which looked as though they were chained. He passed the scope to Hadzic, who swore softly under his breath.

'Something's moving out there,' Razor whispered in Docherty's ear, pointing out to the left. Through the scope the mere impression of movement focused into two men pushing bicycles. Each had a rifle slung across his shoulder, and one was carrying what looked like a billy-can. Steam was escaping from around its lid into the freezing air, looking through the PNGs like a cloud of green gas rising up from a witch's cauldron.

The men were obviously expected. The two guards unchained the glass doors to let them in, and an indecipherable murmur of conversation drifted across the snowy ground before the new arrivals, complete with pot, disappeared into the building.

'Food for a sniper,' Hadzic said, his voice brimming with suppressed triumph. 'The bastard's up there all right.' He turned to Docherty, a knowing look on his face. 'But we must still find a way in without waking up the whole neighbourhood. I think maybe this is where you Englishmen show your skills.'

Docherty looked at Hadzic, just to make sure he was serious. He was. He then examined the two soldiers once more through the nightscope. They were little more than faint silhouettes: certainly there was no way Docherty could see their faces.

Which was fitting enough, he thought. If they wanted the Bosnians' help in rescuing Nena, then he had no choice but to order the killing of these two men, whom he knew nothing about, whom he had never seen before. They were enemies of his friends, that was for sure. And they were holding guns in a war zone, which he guessed made them fair game. It might not be the SAS's war, but tonight they seemed to be making a guest appearance.

'*Nema problema*,' he said softly. It was the only Serbo-Croat phrase he'd picked up so far.

The four SAS men squatted together to discuss how. 'There's only one safe approach,' Chris said, 'on our bellies until we're level with the front of the building, then we can move in from the side.'

'They haven't rechained the door,' Razor said, 'but there's no way of knowing how thick the glass is, and I don't reckon our chances of getting them both before they get a shot off. These guys' – he patted the silenced MP5 – 'just don't have the muzzle velocity.'

'We'll have to get them outside,' the Dame said thoughtfully.

'How?' Docherty asked.

'Curiosity,' Chris said, his eyes suddenly lighting up. 'And maybe hunger. Let the Dame and I handle it. OK, boss?'

Docherty hesitated, reluctant to let the two youngest men bear the burden of starting this undeclared war, but from the barely concealed eagerness on their faces it was clear that they had no such doubts. And their youth would come in handy when it came to crawling swiftly and unobserved through a hundred yards of snow. 'OK,' he agreed, and went back to brief Hadzic.

Ten minutes later, Chris and the Dame were standing against the wall of the target building, around the corner from the doorway, having successfully worked their bodies across the snow-covered concrete. Watching through the nightscope,

Docherty saw Chris take something out of his pocket, but couldn't make out what it was. He put it to his lips and the noise of a duck quacking came wafting across on the night air.

The two guards inside the vestibule heard it too. They looked at each other, then out into the darkness. One came to the door and pushed it open.

'Quack, quack,' Chris went.

The man went back for his rifle, said something to his companion, and emerged into the night. He stood still, waiting for directions from his intended prey.

'Quack, quack.'

Chris was moving away from the building now, trying to convince the guard his potential supper was getting away.

It worked. As the Serb reached the corner of the block a hand reached out, and something flashed bright green in Docherty's PNGs. The man's hand flew up, then just as swiftly fell lifeless beside him, and he slumped forward into the snow, making only the slightest 'whumpf' as he did so.

'Quack, quack, quack, quaaaaack!'

The other man emerged from the doorway, and seemed to hesitate. Standing motionless by the wall, virtually invisible to the guard, the Dame tightened his finger on the MP5's trigger, prepared to risk only wounding the man with a silenced shot rather than let him re-enter the building.

'Radic?' the figure said, almost apologetically. 'Where the fuck are you?' he added, stepping forward into the darkness, holding his rifle at the ready.

Wanting to be sure, the Dame waited, the extended stock of the silenced MP5 pressing into his shoulder, until the man was within twenty feet of him. Then, his training instructor's voice sounding in his head, he aligned the sight on the centre of the Serb's head and squeezed the trigger, maintaining the squeeze while firing and for a moment more. The man's head flew back, his feet seemed to almost paw at the snow, and he collapsed awkwardly on to the ground.

The Dame walked swiftly forward, confirmed that the Serb was dead, and signalled to Docherty that the way was clear. Then he and Chris went in through the glass doors, and took up station at the bottom of the stairs. There were no signs of life in the stairwell, no indication that the men who had brought the food were on their way back down.

The rest of the group joined them a few minutes later. 'Who will go up?' one of the Bosnians asked Hadzic.

'All of us. We don't know how many there are up there. It is probably just the three of them, but it could be a unit of ten. But there is no need for our English friends to tire themselves out,' he added. 'They have done their bit.'

'We wouldn't miss the climax,' Docherty said.

All ten started climbing, as silently as they could manage. At each landing they stopped for a few seconds, ears straining in vain for the sound of footsteps coming down. On the eighth floor they waited for longer, while Lujinovic scouted out the lay of the land. He returned five minutes later with the news that all the rooms seemed empty save the one in question. That one, number 96, had its door closed. There was music playing inside, and men talking as well, though he hadn't been able to tell what they were saying.

Hadzic's grin was visible even in the dark.

They climbed the last flight of stairs, and walked down the corridor towards the sound of the music. It was Prince, the Dame realized, singing 'Little Red Corvette'. One of his sisters had the CD back in Sunderland.

Hadzic and Began positioned themselves either side of the apartment door, like cops in an American TV series. 'Need to find a love that's gonna last,' Prince sang, as Kaltak launched his foot against the door, and the chorus was drowned in splintering wood as the three Bosnian soldiers burst into the room.

No gunfire greeted them. By the time Docherty and the other SAS men reached the front room three frightened-looking Serbs were being held at gunpoint. There was a heavy smell of marijuana in the air and several roaches in an ashtray that was overflowing on to the pink carpet. A large tarpaulin had been hung across the window, with a narrow opening for sighting and firing through.

The two men who had brought the food were still wearing their coats, while the sniper seemed to be wearing about five layers of sundry T-shirts and sweatshirts. The top one bore the logo 'Alice in Chains', and featured Lewis Carroll's Alice hanging from a noose. The fourfold Cyrillic C logo – 'Only solidarity will save the Serbs' – was tattooed on his right hand. The pupils in his pale-blue eyes were remarkably dilated.

One of the Bosnians was tearing down the tarpaulin, revealing two broken windows. Then Began and Kaltak suddenly grasped the sniper's hands, pulling them back behind his head, causing some reaction at last in the lifeless eyes. His legs squirmed away from the hands that were trying to grasp them, but only for a moment.

'Shoot me,' he cried out desperately. 'I only shot people. Shoot me.'

The Bosnians ignored him. Grim-mouthed, they carried him to the window, where, since they neglected to impart any energy into the process, it was not so much a matter of throwing the sniper into the night as of simply tipping him out. His wail faded into a faint but sickening sound, like that made by a boot crushing a ripe fruit.

The other two captives both started talking at once. Hadzic stepped forward and shot one in the head, then the other.

Nena Reeve sat in the gymnasium of the Partisan Sports Hall in Vogosca, remembering good things about her estranged husband. Perhaps it was more than a little perverse to choose this place and time to remind herself of his better side, but she enjoyed the ludicrousness of it all. Soon after arriving at Vogosca, Nena had decided that only her sense of the absurd would get her through such an experience. Take it all straight, and she'd go mad.

Mad with outrage, mad with sadness, just mad.

Across the gym two women were softly crying, like violins intertwining a melody.

John, she told herself, think about John. Why had she left him, really? Because he was impossible. And why was that? Because he didn't listen – that was what it all came down to. He loved her, she knew that. He loved looking after her, but always on his own terms. It was the same with the children. He'd be wonderful with them right up to the moment when they had wills and lives of their own, and then he wouldn't know how to deal with them at all.

The recurrent thought that the children might be dead crossed her mind. Though she'd always thought she'd know if anything happened to either of them. And John might be dead too. The thought brought a sinking feeling to her stomach. Whatever their differences, they were not finished as a couple. Not if they both managed to survive this.

One of the women had stopped crying, but the other carried on, making a low, moaning sound, as if she was mourning a death.

Perhaps she was. Almost all of these women and girls would have had men in their lives: husbands, fathers, lovers, brothers.

Where were they now? Some were known to be dead. Some had been put to death in front of their wives and daughters, often after witnessing their violation. Some would be in labour camps, and a few might have escaped, across mountains, across borders to God knew where. Whatever had happened to them, wherever they might be, they were lost to these women.

Talking was not allowed in the gym, but the guards were not always inclined to enforce the rule, and the need for conversation, for contact, often outweighed the risk of one more bruise. Over the last few days Nena had spoken to most of her fellow prisoners, heard the stories of their abduction and humiliation. All of them were Muslims, and all but Nena herself were from villages that had been taken over by Serb irregulars since the summer. Separated from their families, they had been loaded on buses like the one which had brought Nena, and brought here to service the local fighters. The lucky ones were taken out at night to a nearby motel where they were raped by between one and a dozen men, and returned, crying, a few hours later. The younger ones had almost all been virgins, and thought that their chances of ever finding a husband were now over. They didn't believe that any man would believe that they had had no choice.

The unlucky ones were taken out and not returned.

Usually, according to the few women prepared to talk about it, the rapes were speechless affairs: the men were using the women to demonstrate their dominance and as substitutes for masturbation. Nena heard several accounts of men who couldn't get an erection seeking compensation by urinating on the woman.

She herself had not been molested since her arrival, and supposed she owed such tender mercy to her age. Hoping to encourage such neglect she had tied her blonde hair back in

125

a tight bun. And every night when they came and took other women away she felt guilty for her own good fortune.

But not on this night. The man came with his torch, moving along the wall from face to face, picking out one girl who seemed to be always chosen, another who was selected almost as often, and finally, almost hesitantly, bathing Nena's face in the beam.

'A blend of youth and experience,' he muttered to himself, like a football coach.

Nena's first reaction was surprise, her second a sense of emptiness that came close to panic. In the back of the van she told herself she had survived the four men in the mountains, and she could survive as many more here as she had to. This had nothing to do with her. It was like being shot by a total stranger: it might hurt like hell, but if the bullet didn't kill you, then the wound would heal. There was no need for her mind to get involved. Just turn off, she told herself, looking at the blank faces of the two younger women. Just turn off.

And it worked as well as anything could have worked, at least until the sixth and last man came into the motel room. He was no younger than the rest of them – in his early twenties – but he seemed to lack his comrades' macho shell of assurance. Seeing her laid out naked on the bed, fresh bruises growing on her breasts and bloody between the legs, he hesitated before reaching to undo his belt.

'Why are you doing this?' she asked, breaking her own rule of silence, and cursing herself for doing it.

'Your people are doing the same to our women,' he said, but not with any great conviction.

He might well believe it, she thought, but he didn't seem to find it a good enough reason to reply in kind. 'Does that make it right?' she asked him. 'What do you think your mother and sisters would say if they could see you now?'

'I don't have any sisters,' he said. The belt was undone, but he had made no move to drop his trousers.

'You have a mother,' she said.

'I have no choice,' he said, 'I don't *want* to . . .'

'Then don't.'

'We have to,' he whispered fiercely.

'No one will know,' Nena said. 'Think of your future. How will you ever know love if this picture is in the back of your mind?'

He closed his eyes. 'Shut up,' he said. 'Just shut up.'

9

The unit got back to the Hotel Starigrad shortly after dawn, tired but mostly satisfied with the night's work. Hadzic and Docherty agreed that their combined unit would leave for Vogosca an hour before midnight the following day. The next thirty-six hours would need to be spent gathering intelligence on the military situation between Sarajevo and their destination, working out the safest route and possible assault plans, and making sure that they had everything they needed, both for this op and the subsequent mission to Zavik.

Razor and Hajrija were charged with acquiring the necessary maps, and with interviewing refugees who knew anything of the current situation in Zavik or its surrounding region. Chris and the Dame were put to work securing supplies. Extra emergency rations would be needed for the Bosnians, and since the party would have to spend at least one night camping out in the snow, digging tools of some sort would also be necessary. Vogosca might be only four or five miles away as the crow flew, but there was a Serb-held mountain ridge in the way, and no chance of reaching the town, doing a proper recce, launching a rescue and getting back to Sarajevo, all in one night. The unit would have to spend a whole day hidden up in the hills above Vogosca, ready to launch their assault early the following night.

Docherty himself went to see Brindley at the HQ of the British UN contingent. The major's makeshift desk was overflowing with pending paperwork, and he seemed only too pleased for a chance to take a break. He led Docherty across a car park crammed with white UN vehicles and into the steamy Portakabin which did duty as the unit's mess. The coffee was even worse than Docherty expected, despite the generous nip of whisky from Brindley's hip-flask.

'So what have you lot been doing with yourselves?' the major asked.

'Oh, just getting acclimatized,' Docherty replied, wondering exactly how much he should be telling the other man.

'Have you found the woman?'

'We've found out where she is.'

'That's good.'

'Not really. She's in a Serb brothel in Vogosca.'

'Oh Jesus . . .'

'But not for long, we hope. We're going after her . . .'

Brindley's eyes widened. 'Is that . . .' he started to say.

'Is that what we're here for?' Docherty completed for him. 'Probably not. And that's why I'm here.' He paused, ordering his thoughts. 'You know how hard it is for the UN to be involved in a war and still not take sides . . .'

'You're not kidding.'

'Well, I don't think there's any chance of us keeping our hands as clean as you lot have to. If we're going to have any chance of doing what it was we were sent out here to do, then we can't afford to be choosy about accepting help. So our trip to Vogosca is a joint op involving men from a Bosnian Army anti-sniper unit . . .'

'Oh boy,' Brindley said with a smile.

Docherty smiled back. 'I wanted someone to know,' he said, 'and you've been selected. If we don't come back, at least they'll be some facts for the Regimental magazine.'

'And after Vogosca?'

'Then we head for Zavik. Just the four of us and Nena Reeve – assuming we've found her and she's willing to go.'

'And then?'

'Depends what we find when we get there. But I've no intention of making it my permanent address. If we say two days to Vogosca, another three to Zavik and a couple of days there, then add three or four to reach the coast . . . I'd like to be in Split again around two weeks from now.'

Brindley nodded. 'OK,' he said. 'I take it you haven't called Hereford since you got here. I could fix it,' he added. 'It might take a while, but there are ways . . .'

'We could call them ourselves,' Docherty said, 'but they know nothing about the situation here, and there's nothing they can do to help us. Anyway,' he added with a grin, 'they don't like to be bothered.'

Brindley wished them good luck as he and Docherty parted again in the vehicle park.

The PC made his way back to the Holiday Inn, wondering what Barney Davies would make of the decisions he was taking. There was no way he could officially agree to joint action with local forces, Docherty knew, so there was no point in telling him. The fact that HQ had made no attempt to reach them since their arrival in Sarajevo seemed to suggest that the CO had an equally firm grip on reality.

The combined unit's jump-off point was a house on the road to the mountain village of Nahorevo, just inside the city's northern boundary. The ten soldiers arrived in dribs and drabs throughout the day, so as not to tip off any watchers in the hills that an operation was imminent. They sat around drinking dandelion tea, smoking cigarettes, rechecking their equipment and reading one of several hundred copies of *Mad* magazine. The house's owner, a member of the anti-sniper unit who had been killed a few weeks earlier, had obviously been a subscriber.

They left the house at 2200 hours, following the Nahorevo road uphill for a few hundred yards before turning on to a path which ran diagonally up across the slope of the hillside. The ridge-line was still some five hundred yards above them. And up there were some of the Serbian guns that continued to pound what remained of Sarajevo.

There would also be some sort of encircling ring of troops, deployed to prevent goods and men from either entering or leaving the besieged city, but opinions in Sarajevo had differed as to how thick or thin this cordon would be. Hadzic was gloomy on the subject, and feared that they might not find a way through without alerting the enemy. His main hope lay in the silenced MP5s.

Docherty was of a different opinion. His experience told him that such cordons often existed mostly in the mind, and only needed minimal manning to reinforce a false impression of impregnability. Historically, in most sieges, both sides tended to become stuck in the roles of besieger and besieged, to the point where neither felt able to cross the line between them. The Serbs up above, Docherty thought, would not be expecting anyone to try what they were trying. Consequently, they would not be expending scarce manpower on blocking off such a possibility.

Or so he hoped. At least they were on the move, and in the right direction, away from Sarajevo. The evening before, in the bar of the Holiday Inn, he had got into a conversation with a fellow Scot, a journalist with one of the quality Sundays. The man, who looked around forty-five, had been pleasantly drunk, and most of the conversation had been small talk, ranging from Celtic's fall from grace to the fate of the SNP. But like a cloud-laden sky parting briefly for sunshine, their good-natured banter had parted to reveal a glimpse of something close to despair. 'Say what you like,' the journalist had said, 'but what has died in this city is the belief that humans have learnt anything from this century.'

Docherty had wanted to disagree, but could think of no reasons for doing so. Nor could he now, climbing the dark path behind Hadzic and Hajrija. And with that realization came another question: if the world was up shit creek without a paddle, then what the hell was he risking his life for?

A friend? He liked Reeve, but he had no sense of obligation to the man that would outweigh his responsibility to Isabel and the children.

Regimental duty? He'd done his share of duty. The SAS wasn't a religion, and Barney Davies wasn't the high priest. No, he'd accepted this job almost out of habit. And out of curiosity. And now he was beginning to wonder whether it had been the stupidest decision of his life.

A couple of Bosnians behind him, Chris was not wondering about what might have been. He rarely did. In this life, he reckoned, you opened doors and then dealt with what was on the other side. And he loved opening them. Of course there was always the chance that he'd not beat the clock on this one, the way Eddie and Anderson had failed to beat it in Colombia, but that was the chance you had to take. Knowing that was the one thing he and Eddie had had in common, but it was so basic that it had made up for all the things they had disagreed on.

Eddie had loved moments like this, walking across a mountain in almost total darkness, senses attuned to every little noise, utterly alive in every respect. Chris did too. He loved the idea that every place they got to was somewhere he'd never been before. Even Sarajevo had been incredible. Downright tragic, certainly, but fascinating. It hadn't looked like he'd imagined it, but then places never did.

So far, his only regrets regarding this op concerned the paucity of birds he'd been able to see. There had been the usual Mediterranean coastal types around Split, but since their arrival in Sarajevo he'd hardly seen any at all. That said a lot for their intelligence, Chris thought. What birds in their right minds would want to winter in a city pounded by sustained artillery fire? Once they started out for Zavik, though, who knew what he might see. Maybe a booted eagle, or even a Bonelli's eagle.

Twenty yards ahead, Razor was thinking about a different kind of bird. Hajrija was walking in front of him, and, even bundled up like a bear, she was offering the Londoner more than enough food for his fantasies. No amount of clothing or equipment could quite disguise the grace of her walk, and the long wisps of hair escaping from the woollen balaclava seemed unbelievably feminine. Physically she reminded him a little of Maureen, which wasn't the best of omens.

Maureen had been a couple of years older than Hajrija, a divorced occupational therapist who lived in Hereford with her six-year-old son. She and Razor had met in a pub, and taken to each other immediately. They didn't have any interests in common, but the sex was great and he got on well with the kid. Within three months they had arranged to get married. He couldn't remember ever having been happier. Even his mother's announcement that she was remarrying, and going off to Australia for at least three years, had failed to really upset him.

Then the roof had fallen in. Maureen had called off the wedding a month before it was due to take place, and announced that, for the boy's sake, she was going back to his father. Razor had thought the man lived in London, but it turned out he had been back in Hereford for several months.

Six weeks later his mother, to whom he'd always been close, left for Australia. For the first time in his life Razor had felt uncertain of his own judgement, rootless, and mortal.

That had been two years ago, and things had not changed much in the intervening period. He had acquired a sense of time passing, and a tendency to reflect on the past, which he had never had before. His job in the Training Wing was interesting, even challenging, but seemed to be leading to nothing more than a distant retirement. And there was always the chance that the loss of his happy-go-lucky self had made him less of a soldier.

So far, though, he could detect no signs that it had. And maybe it was the presence of Docherty, but he could feel all the old excitement at setting out on an operation. Hell, he thought, Docherty got the woman in Argentina – this time it's my turn. Hajrija, you're going to be mine, he silently told her back, and at that moment, right on cue, she turned her head to give him a quick smile. Razor thought how much he'd like to see her in sunshine, with considerably fewer articles of clothing on.

Towards the rear of the column, the Dame was enjoying the darkness. He had always preferred the city to the country, and the sort of vast terrain which made many people gasp with wonder tended to make him feel uneasy. It was all too much, somehow. It was so fucking eternal. He preferred not to have to look at it.

He thought about the other night, and the two men he'd killed beneath the high-rise. They'd never know who won this war, never know anything more. They wouldn't catch Bosnia's first appearance on the fucking Eurovision Song Contest. Life had just ended for them – just like that.

But where were they now? It was hard to imagine those men in heaven, but he doubted if they'd done anything bad enough to warrant endless torture by fire.

At the Holiday Inn he'd come across a guide to Yugoslavia, and one of the bits he'd read had been about a place called Medugorje, which was fifty miles or so to the south. In 1981 six of the village's teenagers had seen an apparition of the Virgin Mary, and the place had suddenly become a place of pilgrimage, not to mention a tourist attraction.

The Dame found it hard to believe that anyone had seen such an apparition, but then it wasn't much easier believing six kids from a dirt-poor village had conspired to make the whole story up. And apparently the apparitions had continued on a regular basis, usually on Mondays and Fridays.

He had laughed when he read that – it seemed such bullshit – but then it occurred to him that if there were no apparitions then why had none of the thousands of witnesses not blown the whistle on it all, and exposed the whole business as a fucking rip-off? Maybe it wasn't, or maybe they were all so desperate to see something that they had. Maybe that's what faith was, a sort of desperation. He could understand that. He knew death wasn't the end of everything – it couldn't be, or what was the point? There had to be a reckoning, a time to answer for what you had done. There had to be somewhere to wipe yourself clean.

* * *

The path led them slowly but remorselessly upwards, winding around the rims of indentations in the mountainside, passing through large stands of conifers that clung to the slopes. The snow was deeper the higher they went, and the trail they left became ever more marked. The good news was that no one else had used this path lately, or at least not since the last snowfall two days before.

About two hours into their journey Docherty and Hadzic agreed to call a halt. The column was now only some two hundred feet from the ridge top, and the two leaders thought it prudent to send scouts forward to check the situation. Chris and Kaltak were dispatched.

They returned less than fifteen minutes later with some welcome intelligence. Each Serb gun emplacement was obviously allowed a fire for cooking and warmth just behind the ridge top, out of sight of the city below. The two nearest fires were a couple of hundred yards to the west of their path, and rather more than that to the east. They should have no trouble slipping through.

The march resumed, with Chris out in front as lead scout. Five minutes later they crested the rise, and crossed what was obviously a much-used path along the top of the ridge. To left and right each of them could see the line of fires stretching into the distance. Ahead and below there was nothing but the ghostly light of the snow-covered slope falling away into darkness.

They worked their way down it, using what looked like a snowed-over stream bed to make their tracks less obvious, and eventually reached the trees. This side of the mountain, unlike the slopes looking down on Sarajevo, was mostly covered in forest, and their hopes were high that they could find a suitable observation point overlooking Vogosca without leaving the shelter of the trees.

It was almost two in the morning when they gave up any idea of finding such a spot. There just wasn't enough light. They were relying on the Bosnians' knowledge rather than eyesight to gauge where the small town was, and there was no way of judging what would be visible when daylight came. It was decided to make camp deep in the trees, and send a two-man team forward to set up an observation post just before dawn.

For the moment the SAS men concentrated on seeking out and enlarging spaces beneath the lower branches of conifers where snow had built up around them, leaving a pocket of air beneath. The Bosnians watched with initial astonishment as the SAS men dug into the snow beneath the spreading branches on the lee side of the trees, and unearthed these living quarters.

'Where do you learn this?' Hajrija asked Razor. 'There is no snow in England.'

'Norway,' he said. 'NATO exercises.'

An hour later two buttressed snow caves had been excavated, complete with removable doors. There were too many tracks for the hides to be completely secure, but they would only have to remain undetected for the nine or so hours of daylight.

There remained the matter of choosing the recce team. Hadzic picked Hajrija, and Docherty named Razor, repressing a smile as he did so. 'You know what we want,' he told his second in command. 'We'll see you at dusk. Be good,' he added in parting.

She seemed pleased it was him, Razor thought, as they made their way back down through the trees, aiming for the spot which their map had suggested would be the most promising. Walking down, he couldn't remember ever being in a darker place: the thick cloud cover, and lack of any moon, gave the snow nothing to reflect. The PNGs enabled them to avoid trees, but not much more, and he had to rely on all his dead-reckoning skills. Even then, once they had reached what he gauged was the correct location, there was nothing much to reinforce the supposition. Ahead of them the trees gave way to nothing but blackness; they could be staring out across the hollow which held Vogosca, or just gazing into an empty meadow. Only the dawn would tell.

It was still something between ten and twenty minutes away, so Razor suggested they use the time digging out the blocks of frozen snow they would need to cover the observation trench. Hajrija agreed and, following his example, used the spade to cut out blocks of snow half a yard square and roughly four inches thick. Once they had a dozen, Razor called a halt.

The faintest glimmer of light was now showing in the eastern sky, and they both squatted on their haunches watching the blackness in front of them slowly fade into browns, and the scene gradually swim into focus. It was the town, and their positioning was almost perfect. Razor selected a sight some ten yards to their left and just inside the line of trees, which gave them an overall view of not only the town but both major access roads, and started furiously digging their trench.

Hajrija carried the thick snow tiles across and then helped with the digging. Ten minutes later, with sweat running freely inside their winter clothing, they had a trench about eight feet long and about two and a half feet wide. Razor used the spade to cut a ledge along both sides just below the upper lip, and between them they balanced pairs of snow tiles against one another to make their roof. Once this was completed they used loose snow from the drifts beneath the trees to smooth out the angular outline of the structure and disguise its rectangular shape. Only twenty minutes had passed since first light when they took up residence, lying closely together side by side, their eyes looking out through the observation slit. The trench was designed to sleep one while the other observed, but both were too interested in what lay below for either to countenance sleep.

It was growing light enough now to pick out details. To their left the main road from Sarajevo swung down from the mountain, entering the town between two lines of dwellings and emerging on the far side before swiftly dropping from sight into an unseen valley. What looked like no more than a dirt track wound up into the hills to the east, beyond the river which ran down through the heart of the town.

This had no more than two hundred buildings, sprinkled apparently at random around the church in the centre. The only signs of socialist-style construction were two four-storey blocks on the western edge of town and a long, single-storey building on the road leading in down the mountain. That had to be the Sonja Motel, where the women were taken.

The Partisan Sports Hall was easy to spot: a large, almost windowless structure on the far side of the town, rising out of a complex between the river and the main road. So far, Razor thought, reality matched their map.

He started a more thorough search with the binoculars, and found his first signs of life, a soldier walking from the motel towards one of the last houses on the road out of town. There seemed to be a few upright chairs under a tree by the road. By day it had to be a checkpoint, he decided.

He trained the binoculars on the road beyond the town and found another, but the dirt track leading up to the right didn't warrant one. The Serbs here weren't expecting any trouble, he thought.

'More men,' Hajrija whispered by his side.

Razor followed the direction of her East German binoculars, down to where several men were gathering in the forecourt of the Sonja Motel. The faint sound of an engine starting drifted up from the town, and a dormobile emerged into view from under the overhang of the motel's roof. The men all climbed aboard, and the vehicle moved out on to the road, turning left, away from the centre of the town. At the checkpoint it slowed, and then accelerated away up the hill.

'The day-shift gunners,' Razor thought out loud. He turned to Hajrija, whose face was uncomfortably close. Her breath smelt faintly of the plum brandy they had all imbibed after completing the shelters back in the forest. Her eyes were dull with fatigue. 'Do you want to sleep first?' he asked.

'OK,' she said. 'But you wake me, yes?'

Razor looked at his watch. 'It will get dark around five,' he said. 'I'll wake you at twelve-thirty.'

'OK,' she said again, yawning.

He listened to her struggle her way into the sleeping bag in the confined space, and then her breathing in the silence. Just when he thought she was asleep, the words 'you make a nice house' emerged faintly from out of the darkness.

'Thank you,' he said, and smiled to himself.

The next four and a half hours he spent struggling to stay awake and alert, and noting down everything that happened in the town below, adding detail to their map. The amount of military traffic did not seem high, and seemed to consist mostly of men returning from or setting out for the Serb positions in the hills above Sarajevo. The exceptions were one lorryload of uniformed troops which arrived from somewhere down the valley and two cars carrying irregulars sporting broad-brimmed hats. Chetniks, Razor guessed, though one brief glimpse was not enough to ascertain whether they wore long beards. Like everyone else they disappeared into the Sonja Motel, which seemed to function as the local barracks.

As for the Partisan Sports Hall, there seemed to be no movement around it at all, and Razor began to wonder whether the women held there had been moved in the week since their informants' release. He could see no sign of guards, but with any luck they were positioned out of sight on the far side of the building. The thought of this mission coming up empty left a sinking feeling in his stomach.

At twelve-thirty he shook Hajrija by the ankle, eliciting what sounded suspiciously like a Serbo-Croat curse. She emerged by his side a few minutes later, bleary-eyed and beautiful.

He concentrated on the job in hand, listing what he'd seen, and sharing his anxiety about the Sports Hall. Her face fell as he did so, but the disappointment quickly turned to anger, and another indecipherable curse escaped her lips as she ran a hand angrily through her tangled hair.

'One day you must tell me what that means,' Razor said.

She shook her head, ran the other hand through her hair, and managed a faint smile. 'One day maybe,' she said, 'now you go sleep.'

'Gladly,' Razor said. He backed himself into the trench, found his way into the sleeping bag, and the next thing he knew she was tugging on his ankle and whispering that it was five o'clock. He lay there for a few seconds wondering where the light had gone and why he still felt dog-tired.

Hajrija's smile of welcome made him feel better for an instant, until he made out the change in the outside world. For the first time since their arrival in Sarajevo the sky was clearing, and the last vestiges of a visible sun were glowing orange above the mountains to the west. 'Shit,' he said succinctly.

'It works for us too,' she said.

'We have PNGs,' Razor said.

'The women have not. I think it will be more easy to get them away from there if there is some light.'

She had a point. 'Maybe you're right,' Razor agreed, 'but we don't even know if they are still here.'

'Some are,' she said. 'Take a look.'

He trained the binoculars on the area of the Sports Hall. A couple of streetlights burned in the growing gloom, and just to one side of them was . . . a bus.

'Ten women come in the bus,' Hajrija said. 'About one hour now. Two men come out and take them into the hall.'

'I suppose that's good news,' Razor said, aware of the irony.

'Yes,' she said, in the same tone.

'OK,' he said. 'What are we going to recommend here? What's the best way in and the best way out?'

'The river to go in,' she said. 'But out – we not know how many people or where we are going. If there are thirty women . . .'

'We shall need the bus,' Razor completed the thought. 'And I agree, the river is the best way in. How much longer do you think we should stay here?'

'Thirty minutes? It will be all dark then.'

'Yeah, and it'll give us a chance to see what the lighting's like down there,' said Razor.

They both watched in silence for the next few minutes.

'Are you married?' she asked out of the blue.

'No,' he said. 'Are you?'

'No.'

He asked a question that he'd been wanting to ask.

'That American journalist Bailey – was he . . . more than a friend?'

'You mean, do I sleep with him?' she asked, surprised.

'No. I mean, were you in love with him?'

'Oh no. But I like him. He is – was,' she corrected herself, 'a nice man. He has innocence, you know?'

So had she slept with him, Razor wondered. He decided to change the subject. 'How did you get involved?' he asked. 'In the Army, I mean?'

'Oh, that is an easy story,' she said. 'I am a student of journalism, and it seems more important to fight for what I believe than write it down.'

'Makes sense.'

'My boyfriend does not think so,' she said. 'He say it is crazy for a woman to do this. I tell him "fuck off".'

'Does he?' Razor asked.

She laughed. 'Who knows? I do not see for a long time. But why I am in the unit, I see children killed in the street and I know I want to fight the bastards who do this.'

'And the men accepted you?'

She grimaced. 'Not at the beginning. But slowly, yes, they realize I can run as good and walk as good and shoot better than any of them. They learn now, I think. I am just one of the boys,' she added sarcastically.

Razor found it hard to take that thought seriously. She might be a better soldier than any of them, but a boy she certainly wasn't.

Half a mile away Docherty was wondering why it seemed harder to sleep when you were older and needed it more. Or at least felt like you did. All these young men he was surrounded by hardly seemed in need of energy conservation, yet they slept like bairns.

He hoped it hadn't been a mistake sending Razor with the woman. The two of them obviously had something brewing

143

between them, whether they knew it or not, and on the spur of the moment he had felt like indulging a romantic whim. Hardly appropriate in retrospect, and he hoped the two of them had risen above the temptation he had wilfully put their way.

Still, something inside him remained unrepentant. The business of being a soldier often involved putting the business of being a human on hold, but there was something about this war and this op, he felt, which made it more important than usual to keep the two men inside him tied closely together. If the human being slowed the soldier down then that was too bad.

As his favourite strategist Liddell Hart had been fond of pointing out, it didn't help to win the war if you lost the peace. And whether Liddell Hart had meant it or not, Docherty had always believed that any decent peace must include the soldier's peace of mind.

It was almost fully dark now, or at least as dark as it was going to get. Docherty pulled himself out through the narrow exit and on to the snow-covered forest floor. As he expected, the patch of sky visible between the treetops showed stars – the sky had cleared during the day. To his left the light seemed brighter, and he walked across to find a clearing no more than thirty yards from their hides. Here a few clouds could be seen scudding across the sky, and the stars seemed as bright as they ever did at this altitude. Deneb flickered like a roseate diamond to the north, and directly above the clearing the Milky Way looked like a jewelled scarf that someone had tossed into the air.

Docherty stood there, revelling in the wonder of it all, thinking about Isabel. She'd be giving the kids their tea about now, and then maybe watching the news while they shared a bath. He could see the kids in his mind's eye, splashing water over each other.

He walked back down to the hides, grateful that they wouldn't be needing the wretched PNGs that night. If the clouds were anything to go by there'd be a stiff breeze blowing out there in the open, and that would make it that much easier to reach their target undetected. In Docherty's experience it was more often sound than sight which gave an attacker away.

He arrived back just in time to see two shadowy figures approaching through the trees, and froze in his tracks, just in case. Then the taller of the two extended an arm into the air – the prearranged signal. It was Razor and Hajrija.

Docherty gestured Razor into the British hide, and invited Hajrija to bring Hadzic over for a conference. Chris and the Dame were awake now and, once the two Bosnians had arrived, all six of them huddled together in the confined space, the much-amended map spread out on the small portion of hardened snow left between them. Three torches illuminated the map and faces surrounding it.

Razor and Hajrija took turns describing what they had discovered, and then he outlined their recommended method of approach.

'OK,' Docherty said. 'But let's start at the end and work backwards – it usually helps. Assuming we get the women out of the hall, where do we take them from there?' He looked at Hadzic. 'Where will they want to go?'

The Bosnian shrugged, or at least tried to. It was difficult when both shoulders were pinned by the person on either side. 'Somewhere safe,' he said drily. 'The way I see it,' he went on, 'there are two choices. The first is to take them back the way we have come, across the mountain to Sarajevo.

But there are reasons not to do this. We don't know what condition the women will be in, and whether they can make such a journey. We do know that Sarajevo is not the best place to be in the world right now. So . . . I think the second choice is better. We take the bus and we drive it west. We will have to go through the Serb lines somewhere between here and Ilijas, but it will be three, four in the morning, and if they are not expecting us our chances will be good . . .'

'That's the main thing,' Docherty agreed. 'We have to get out of Vogosca without raising the alarm. Now, remember what the women told Razor and Hajrija about the lorry coming for them each evening around nine o'clock . . .'

10

'Remember to bring the blonde again – the young one with the big tits,' his friend shouted.

'I'll bring what *I* fancy,' Dragan Kovacevic retorted, climbing unsteadily into the cab and almost knocking his hat from his head.

'Christ, I'd better come with you,' his friend said. 'The state you're in you'll probably come back with our grandmothers.'

He climbed into the driver's seat and belched loudly. 'That's fucking good beer,' he said. 'Hey, I need a piss,' he suddenly realized.

He climbed back down again and sent a long, steaming stream on to the slush-covered gravel, sighing loudly as he did so.

'Come on, get a move on,' Kovacevic said.

'What's your hurry?' his friend wanted to know, lifting himself back into the cab. 'The whores aren't going anywhere, are they?' He untucked his shirt and used it to dry his beard. 'It'll freeze solid,' he explained, as the other man eyed him with amusement.

'I'm going to cut mine off,' Kovacevic said, turning the key in the ignition and letting in the clutch. 'You see those boys from Goradze? They all had lice crawling in theirs. It was disgusting.' He pulled the lorry out of the motel forecourt and on to the road.

'What do you expect from that bunch? They've been living around fucking Muslims too long.'

The lorry rumbled down the road into the dark town, its headlights picking out the twin tracks of clear tarmac in the snow-covered road.

'I wonder what they all do at night,' Kovacevic observed, his eyes roaming across the darkened houses. 'No electricity for TV, no light for doing anything.'

'They probably do what we do,' his friend said with a grunt. 'Except they don't get such a varied menu,' he added, laughing. 'You know, it's gonna be hard to get used to having only one woman after all this is over,' he went on.

'You . . .' Kovacevic started to say. A light was shining on the road ahead, waving to and fro. On the bridge, it looked like. He braked, wondering what sort of idiot could have ordered a checkpoint in the middle of the town.

There only seemed to be one man though, his face shadowed by the hood on his anorak. He didn't appear to be carrying a gun, which was strange for a checkpoint . . . 'What the fuck?' Kovacevic muttered, pulling the lorry to a halt some ten yards from the waving flashlight.

It was the last sound he ever made. The windows imploded as the silenced MP5s raked the cab with automatic fire, leaving an echo of breaking glass to compete with the swift-flowing river in disturbing the night's silence.

Docherty pulled open the cab door and yanked the bearded soldier out and down on to the icy road. Chris was doing the same on the other side. Razor and the Dame had taken up covering positions twenty yards back up the road. No lights had gone on in the nearby houses, but that was presumably because of a lack of electricity. No one had appeared out of the darkness, which suggested either bad hearing or a healthy instinct for survival.

The PC pointed the flashlight up-river, switched it on and off three times, and then set about heaving the Chetnik's body across to the stone parapet. Once there, he lifted the shoulders up across it, and then used the legs to lever the corpse out into space. The splash was barely audible above the sound of the rushing water.

The corpse from Chris's side followed it in, and Docherty had a momentary memory of a Saint book he had read as a youth, in which the hero had come across three men attacking one on a bridge like this in Innsbruck. Being the Saint, he had tipped all three into the icy river, only to belatedly discover that they were policemen trying to arrest a thief. *The Saint's Getaway*. He had loved those books.

The six Bosnians loomed out of the dark like wraiths and, without a word, clambered into the back of the lorry. They were good soldiers, Docherty thought. He checked that all the bergens had survived the journey and then, signalling Razor and the Dame to join the Bosnians, picked up the Chetnik's hat and climbed into the cab. Chris was already waiting at the wheel, broad-brimmed hat perched on his head, looking like anyone's idea of a drunken Australian.

There was a rap on the cab's back window. 'Let's go,' Docherty said. 'And keep it slow.'

Chris obliged, rumbling past the town's neat orthodox church, several official-looking buildings and an apparently empty supermarket with one large window boarded up. The road curved round to the left, and the Sports Hall came into view. 'Where the fuck do they park it?' Chris asked.

'Up against the side of the building,' Docherty suggested. There wasn't anywhere else he could see. 'But where's the fucking bus?' This lorry would do at a pinch, but it would be a real pinch, with thirty women to transport.

'It's round the back,' Chris said, braking to a halt. 'Razor's new girlfriend saw them move it there.'

'OK,' Docherty said. He took a deep breath. 'Ready?'

'Yeah.'

'Then let's do it.'

They got down from the cab, adjusted the hats as low across their faces as they could without looking ridiculous, and started walking towards the corner of the building. The entrance was reportedly on the other side, and they were just rounding the corner when they heard the sound of a door opening. Someone had heard the lorry arrive.

A man stepped out through the doorway, silhouetted against the dim light that came from within. Docherty didn't break step.

'*Zdravo*,' the man said.

'*Dobro vecer*,' Chris replied.

They were only a few yards apart.

'*Koja* . . .' the man began, suddenly suspicious.

Docherty flicked open his coat and fired the MP5 from the hip. The man was still falling as Docherty sped in through the doorway. Another two men, both well into middle age, were looking up from a makeshift table, cards spread around the yellow-glowing kerosene lamp. Docherty's finger tightened on the trigger, and then slowly unclenched itself.

'Tell them we're looking for a reason to kill them,' he said to Chris. 'And find out where the women are.' He went back outside, dragged the body off into the shadows, and went to get the rest of the unit.

'The bus is round the corner,' he told the Dame, who sped off to check it out.

Lujinovic and Began started off up the road back into town; their job was to provide early warning of any enemy approach. Docherty didn't know how long the Serbs at the motel would be prepared to wait for their victims, but, always assuming they weren't all too drunk to notice, he doubted if their patience would survive much more than half an hour.

Abdulahu and Kaltak had clambered into the lorry's cab, with Razor still seated in the back. They were waiting to move off in the opposite direction, towards the checkpoint a few hundred yards further down the road, once any problems in the Sports Hall had been dealt with.

Docherty led Hajrija and Hadzic round to the entrance. Chris was standing over the two Serbs, whom he'd ordered to lie flat on the wooden floor. 'In there,' he said, pointing towards double doors further down the corridor. 'This is the key,' he added, handing it to Docherty.

'Look after those two,' the PC said. He passed the key to Hadzic, and followed the Bosnian commander and Hajrija down the corridor. The Bosnian turned the key and opened the door on to the darkened gym. Almost immediately, it seemed, several invisible people started to cry.

Hadzic stepped in with his torch, and the wailing seemed to go up a notch in volume.

Sensing what was happening, Docherty went back outside to collect the kerosene lamp.

'We are here to rescue you,' Hadzic said in his native tongue, but there was no response, save perhaps a muting of the keening sound.

'Nena, are you there?' Hajrija asked, as Docherty came back in with the marginally brighter light.

A sound like a sob escaped from Nena Reeve's lips. 'Hajrija?' she said disbelievingly.

Hajrija shone the torch into her own face. 'It's me. We've come to take everyone away from here.'

Nena pushed herself up from the wall and walked across towards her friend, slowly, as if she feared speed would dissolve the mirage. 'I can't believe it,' she said, and at that moment she caught sight of Docherty.

'This is a dream,' she said.

'Hello, Nena,' Docherty said.

Outside in the parking area the Dame had found the bus. The destination board read Foca, but presumably hadn't been changed since the war began. The tyres were worn, but snow-chains had been fitted, which more than made up for them. There was no key in the ignition. He set about trying to hot-wire the vehicle, and a few minutes later was rewarded with the motor chugging noisily into life.

Rather too noisily. The Dame checked the petrol gauge, which seemed to be hovering between a quarter and half full, before switching off the engine and stepping back down to the ground. He had a momentary glimpse of a slim moon rising above the mountain before someone started shouting at him in a language he didn't understand.

A uniformed soldier was hurrying towards him, doing up his coat as he came. The Dame just stood there, his mind utterly calm, as the man strode up. He watched the soldier's face turn from anger to surprise, the body try and fail to apply the brakes, and then he stepped in like a ballet dancer, taking the man around the neck with one arm and pulling back, his knife slicing across the outstretched throat.

The warm blood gushed across his hand, and he let the body gently down to the ground, before doing a panoramic turn, eyes searching the shadows for other sources of trouble.

Satisfied there was none, he pulled the body into the deeper shadow beneath the wall, and washed his hand in a small drift of snow. Looking down he had the momentary illusion that the stain was spreading towards him.

Once Chris had given him the green light, Kaltak had started the lorry down the road in the direction of the checkpoint. They quickly left the town behind, the road running between the river and a narrow meadow, aiming for the mouth of the valley. The lone house ahead was unlit, but beside it a yellow light seemed to be hanging in the air just above the road. As they approached, it revealed itself as a kerosene lamp perched on a wooden bench that was placed across the highway.

The lorry slowed, one of the Bosnians rapped his knuckles on the cab's window, and Razor leapt nimbly down to the road. He reached the bank of the river as the lorry came to a halt in front of the makeshift barricade. There was still no sign of life inside the house.

The Bosnians climbed down, and stood there waiting for a moment, wondering what to do. Razor asked himself whether they could trust the men inside the house – always assuming there were some – not to wake up at any time in the next hour. The answer, unfortunately, was no.

Kaltak and Abdulahu had obviously reached the same conclusion. The latter climbed on to the lorry's running board, reached in, and blew a short blast on the horn. It sounded almost deafening to Razor, but he doubted whether the noise had travelled across town to the motel.

For a moment it even seemed that the blast had failed to rouse anyone inside the house, but the door abruptly banged open, and a man stepped out, complaining loudly. He had no hat on, but the bottom half of his face was darkened by a beard.

Razor waited until he was out in the open before knocking him down with a three-shot burst of the silenced MP5.

At the same moment another man came through the doorway, also apparently complaining, and ducked back instantly the moment he saw his comrade fall. Razor cursed and went after him, his mind registering the fleeting impression that the man had not been carrying a weapon. He leapt on to the low veranda and rushed in through the doorway, moving swiftly to his right to avoid being silhouetted against the lighter outside world.

He could hear the man running up the stairs, and restrained himself from instant pursuit. Five seconds, ten, and his eyes were more accustomed to the dark. As he made out the foot of the staircase there were raised voices upstairs, the thud of moving feet on the ceiling above.

Razor went for the stairs, climbing as swiftly and silently as he could manage. There was a faint light above, and three voices talking excitedly to each other, or maybe only two. The thought flashed through his mind that this was a modern house, probably someone's pride and joy before the present war. He wondered what had happened to the people who had lived there.

Thumping footsteps gave the Chetnik away before his silhouette appeared at the head of the stairs. The SAS man fired an automatic burst, and the man crashed backwards, his weapon bouncing past Razor down the stairs. By the time it reached the bottom another man had died. Driven into view by his own inertia, unable to find a target for his AK47, this Serb managed one shot before the MP5 took out his left eye and threw him back on to his partner's body.

The sound of the shot echoed round the house, dying into silence. Razor advanced carefully, ears straining for evidence that there was a third man present. He heard a whimpering noise, which was suddenly drowned out by the entrance of his two Bosnian allies downstairs.

Razor put an eye cautiously round the top of the stairs. The dim light was coming from the room across the landing. There were two other doors, both shut.

He edged his way on all fours towards the half-open door, and gently pushed it wide. The whimpering grew louder, but no shots came out.

'You OK, English?' one of the Bosnians whispered loudly from the bottom of the stairs.

'*Da*,' Razor whispered back, using half of his Serbo-Croat vocabulary and wishing the other half was the Serbo-Croat for 'wait'. The whimpering inside stopped suddenly, and for a few seconds the only sounds to break the silence were his own breathing. Then the shot resounded inside the room, followed in quick succession by the sharp thunk of something metallic hitting the floor and the duller thump of something bigger.

Razor put his eye to the crack between door and frame, and then wearily climbed to his feet. 'It's OK,' he shouted down the stairs. Inside the room he found the youth – he was about fifteen, he guessed – crumpled on the floor. The half of his head that was missing was still sliding down the wall. The AK47 which had put it there was lying in the middle of the room.

Why? Razor asked himself. He turned his head away, and found the answer. A young girl, younger even than the boy, was stretched out on the bed, naked but for the sock stuffed in her mouth and the scarf that had been tightly looped around her neck.

He yanked out the sock and undid the scarf, almost in a frenzy, wanting to cry out something, anything.

He reached for the carotid artery and felt life. The pulse was slight, but she was breathing, almost desperately now, and even in this light there was a blueness around the lips. There seemed no external injuries other than a redness around the vagina, and Razor turned her over, moving one arm and leg outwards to stop her lying flat. The breathing seemed to ease.

Abdulahu appeared in the doorway, took in the scene and said something in his own language, something that seemed to encompass surprise, resignation and sadness. He squatted down next to Razor by the bed. 'She OK?' he asked.

As if in answer the girl's eyes opened, slowly at first and then wide with fright.

Abdulahu said something and took her hand. She began shivering.

Razor looked round for her clothes, but could see none. He yanked the curtain violently down from the window and covered her with that, as her eyes seemed to search his face for understanding. He turned away and stood there for a minute, thinking furiously. 'You stay with her,' he told the Bosnian, miming to reinforce the other man's understanding.

Abdulahu nodded. 'She come with us,' he said.

Razor walked out of the room to where the two dead men lay twisted together and, on an impulse too strong to resist, lashed out a foot at the nearest body. Then, for the first time that he could remember in his adult life, he simply lost control, kicking and kicking the lifeless heads until Abdulahu gently pulled him away.

Back at the Sports Hall Docherty had heard the two shots in the distance, but only faintly. He very much doubted that they would have been heard across the town, and his only real worry was that Razor or one of the Bosnians had been on the receiving end.

In the gymnasium Hajrija and Nena were going from woman to woman, explaining what was happening and where they were being taken. It seemed to be taking a lot of time, but Docherty knew that he couldn't hurry the process. As Nena had explained it, slowly and carefully, as if she was talking to a child: 'These women were put into buses once, given no explanation, and they ended up here – there's no way we can just put them in another bus without telling them why and where they're going.'

The reactions of the women, as far as he could see, varied greatly. Some seemed in shock, blanked out, like mental patients. Others seemed simply tired, as if they'd been awake for days on end. Many were distraught, and found it hard to understand what they were being told. A few were simply brimming with anger.

Nena's state of mind was hard to gauge. Docherty remembered her mostly as a woman with a ready laugh, a bundle of enthusiasms, and a defiant willingness to wear her emotions on her sleeve. He had always known she must have a more introverted side – he knew from Reeve how seriously she took being a doctor – but it had rarely surfaced in her social persona. The woman he could now see across the dimly lit gymnasium bore little obvious relation to the woman he had known.

What sort of people could do something like this? Docherty asked himself. He had always drawn a blank when trying to imagine the thought-processes of the men who had run the German concentration camps, and he found this no easier to understand. Anyone could turn off their humanity in the heat of the moment, or in longer periods of extreme stress, but this was something else. Evil was the word that came to mind, but it was only a word – it didn't explain anything.

'Boss,' Chris said at his shoulder, 'Kaltak just came back. The checkpoint's ours, but they found a girl there – in bad shape. She'll have to come with us.'

157

Docherty cupped his hands round his nose. 'Right,' he said, and took the hands away. 'How's the Dame doing?'

'He and Hadzic just got back with some petrol they stole from somewhere. They're putting it into the bus now. They've taken out the lights. How are we doing here?'

'Almost ready, I think.' He looked at his watch. 'The Serbs must be wondering where their women are.'

'It's a pity we don't have time to raze that motel to the ground,' Chris said.

'Yeah.'

'Who's going in what, boss?'

'I want Razor driving the bus – he's the maddest driver I've ever come across, and the best. And I think the Dame should ride shotgun. You and I'll go in the lorry with the Bosnian laddies. And I guess we'll have to take the two prisoners with us.' He rubbed his eyes. 'We'll all have to take the bus up to the checkpoint.'

Hajrija was walking towards them. 'We are ready,' she said, almost accusingly. 'Are you?'

'Yes,' Docherty said.

She turned and said something to the women, who all started getting to their feet. Hajrija said something more, and they started filing out, silently. The few eyes turned towards the men were full of anger.

Nena brought up the rear. She had shaken her golden mane loose, and looked more like the woman Docherty remembered.

'What are you doing here, Jamie?' she asked. 'Is this just a coincidence, you being here?'

'No,' he said. 'We were looking for you, and we heard you were in this place . . .'

'Why were you looking for me?'

'Because of Reeve.'

She looked at him. She had always liked Docherty, liked his Argentinian wife, and the way the two of them were together. She had even thought about them the other day when she was reflecting on her marriage to Reeve. Isabel and Jamie seemed to have got the crucial balance in any relationship, the one between independence and interdependence, about right. It was a hard thing to do. Certainly, she and Reeve had never managed it.

She looked around at the empty gymnasium. 'Aren't SAS wives allowed to leave their husbands any more?' she murmured, her voice a blend of weariness, flippancy and bitterness.

The bus was ticking over in the Sports Hall car park. The women filed on board, filling up all but four of the forty-two seats. The two prisoners were ordered to sit in the aisle and did so, holding their hands over their heads as if expecting a rain of blows from the women they had guarded. Kaltak took the wheel, leaving the other seven members of the combined unit to squeeze into the seats and space at the front.

As they turned on to the main road Docherty cast a glance back up it, in the direction of the river and the motel. There was no sign of anyone coming to look for the lorry that hadn't returned. Maybe they were in luck: maybe the Serbs were all too drunk or full of pills to care.

They arrived at the checkpoint not much more than a minute later. Razor carried the heavily wrapped girl on board, and passed her on to Hajrija. Nena started to examine her.

'Are you all right?' Docherty asked him.

A bleak smile crossed Razor's face. 'I'm fine,' he said.

He didn't look it, Docherty thought. 'You're driving the bus,' he said.

'Right,' Razor said, his eyes taking in the sea of barely lit women's faces stretching to the back of the vehicle.

'Just follow the lorry,' Docherty said. 'If you think you need a rest, give the Dame a turn.' He gave Razor a few more instructions and then got down off the bus and walked across towards the lorry, noticing that someone had placed a bench and lighted lamp across the road behind them. Presumably it had been that way when they arrived.

He climbed up into the cab where Hadzic and Begam were already waiting, and nodded his assent to the question on the driver's face. The lorry moved away, and in the wing mirror Docherty could pick out the dark shape of the unlit bus following some thirty yards behind. No one seeing the lorry's headlights coming towards them would realize there was a second vehicle behind, not until it was halfway past them.

They were heading down a winding valley now, the road crossing and recrossing the rushing river in the confined space. Somewhere at the bottom of this road they would come across the dividing line between Serb-controlled and Muslim-controlled territories. There would be checkpoints of some sort, maybe physical barriers, maybe even an exchange of fire in progress. And the sooner they reached it the less chance there was that they'd be expected, Docherty thought. He was still surprised that no one had come looking for the lorry in Vogosca. Maybe by now they had, and found nothing but the empty Sports Hall.

He wondered whether they should stop and cut the telephone wires than ran along by the road, and decided it would be a waste of time – even if the telephones were operational, which he doubted, the Serbs would be using radio.

He also wondered whether he should have put the bus in front. If they had to force their way through an unexpected roadblock the rear vehicle would be the most vulnerable. But then again, if they ran into enemy forces . . .

Docherty told himself to stop worrying about decisions already taken.

Behind him Razor was guiding the bus by the lights of the lorry ahead. It was a favourite trick of Docherty's to disguise two vehicles as one, and they'd done something similar in Argentina, during their escape from the town where he and Ben had been taken prisoner. That had been a night to remember, all right. Like this one. Only this was different. Argentina had been hairy enough, but it had felt like an adventure. This one was getting to him. Had got to him.

He glanced across to where the Dame was sitting, MP5 cradled in his lap, face showing no emotion. Razor wondered what was going on beneath the surface. Maybe nothing. Maybe the Dame was like he himself had been for so many years, someone who just let it happen, and dealt with it when it did. He had rather liked being that way.

His mother had used to say to him: 'One day you'll get it.' 'Get what?' he had wanted to know. 'When you get it, you'll know,' she had said, affectionately enough. He knew he had driven her nuts, but she'd kind of liked him that way too.

He took a quick look in the rear-view mirror. Hajrija was sitting with the young girl on her lap, looking out of the window beside her.

He realized he knew no more about her than he had about any of the other women he'd really fancied, and that for once it seemed to matter.

The crescent moon was high in the sky now, shedding its thin light across a wider valley below. Lorry and bus passed under a bridge carrying the railway from Sarajevo, which turned in a long curve to run alongside the highway. On the left the river from Vogosca cascaded over stones to join with the broader Miljacka. On all sides a sharp line separated the darker mountains from the star-strewn sky.

A road sign appeared in the lorry's headlights.

'Which way?' Began asked his commander, slowing down.

'Both roads go to Visoko,' Hadzic told Docherty. 'The main highway will be easier to drive, but we'll probably meet less opposition on the smaller road.'

'Let's get off the highway,' Docherty suggested. He looked at his watch. It was a few minutes past three.

'OK,' Hadzic agreed. He said something in his own language to the driver, who took the right fork.

The road ran across a small stretch of bare meadow and tunnelled into a mostly coniferous forest. Curves and dips followed for several miles, and then the road suddenly emerged above a small town, before descending through a succession of hairpin bends to cross the railway tracks and pass the sign that told them they were entering Semizovac.

The town seemed dead at first, full of houses either burnt out or blown up, but as the lorry swung into the main square a line of military vehicles loomed into view, parked along one side. In the opposite corner a brazier was burning, with a soldier standing either side of it, their illuminated faces turned towards the unexpected arrivals.

Lorry and bus left them staring, burrowing down the town's main street.

'I think this is the last Serb-held town,' Hadzic said in English, than added something in Serbo-Croat to Began, who responded by pressing his foot down on the accelerator. In the wing mirror Docherty could see the bus regaining its normal distance as Razor responded.

They seemed to be almost out of the town now, the road dipping suddenly to pass under the railway tracks. As they emerged from the underpass a tank loomed into view, its gun pointed down at the ground. Two armoured cars were parked beside it, also apparently devoid of occupants.

On the tracks to their right a line of covered wagons seemed to be serving as barracks. And a couple of hundred yards further down the road two burnt-out cars had been used to narrow the channel for traffic. There were no lights, but moving figures were visible in the gloom. The pinpoint of a torch suddenly appeared, like a star that had slipped out of the sky.

Docherty leant out of the window with his torch in hand and drew a circle in the air. In the bus behind Razor shouted 'Now!' at Hajrija, who passed on the news in Serbo-Croat. Most of the women responded, either burrowing down on to the floor in front of their seats or simply bending their heads down between their knees.

Razor by this time had brought the bus up level with the lorry, the two vehicles accelerating side by side towards the barrier. Seventy yards, sixty . . . and still no flashes erupted from the Serb guns. Fifty, forty . . . and the lorry slowed abruptly, letting the bus into the lead.

A single bullet passed through a window behind him, and he could hear a machine-gun open up, but they were ripping through the gap between the two hulks, metal screaming on metal down both flanks of the bus.

In the lorry behind, Docherty was firing the MP5 blind, his head jammed as far back behind the window as he could get it. He had a flashing glimpse of trees and running men, a concrete building, another armoured car. Beside him Hadzic had his head down beneath the dashboard, but Began was sitting up behind the wheel, with only the look in his eyes to show that he wasn't going on a picnic. As the bus ahead blasted its way through the gap he let out a great whoop, which seemed made up in equal parts of triumph and terror.

His steering wasn't quite as good as Razor's, the lorry missing the car on the right by a foot or so and giving the one on the left an enormous side-swipe. It rocked on the road like a train on bad tracks, righted itself and sped on after the bus, the soldiers in the back still firing at the vanishing checkpoint.

Another half a mile down the road they found the Bosnian Army waiting to welcome them to what, by Bosnian stand-ards, was safe territory.

One woman in the bus had been cut by flying glass, but everyone else was unharmed.

11

The bureaucratic niceties involved in relocating from one tribal patch to another took up the best part of an hour. The local Bosnian commander was not used to British soldiers emerging, guns blazing, from Serb-held territory, and he wanted more explanation than Docherty was prepared to give him. He spent several minutes reading the small print on their UN accreditation and then simply looked at Docherty, eyebrows raised, as if to say: 'Surely you don't take me for that big a fool?'

At this point Hadzic took over, speaking so fast in his own tongue that Chris had trouble understanding what he was saying. At the end of it all the local commander looked at them, sighed, and handed back their papers with slight distaste. 'OK, you can go,' he said.

'What the hell did Hadzic tell him?' Docherty asked Chris.

'I told him you were mercenaries,' the Bosnian said from behind them. 'And that we didn't have so much help from the outside world that we could afford to antagonise men who had just saved thirty of our women from a Serb brothel.'

Docherty laughed. 'I take it the man didn't approve.'

'He was regular army,' Hadzic said. 'Probably had a good career going for him before someone pulled the rug out from under his feet.'

They walked back out to the vehicles, which were empty.

'Where are they all?' Docherty asked Razor and the Dame.

'Having a bath,' was the reply. 'And then some food, I think. I could do with some breakfast myself,' the Londoner added.

They found the unit's mess by following their noses. A train of coaches stood on the nearby railway line, and on the ground in front of them several men were busy keeping up the fire under two large tureens of bean soup. These had presumably been ordered for the women, but there seemed plenty to go round, and the SAS men were soon offered bowls of the thick, steaming liquid. The unit's commander might not like mercenaries, but his cooks seemed more impressed by results than motivation.

There was bread too, stale perhaps, but delicious once softened by the soup. And each man was given a cup of a hot, bitter-sweet liquid that they later discovered was supposed to be coffee.

The women arrived in dribs and drabs, and were taken up into one of the coaches for their food. They all looked cleaner, and some looked readier to take on the world. Many, though, still seemed in shock. Nena was one of the stronger-looking. She glanced across to where Docherty was sipping coffee, perched on a pile of sacking, and a faint smile seemed to cross her lips, as if she was remembering another world.

Light was showing over the rim of the eastern hills as they resumed their journey. It was a bitterly cold morning, but the local commander had donated a recent shipment of blankets

for the women on the unheated bus, and the clear sky prom-
ised a sunny day.

It was only about ten miles to Visoko as the crow flew,
but the actual driving distance was more than twice that, and
the drivers could rarely exceed twenty miles an hour on the
winding snow-covered road. The sun had cleared the high
horizon before they arrived, transforming the countryside for
the four SAS men, who had only seen Bosnia under cloud.

Docherty was reminded of the area around Aviemore in
Scotland, until the road wound down into Visoko, where a
tall minaret broke the surface of the steep-roofed houses.

The cobbled town square would have looked untouched
by the war, if the local military hadn't picked the old town
hall for its HQ. They drew up their vehicles in front of it,
and sat waiting while Hadzic went in to report their arrival.

Their last hosts had radioed ahead, and they were expected,
though no mention seemed to have been made of British
soldiers, mercenary or otherwise. A group of local women
were waiting to take care of those rescued from Vogosca and
their rescuers had been allocated a billet a hundred yards or
so from the square.

It was an old stone house, probably dating back to the
days of the Austro-Hungarian Empire. 'Serbs lived here,'
Hadzic told Docherty as they pushed in through the unlocked
front door, but he either didn't know or wouldn't say what
had happened to them. Wherever the Serbs were now, most
of their possessions remained in the house. There was a three-
month-old newspaper lying open on the table in the kitchen.

Hajrija having stayed with the women, the Bosnian men
divided up the two bedrooms between them, leaving the SAS
men to spread out their sleeping bags in the single large
downstairs room. All were exhausted, but sleep only came

easily for Chris. Each of the others found it hard to turn off their minds, which seemed intent on running endless replays of the previous night's events.

As usual Docherty woke first, at around two o'clock in the afternoon, and went in search of a toilet. He found it occupied by a whistling Bosnian, and ducked out through the back door in search of an alternative. There he found Hadzic cheerfully pissing against a wall, eyes squinting against the smoke from the upturned cigarette between his lips.

It was a beautiful day, the sun high in a clear blue sky. Through a gap in the houses ahead, mountains rose across the valley, while above the roofs behind, a rock face rose almost sheer behind the town, before flattening out into pine-covered slopes. Some two hundred yards away the top of the minaret peeked up through the red-tiled roofs, looking strangely like a fairground rocket.

'You come with me now to see the General?' Hadzic asked.

Docherty reluctantly turned his eyes away from the illusion of a world at peace. 'Aye,' he said.

The two men walked down the narrow street to the square. There were not many people on the street, but there were some, and Docherty was thinking that at least some semblance of normal life had been preserved here. The distant sound of a hundred children shouting and screaming suggested a school that was actually functioning.

They found the 'General' in a small room at the back of the old town hall. He turned out to be a handsome young Bosnian named Ajanovic, with wavy, light-brown hair and green eyes. He was about twenty-eight, Docherty guessed, and had probably been a lieutenant in the old Yugoslav Army. He also, it turned out, spoke excellent English, thanks to a six-month stint in Australia, where half his family had long since emigrated. Docherty took to him instantly, without knowing why, and was

168

pleased to see his judgement vindicated over the course of their discussion.

Hadzic went through the events of the last few days: the discovery that Nena Reeve was in Vogosca, the idea for a joint rescue mission, the rescue itself. Ajanovic listened with great interest, offered them both cigarettes, and said that all of that was very clear, but what were Docherty and Co. doing in Sarajevo in the first place? Who were they?

Hadzic looked at Docherty, who decided to take a chance. They were regular British soldiers, he said, and they'd been sent in to make contact with another British soldier, who was apparently leading a small army of irregulars in the vicinity of Zavik . . .

'That's in Serb-held territory,' Ajanovic said in his Australian-accented English.

'We know.'

Ajanovic looked at him and smiled boyishly. 'What a war,' he said.

The UN wanted Reeve out, Docherty went on, and the Croats, and the Serbs. 'And your Government,' he added diplomatically. 'Everyone is saying he makes it harder to get peace. And even if that only means he's everyone's excuse for continuing to fight, then it makes sense to get him out.'

'Are you supposed to kill him?' Ajanovic asked. 'Terminate him with extreme prejudice,' he enunciated carefully. 'I saw that movie in Sydney. And this war is even crazier,' he added.

'He's a friend,' Docherty said simply.

'Ah, I'm sorry. And his name is Reeve, so the woman is his wife, yes?'

'Yes.'

Ajanovic leaned back in his chair. 'OK,' he said. 'So what do you want from me?'

'Three things, if possible. Some sort of authorization to get us as far as Serb territory, any intelligence you have of the military situation between here and Zavik, and a vehicle of some kind. The lorry we came in if nothing else. Something a bit smaller and more manoeuvrable would be better.'

'You know the British UN base is only forty kilometres up the road, in Vitez?'

'Aye. I was hoping to avoid involving them. You see . . .'

'Yes, yes, I can see why,' Ajanovic agreed. 'But you do understand – what you are doing may be for the good of us all, but it will not help my people in this war, and it is hard to justify giving away anything which we might find useful.'

'Aye, I understand that,' Docherty said. He would have felt the same in the other man's shoes.

'But,' Ajanovic continued, 'there is a – what do you call it? – a transit van? A van with seats . . .'

'Sounds ideal . . .'

'Ah, there is a catch. It needs repair, and we have lost our mechanic. If you have one . . .'

'We do.'

'OK, it is of no use to us. As for the other things, I could write you a hundred authorizations but it would do you no good. I am the commander for this district, and that is all. I have no superiors giving me orders from outside, and no one outside will accept my orders. This is a war in compartments, yes? The next commander you meet may have you shot as spies.' He shrugged and laughed. 'I like the English,' he said, 'and I am grateful on my country's behalf that you risked your lives for our women. So any information we have is yours. But your own people in Vitez will know more.

'I will give you one more piece of advice. If you could travel as something other than what you are, it will be safer

170

for you. Perhaps your people at Vitez can arrange for you to have journalists' papers.'

Docherty thanked him, but didn't see any reason to admit that they already had the various such accreditations Thornton had provided in Sarajevo. He asked where the van was, hoping it had the right number of wheels and an engine. Ajanovic left the room and came back a couple of minutes later with another uniformed soldier, this one barely out of his teens. 'Kemal will show your man the vehicle,' he said. 'And our intelligence man works in the office next to this. His name is Akim, and I have told him to give you any information he has that you need. Do you know when you will be leaving?'

'That depends on how good our mechanic is,' Docherty said.

'Then we may meet again.' Ajanovic offered his hand, and the two men shook. Docherty found himself hoping this man survived the war.

He and Hadzic walked back to the house, where the SAS men were in various stages of getting up. Razor was shaving, Chris rummaging through his bergen for a clean shirt, the Dame leaned up against the wall in his sleeping bag reading a Yugoslav tourist guide. 'Having a nice holiday, are we?' Docherty asked them.

'This is a good B&B, boss,' Razor observed, 'except for the lack of beds and breakfast.'

'Been out sightseeing, boss?' Chris asked.

Docherty told them whom he'd seen. 'There's a boy out here wants to show you a van,' he told the Dame. 'It needs some sort of fixing, but I don't know what. See what can you do.'

'What if it's unfixable?' Razor asked.

Docherty shrugged. 'I guess we fight Hadzic and his boys for the lorry.'

'I'm game,' Razor said.

171

'Yeah, we all know which of his boys you'd like to wrestle,' Chris murmured.

As if on cue, Hajrija appeared in the doorway. 'Nena is here,' she told Docherty. 'She likes to talk to you.'

'Where is she?'

'In the street.'

Docherty walked out to find her leaning up against a wall, apparently lost in thought. She was wearing the jeans they had found her in, and a large coat that she had since acquired from somewhere. She looked cold.

'Are you coming in?' Docherty asked her.

'No, I . . . I feel like being outside in the sunshine. You know? Can we walk?'

'Aye, of course. Just let me tell the lads.' He slipped back inside, told Chris and Razor to see Akim at the town hall and to start planning their route to Zavik, and re-emerged half a minute later to find her in the same position.

'This way?' he suggested, looking down the road towards the far-off mountains.

They started walking, in silence at first.

'I don't know what to say,' he eventually said. 'I can only try and imagine what you've been through . . . If you want to talk, I can listen.'

'No,' she said, 'I don't want to talk about it. Not to a man. Not even to a good man,' she added, looking straight ahead. 'Tell me what you are doing here. Hajrija told me some of it, but I'm not sure she understands it completely.'

Docherty went through it all again, from the moment he had picked up the phone and heard Barney Davies talking to him over the bar chatter at Glasgow Central.

She listened in silence, and when he had finished turned to him with a perplexed look in her eyes. 'Why did you say yes, Jamie?' she wanted to know. 'Why did Isabel let you?'

'I've been asking myself the same thing,' he said. 'And you know, there's a voice in my head saying "OK, you've been a soldier, you think you know what war is, well, you don't. You've just been through soldiers' games like Oman and the Falklands and Northern Ireland. You've been through wars where the rules get bent. But this is a war where there aren't any rules." I . . .' He stopped himself. 'I'm sorry,' he said, 'this is not what you need to hear right now.'

'I asked the question,' she said.

They walked on for another minute in silence. 'You'll take me to Zavik, then?' she asked eventually.

'Only if you're sure you want to go.'

'I've already tried to get there once.'

He wondered how long the bitterness would colour her voice, and thought about Isabel. It had left his wife's voice, but it had only been an outward manifestation of the breakages within. Her experience with the torturers would always be part of her.

They were almost at the edge of town. A hundred yards ahead their road joined the main highway, which bypassed Visoko to the north. Beyond that the wall of mountains bathed in the afternoon sunshine.

She shivered. 'When do we go?' she asked.

'I don't know yet,' he said. 'Maybe tomorrow.'

'That's an Everly Brothers song,' she said. 'You remember Reeve loves the Everly Brothers?'

'Aye.' The idiot had sung 'All I Have to Do Is Dream' at his own wedding reception. Badly.

'I can't believe he is doing what they say he is doing,' she said.

'No,' Docherty agreed, but a small doubt nestled in the back of his mind. He knew what this war had done to him in a week. God only knew what it had done to Reeve in nine months.

After Docherty's departure with Nena, Razor had found Hajrija standing in the garden, staring into space.

'Hajrija,' he said gently, but she jumped anyway.

'Don't do that,' she said angrily when she saw it was him.

'I'm sorry,' he said. 'I . . .' He shrugged helplessly.

'No, I am sorry,' she said. She pushed her hair back from her eyes in characteristic fashion. 'It is hard,' she said, looking at him almost pleadingly. 'To be with those girls after what happens to them. It breaks my heart. But I must be strong and make them happy, you understand.'

'Yeah,' he said, 'you need a hug.' He opened his arms. 'Come on,' he said, and she burrowed her head into his neck, her tears running down inside his shirt.

'Thank you,' she said after a couple of minutes, pulling herself gently away.

'You're welcome,' he said, thinking he'd never seen anyone he desired half as much. 'How's the girl?' he asked. 'The one from the house . . .'

Hajrija looked distraught again. 'Satka,' she said. 'Her name is Satka, and I forget to tell you – she wants to see you, "the man with the funny face" she calls you. She is . . . She is OK, I think. You know? Not sick.'

'I know,' he said. Not sick perhaps, but who knew what damage had been done?

'We can go now,' she said. 'It is not far. Two streets.'

'Why not.'

They went back into the house, where Chris was looking through his bird book as he waited for Razor.

'I've got a house call to make,' Razor told him. 'I'll meet you at the town hall in half an hour or so.'

Chris nodded and smiled knowingly at him.

'I'm the man with the funny face,' Razor shouted back over his shoulder as they left the house.

He didn't feel like cracking any jokes once they reached the place where the women had been temporarily housed. It was a large building next to the mosque, part of a religious school, as Hajrija explained. Satka, along with nine of the youngest women, was sharing one of five mattresses in an upstairs room. When Razor arrived all the other women seemed to shrink away from him, despite the presence of Hajrija.

Satka, though, was pleased to see him, and they talked for ten minutes, with Hajrija translating. She was twelve, she said, and when the men had come to their village her mother had told her to hide. When she came out everyone was gone, and all the houses were burning. She'd stayed there for a couple of days but no one had come back, so she'd tried walking to the next village, and that was when the other men had found her and made her go with them in their car.

Up to this point she told the story almost as if entranced by her own narrative flow, but then abruptly she shifted into the third person, using 'she' instead of 'I' when describing how the men had hurt her and kept her tied up, right up to the moment when 'she' was rescued by the 'man with the funny face'.

Razor listened, smiling encouragingly, and thought that never before had he fully understood the meaning of the phrase 'a broken heart'. He wanted to promise this girl that he'd take her to England that very minute, but he knew that he couldn't, and even that he shouldn't.

At least she was alive, he thought, as they walked back down to the building's courtyard. It wasn't enough.

'I think you need hug now,' Hajrija told him, putting her arms round his neck.

After parting with Nena, Docherty let his feet carry him round the town. The temptation to stay another day was strong, and he could think of at least one good reason to reinforce the desire. They needed the rest, not so much from the physical stresses as from the emotional ones. None of them had ever been through anything like this before. So far the other three had performed in exemplary fashion, but the danger signs were there: a lack of jokes from Razor, almost total silence from the Dame, and his own tendency to let things slide, as evidenced by the fact that he was strolling round the town rather than doing what needed to be done.

Only Chris seemed to be taking it all in his stride. Maybe they should all take up bird-watching.

His stomach suddenly let loose an angry rumble, reminding him that he hadn't eaten for about twelve hours. And presumably neither had the others. 'The least you can do is keep your men fed, Docherty,' he told himself out loud.

Back at their lodging he found Begar brewing tea in the kitchen. 'Where is Hadzic?' Docherty asked. Began grinned and shrugged.

Docherty came out of the kitchen door just as Hajrija came in through the front. 'Ah, I need you,' she said.

'I'm spoken for, love.'

She looked at him questioningly.

'What do you need me for?' he asked.

'I need to say I come to Zavik with you, yes?'

Docherty's first thought was that this would make Razor's day. His second was that it was impossibly irregular, his third that she'd be invaluable in several ways. His fourth, he expressed out loud: 'Will Hadzic let you go?'

'Of course,' she said. 'I join up, I leave. No problems.'

'It doesn't quite work like that in the British Army,' he said, 'but if it's OK with your boss, we'd love to have you along.'

She beamed at him. 'That is good.'

'You can ask Hadzic now,' Docherty said, catching sight of the Bosnian commander through the open door, crossing the street towards them.

Hadzic seemed rather less sanguine about letting her go than Hajrija had led Docherty to believe, but after an animated five-minute exchange of opinions in Serbo-Croat he reluctantly acquiesced in the transfer of her loyalties.

'Is there any spare food in this town?' Docherty asked them both when they'd finished, 'or do we have to break open some emergency rations?'

'There is a place for soup,' Hadzic said. 'You want to go there now?'

'When the others get back.'

Began called out something from the kitchen.

'Who wants tea?' Hadzic translated.

'We do,' Razor said from the doorway. Chris was behind him.

'I come back later,' Hajrija told them all, on her way out.

The three SAS men took their mugs of tea and sat round a large-scale map of the region, discussing the information Razor and Chris had managed to glean at the town hall. Zavik was about ninety twisting miles away, all but twenty-five of them through allegedly safe territory. The first thirty miles to Vitez followed the main highway, and the road south from there to Gornji Vakuf was apparently being kept open by the British UN contingent of Cheshires as a supply route for themselves.

'With any luck we can hijack a Mars Bar shipment,' Chris said.

Razor grunted. 'The problems begin after that,' he said. 'The road to Bugojno is supposedly open, but the town's probably being bombarded by the Serbs. Beyond there, we have a very dicey road to Kupres, which the Serbs seem to hold, and then the last stretch to Zavik, right up in the mountains. I'm beginning to think even an HAHO drop would be preferable to driving this fucker.'

'We don't seem to have that option,' Chris said.

'That's why he's suggesting it,' Docherty said with a grin. 'By the way, Hajrija is coming along for the ride.'

Chris shook his head. 'The man's in danger of charisma overload,' he said.

Razor, though, didn't seem so pleased. 'Why, boss?' he asked seriously.

'She asked. I guess she wants to keep Nena company.'

'And why did you agree?'

'I think it will be good for Nena to have another woman along. And Hajrija knows Zavik. We already know she's a good soldier.'

'OK, boss.'

'If you think I've made a wrong decision, say so.'

Razor smiled. 'No, boss, I don't think you made a wrong decision. I guess I just don't like the thought . . . you know what I mean.'

'Aye.'

'If we're gonna be walking over snow-covered mountains she'll need some better gear than what she's been wearing,' Chris said.

'Aye, so will Nena. I have a horrible feeling we're going to have to visit the Cheshires after all.'

'Maybe they'll lend us a Warrior,' the Dame said from the doorway.

'No joy with the van?' Razor asked.

'It's outside,' the Dame said.

They filed out into the street, where a sorry-looking vehicle greeted their eyes. The VW Microbus had obviously seen some action, though whether in a war or a demolition derby was impossible to tell. The various wounds it had suffered had all been duly painted over, in a veritable kaleidoscope of different shades. The overall effect was of a mottled, rusty, hippie camper.

'Far out,' Razor said sarcastically.

'The motor's OK,' the Dame said. 'And it does about seventy.'

The interior had been customized, presumably to improve its troop-carrying capacity. Behind the solid front seat two wooden benches ran along either side of the vehicle. It was roomy enough, Docherty thought. Not as sturdy as the lorry perhaps, but easier on petrol and more manoeuvrable.

And a much more likely-looking transport for a group of journalists. From what Razor and Chris had discovered it was beginning to look as though the last stage of the trip was going to be difficult enough without Serb opposition, let alone with it.

'What do you think?' he asked the Dame. 'Does the engine seem reliable?'

The Dame looked at it. 'Yeah,' he said, 'I think so. And I wouldn't say the same for the lorry you lot came in.'

'That settles it,' Docherty said. 'We'll get off tomorrow morning at first light, and have lunch with our fellow Brits in Vitez.'

'I think we should call it Woodstock,' Razor said, staring at the Microbus.

Docherty had a sudden image of them all riding round Bosnia, flashing peace signs at burnt-out villages.

Two streets away, their positions of a fortnight before strangely reversed, Nena was trying to persuade Hajrija not to make the journey. 'It's because of him, isn't it?' she asked. 'Rija, this is no time to go chasing after a man.'

'I am not chasing after a man,' Hajrija shouted back, thoroughly angry. 'I am coming with you because you are my friend, and the last time I let you go off alone . . .' She stopped herself. 'OK, I like him, but that's just a bonus. It is *not* why I am coming. Zavik is my home too, you know . . .'

'You have no family there any more.'

'I have friends. It's my home. I have a right to know what's going on there . . .'

'OK, enough,' Nena said. 'I just don't want you to put yourself in danger, for me or the Englishman . . .'

Hajrija burst out laughing. 'What do you think I was doing in Sarajevo,' she wanted to know, 'modelling swimsuits?'

12

They left Visoko at dawn the next day, with Razor in the driving seat, Docherty beside him, and the other four in the back with their gear. The previous day's clear skies had been filled with hurrying clouds, and except for those few occasions when the sun shone through, the road down the Bosna valley twisted and turned in perpetual twilight.

There was not much conversation to lighten the journey, with each of the travellers engrossed in thoughts of what had passed and what was to come. But neither were there any roadblocks to slow their passage. Traffic was virtually non-existent on the main highway – only two lorries went up the valley as they went down – and the signs of life were few: smoke from a farmstead on the other side of the river, a man trudging through snow high on the valley slope, a dog barking outside an abandoned roadside café.

After driving about twenty miles they left the Bosna valley and its highway, turning left up the Lasva valley. Nearly ten miles of steady climbing later they came into the small town of Vitez, where the British UN Protection Force was based. The depot was on the higher side of the town, an affair of temporary barracks and vehicle pound, surrounded by wire fencing still new enough to gleam.

Razor pulled up at the gate, where two Cheshires in UN berets waited, their SA80s held pointedly close to the firing position. Through the gates the new arrivals could see Warrior infantry carriers and Scimitar armoured reconnaissance vehicles, all painted UN white.

Docherty climbed slowly out of the van, approached the two sentries and introduced himself. They were impressed enough by the SAS credentials to let him through to see the duty officer, but insisted on the vehicle and its other five occupants remaining outside the gate. Serving under the UN flag did not seem to have filled these soldiers with a warm glow of security.

Five minutes and two go-betweens later Docherty reached the office of the unit commander, Lieutenant-Colonel William Stewart, a tall, fair-haired Yorkshireman. As luck would have it he was also an ex-SAS officer, whom Docherty had served with nearly twenty years earlier in Oman, when Stewart was a hyperactive young lieutenant who had only just been badged.

'Docherty!' he exclaimed. 'What the hell are you doing here? I heard they'd put you out to grass months ago.'

Even in his forties, Stewart found it impossible to sit or stand still. As Docherty explained that his SAS patrol was on an undercover mission, and that they would appreciate some unofficial help, Stewart paced up and down his cramped little office like a caged tiger. 'We need Arctic gear for two, and the latest intelligence on the roads between Vitez and Bugojno,' Docherty said. 'And some breakfast wouldn't go amiss,' he added.

'I dare say we can manage all that without breaking the UN Charter,' Stewart said. 'I don't suppose you're going to tell me what you're up to in this neck of the woods?'

The answer should have been no, but Docherty told him anyway.

Stewart was envious. 'We spend most of our time here wishing we could do more than just watch it all happen. It's like holding the coats of two men who've decided to beat each other to death.' He reached for the door. 'Let's go and fill your order.'

An hour later they were on their way again, having been supplied with Arctic clothing for the two women – both of whom, fortunately, were tall – an optimistic assessment of their road as far as Gornji Vakuf, and a fry-up in the Cheshires' mess. Cholesterol-rich it definitely was, but the men hadn't had a better meal since Split, and the two women hadn't eaten as well for months. A couple of Cheshires at the next table couldn't keep from commenting on the two women's appetite, and were met with looks from the SAS men which would have silenced Cilla Black.

Razor's benign mood had been further lifted by the news that Tottenham had won on the previous Saturday. Sunderland and Celtic, however, had both lost.

'I don't suppose you remember Tottenham's games against Rangers in '62?' Docherty asked Razor, as the latter steered the Microbus up the long incline leading out of town.

'I was only four, boss.'

'I was eleven. I can't remember which European competition it was, but they were really big games. English and Scottish club teams had hardly ever played each other before then, and then those two were drawn against each other and there was this enormous expectation, enormous curiosity, because no one really knew whether English teams were much better than Scottish teams, or much the same, or vice versa.'

'I take it we won.'

'Oh aye, you won all right. Five-two, I think, down in London. But Rangers played well enough to make people think they could turn it round at Ibrox. They had some great players then – Willie Henderson, Jim Baxter. And then the second leg was only about five minutes old when Jimmy Greaves ran half the length of the field and scored. People who were there said the silence was so deep you could hear sheep farting in the Outer Hebrides. Spurs won that one three-two.' Docherty smiled to himself. 'I always remembered those games because I felt so torn. Being a Scot I wanted Rangers to win, and being a Celtic supporter I wanted to see them thrashed. I guess it was the first time I understood how loyalties could cut across each other.' He looked out of the window. 'But it was a long time before I realized what a good thing it was that they did. Because people with only one loyalty have nothing to restrain them.'

'Like here in sunny Bosnia?'

'Aye.'

A few miles further on they turned left, on to a small road which climbed across the mountains towards Bugojno. In normal times this would have been closed to traffic, but the UN Protection Force needed it open for resupply purposes, and the necessary vehicles and equipment had been brought up by road from Split two months earlier. Piled snow on either side of the twisting road offered evidence of the use to which they had been put.

In the back of the Microbus the euphoria provided by breakfast soon dissipated. As they got nearer to their destination Nena was finding her anxiety for her children beginning to grow, and Hajrija was finding no reason to worry less about Nena. Her friend still seemed locked inside that mental shell she had grown to protect herself during captivity, and Hajrija didn't know how to react. Should she try breaking it open from the outside or wait for Nena to free herself?

And there was also the Englishman to think about. Feeling desire for a man didn't seem very appropriate after what her best friend had just been through.

Sitting opposite each other by the back door, Chris and the Dame were also in very different states of mind. Since the bus ride from Vogosca the Dame had been unable to shake the picture of all those traumatized women and girls out of his head. Memories of his sister's wedding reception kept coming back to haunt him with their pettiness. If people only knew how bad it could get, then they wouldn't waste love in the stupid way they did. They would cherish it, look after each other, thank God that their sisters and wives were not on a bus to somewhere like Vogosca.

Facing him, Chris was watching the sky above the snow-covered moorland, and occasionally catching sight of a hovering bird of prey too far off to identify. He wanted to stop the van, get out and climb into these unknown hills, and feel as free as the birds that circled above them.

They reached Gornji Vakuf around eleven and turned off the main road to Split, following another, wider road north-west towards Bugojno. The most recent hard intelligence available at Vitez had placed the Serbs within a few miles of Bugojno, and there was an unconfirmed report that long-range shelling of the town had begun in the last few hours. The small UN unit stationed there had been incommunicado for almost twenty-four.

The SAS men found out why a few miles short of the town, when they came upon the UN unit's two vehicles and five men eating an early lunch in a convenient picnic spot beside the highway. The town, the men from the Cheshires told them, was now under almost continuous bombardment by Serb artillery, and they had been ordered out by the overall UN command. The five Cheshires seemed pleased enough to be out of immediate harm's way, but, as one of the younger men put it succinctly: 'What's the fuckin' point of it all?'

The major in charge had more recent information on Serb movements in the area, but warned them not to take anything for granted. 'The bastards could be in the town square by now,' he said cheerfully. When Docherty asked him about Zavik the major raised a knowing eyebrow, and said that there had been no news of the town for weeks. 'Which could mean that they're all still hung over from Christmas, or it could mean that the Serbs have burned the place to the ground. Who knows? I just want to get back to the Falls Road,' he concluded, with only the faintest trace of irony.

Another few miles down the valley they could hear the big guns firing up ahead. Razor stopped the Microbus on a convenient rise and all six of them got out on to the road for a panoramic view of the distant town. Smoke was already rising from half a dozen buildings, and every few minutes another flash of white light would be followed by the sound of a shell exploding.

'I don't suppose there's a way round,' Razor muttered.

'Not on this map,' Docherty replied.

'The shells are landing about every three minutes,' Chris said, looking up from his watch as another white flash erupted, 'and they just seem to be lobbing them in at random. Our chances of being hit by one are not much worse than our chances of being knocked down by a London bus.'

'Oh well, that's all right then,' Razor said sarcastically. He looked round at the Microbus. 'Boss,' he said more seriously, 'I think everyone should get in the back with the bergens up against the windows. And keep your heads down, no matter how good the architecture down there used to be. If I see a one-winged, purple-crested parrot flying out of the smoke I'll give you a shout,' he told Chris. 'OK?'

They did as he suggested, and huddled together between the rows of seats in the back. Razor started off down the hill, trying to gauge times and distances. The town didn't look so big, and it shouldn't take much more than five minutes to reach its centre, find the road which they wanted, and drive back out again. If he entered the town just after a shell landed, then with any luck there would only be one to avoid before they made their exit.

'You're a genius, Razor,' he murmured to himself, easing his foot down on the brake as the Microbus drove past the first houses. At that moment there was a loud explosion, a far louder one than he'd expected, and half a house not fifty yards away seemed to rear and crash down into the street ahead. Razor moved slowly forward, poised on the accelerator, and when the dust had cleared sufficiently for him to see a path through the rubble, rammed his foot down. And then he was racing along the empty street towards the town centre, where a mosque's minaret contested the sky with a Christian spire.

The road signs were still up, and he was swinging across the small square towards the Kupres road, thinking the worst was over when several bees seemed to whizz past his head. Pretty solidly built bees, to judge by the holes they had left in the windscreen.

Razor pulled down the steering wheel, first one way and then the other, careering in violent curves down the road away from the square. He thought he heard other shots, but no more bees came through the cab, and a minute later the Microbus was back in open country, beginning a slow climb towards a distant cleft in the valley's side.

He could feel the adrenalin pumping through his veins. 'Is everyone OK back there?' he called out anxiously, risking a glance in the rear-view mirror in search of Hajrija. She was there. And everyone else.

'What did you see?' Docherty wanted to know.

'Nothing. Not a soul,' said Razor. 'Maybe they were all in their basements, or maybe the Serbs are just firing at an empty town.'

'Who fired at us?'

'No idea. Didn't see them either.'

'We'd better stop and make sure there's no real damage.'

Razor brought the van to a halt just above a hairpin bend, and they got down to make an examination. Three bullets had passed through the vehicle, all of them in through one of the door windows at the back and out through the windscreen to Razor's right. If Docherty had still been sitting in the passenger seat there wouldn't have been much left of his head. As it was, the only lasting consequences of the attack were an increased draught of cold air and an obscuring of the view through the affected windows.

They got back on board, Docherty resuming his front seat. For the next six miles the road clambered out of the valley in ever-tightening spirals, the Microbus's wheels slipping and sliding far more than Razor liked. The way down was even more treacherous, and their progress often slowed to no more than a crawl. It was only when they reached their intended turn-off that the way became easier, and not for a very comforting reason. Tracked vehicles had used this road not long previously; the Microbus had obviously entered Serb-controlled – or at best Serb-contested – territory.

According to the Cheshires they had met outside Bugojno there was a checkpoint in the village of Dragnic, another six miles up this road. They were planning to abandon the Microbus half a mile short of the village and take to the hills, literally. It would be a twenty-mile hike to Zavik, across a 6000-foot range of snow-covered mountains, but Docherty had no doubt that Hajrija and the four men could cover the distance in reasonable time. Nena, though, was a different matter. She had told him she could do it, but . . .

He was still worrying this over in his mind when the tell-tale drift of smoke came into view, curling up above the next rise.

'I see it,' Razor said, as Docherty pointed forward.

'Stop short of the next crest,' the PC said. 'And we'll go take a look.'

They did, inching their heads above the skyline to see the roadblock a quarter of a mile ahead: a car and a transit van nose to nose in the middle of a river bridge, and on the bank beyond a blazing fire surrounded by several men in the familiar broad-brimmed hats.

'I love barbecues,' Razor said.

'Shit,' Docherty muttered. This had added another five or six miles to their walk.

They had no other choices. They couldn't ram a path through this roadblock, and there was no way they could get within killing distance of the enemy without being seen. At least not before nightfall, and that was five hours away. Who knew what might appear on the road behind them in the meantime?

Docherty glanced to the right, where the ground fell brokenly towards the same river, and then rose up beyond it in pine-covered slopes. That was the way they had to go.

He and Razor inched their way back from the crest, then hurried back down to the van. 'Bad news, folks,' Docherty said. 'We're on foot from here on.'

They unloaded their gear.

'What about Woodstock?' Razor asked.

Docherty thought for a moment, wondering whether to bury the Microbus in a snowdrift, or drive it back to the top of the last rise and give it a push. 'We'll leave it here,' he decided. 'They're not going to follow us across country.'

'Ready?' he asked, looking round at them all. Chris was smiling with anticipation, the Dame poker-faced as ever, the two women tensely determined. 'Dame, you take lead scout,' Docherty said. 'Chris, you're Tail-end Charlie. Nena, I want you and Hajrija between me and Razor, OK?'

They hoisted the bergens on to their backs and started off in order of march across the sloping meadow, all but Nena holding an SMG cradled in their arms. The snow was about a foot deep, and the going was slow. At this rate, Docherty thought, it would take about a week to reach Zavik. He hoped the forest would be easier walking.

They found a dry way across the river without much difficulty, and were soon under the cover of the trees, where the going was not appreciably easier. After half an hour they seemed to have covered only about a quarter of a mile.

Docherty called a halt. 'Any ideas?' he asked.

'The plan was to get off the road about six miles further up, right?' Chris said. 'And then take this track Hajrija knows across the mountains and in through Zavik's back door?'

'Right.'

'So why not work our way round the roadblock we know is there, wait for dark, and then walk up the road?'

It was so obvious Docherty wondered why he hadn't thought of it. He consoled himself with the thought that the Incas hadn't managed to come up with the wheel. 'Can anyone see a flaw in that that I can't?' he asked.

'Sounds good to me,' Razor said.

'There is one problem,' the Dame said slowly. 'If we have to hang around somewhere until it gets dark then anyone following our tracks will have time to catch us up.'

'Good point,' Docherty agreed. 'We'll have to keep our eyes open.'

As it happened, it took them most of the remaining daylight hours to work their way around the Serb roadblock, and anyone following their tracks would presumably be making no better progress. They eventually reached a position on the edge of the trees just above the road, which was now hugging the eastern side of the valley. Chris was sent back fifty yards along their tracks to provide any advance warning of pursuit, while the other five retreated further into the trees for rest and refreshment. Since it was still light Docherty risked using the hexamine stoves to boil water for soup and tea.

They needed all the warmth they could get. The sky was clearing once more, and the temperature seemed to be dropping like a stone. After their struggle through the snow their limbs needed rest, but there was no doubting that it was warmer on the move, and once darkness had fallen they lost no time in getting started once more.

About twenty minutes later the sound of a vehicle on the road behind caused them to scurry up the bank and into the trees. A few moments later a lorry rumbled by, with two men sitting in the cab and another half dozen or so barely visible in the rear, their cigarettes glowing like fireflies.

'Our chums from the roadblock,' Razor observed.

'Pigs,' Hajrija said contemptuously.

They continued their march up the long road, the stars shining in the sky above the valley, the river singing its way across the stones. In any other circumstances, Docherty thought, this would be almost magical. He could be walking down a glen on New Year's Eve, on his way to visit a warm and welcoming pub by the side of the loch.

Some hope. He turned to check on Nena, walking some five yards behind him. She seemed steady enough on her feet, and even managed a faint smile in his direction. She was strong, Docherty knew, and as far as he could tell her experience didn't seem to have taken any great toll on her body. The mind was a different matter. He wondered how Reeve was going to react to the news that his wife had been repeatedly subjected to multiple rape, and realized that he didn't have much of a clue. Reeve had often surprised him in the past, behaving badly when expected to behave well, rising above his usual self when Docherty had expected the worst. He hoped this would be one of the latter cases. The woman had been through more than enough already.

Four hours and twelve miles later they had skirted round two small villages – though no lights shone to suggest there might be anyone to watch or listen – and carefully approached the location of the roadblock they had been told about, only to find an empty stretch of road. Soon after they reached the spot where Hajrija's track took off to the east, and started following it up a wider valley towards the first village, which she said was only a couple of kilometres away. She knew some of the people who lived there, and hoped for news of what was happening in Zavik.

They reached a slight rise overlooking the village about half an hour later. The moon was up now, reflecting in the tiles of the roofs and the bend of the river which enclosed most of the dwellings. There were no lights shining, but none could be expected at such an hour.

They walked carefully down towards the first house, keeping to the shadows beside the road. A burnt-out Lada by the side of the house offered proof that the war had come to call. The whole place felt dead, Docherty thought. He remembered villages in Dhofar which had felt as empty as this.

The door of the first house was open. Razor entered cautiously, and walked through the house, sweeping it with his torch. There was no one there – alive or dead.

They went through the next two houses with the same result.

'They've gone,' Hajrija said.

'There's no point in going through every house,' Docherty decided. 'We'll just borrow one for a few hours, get some sleep, and move on at first light. We should be in Zavik by noon.'

Chris had the penultimate watch, and, when Docherty came to relieve him half an hour or so before dawn, he decided to walk up through the forest rather than try for a few minutes' more sleep. Some chaffinches were soon chirping in the trees around him, but the dawn chorus as a whole was disappointing. Chris emerged from the forest above the other side of the village, and stopped for a moment in the shelter of the trees to check that there were no signs of life below. There were not, but several huge birds were lazily circling in the dawn sky. He fixed the binoculars on one of them, and saw a pale-grey head which hardly protruded at all from the yellow-brown body. A large, hooked beak adorned the head, while the tail was short, dark and square. It was a griffon vulture.

He watched it through the binoculars for a few moments, marvelling at the sheer size of the bird. Then the realization dawned – these creatures only came together for carrion. Chris started walking down through the houses, towards the centre of the village, above which the predators were circling.

He found a space where a building had been, and the charred wooden moon and star lying half-buried in the snow told him what it had been. He walked forward, expecting the worst, and found it. The snow lay across a pile of charred and half-consumed corpses. A large metal padlock, still locked around the two halves of an iron hasp, lay where the entrance had been.

Time and winter had taken the smell away from the vultures' refrigerator. He walked round the site, conscious of the huge birds hissing in the sky above. At least fifty bodies, he reckoned. The whole village, perhaps.

Chris walked back down the road to the house they had borrowed for the night, and told Docherty what he had found. The PC closed his eyes for a second, then looked at the ground. 'How long ago?' he asked.

'Hard to say. Weeks, at least. Maybe months.'

Twenty minutes later the whole party was staring dull-eyed at the scene of the massacre. There was no time to sift through the wreckage, or to disentangle what remained for burial. If the time for grieving ever passed, Docherty thought, then it had passed for those who had perished here.

They walked up the dirt track that led out of the village, into the innocence of the forest. The morning sunshine slanted down through the tall pines and lit the virgin snow that covered the more open parts of the forest floor, giving the Dame, again leading the way, the impression that he was walking through a huge cathedral. Images of the burnt mosque back in the village, the women on the bus, the sniper flung from the window . . . all passed through his mind and were somehow consumed by the beauty of the forest, like the heavenly sound of interweaving requiems.

Ten yards behind him, Docherty felt numb. This is Europe, he told himself. The house they had stayed in had been a

European house, connected to an electricity grid, plugged in by radio and TV and cars to the rest of the continent. There had been a record player, and records ranging from Rachmaninov to Elton John. And the family who had listened to 'Crocodile Rock' had probably been among those herded into the time warp, taken back to an age in which they could be herded into a mosque and burnt alive.

Why? he asked himself. What had happened in this country? Were these people so different from all the other peoples of the world who could take the body's needs for granted? Or was this just the place where the surface had cracked to reveal the rotten ooze welling up below?

For the first time in his life Docherty felt a stirring of fellow-feeling with his late father. The old union man hadn't liked the way the world was going; he always said that people were getting more and more of what they wanted, and less and less of what they really needed. And because they were getting what they wanted they couldn't understand why they were so unhappy. And that made them angry.

Docherty wished he could feel angry, but felt something closer to despair.

They walked on through the forest for several miles, to where the track finally emerged in a high valley. They prudently waited for several minutes, scanning the surrounding countryside for signs of an enemy, but in this empty place there were none. They walked on, following an infant stream which trickled down between wide, snow-covered moorland slopes.

For half a mile or so the going was hard, but then they passed across a small crest and down into another, more sheltered valley, where bare trees gathered in the bends of a wider stream. They were now only about a mile from the next and last village on their route, and no one in the party was feeling particularly sanguine about what they would find when they got there.

Of the two women, Hajrija had been more affected by what they had found in the previous village, despite seeing more than her share of death and cruelty in Sarajevo. 'It's different,' she told Nena. 'In the city we are fighters against fighters, and the shelling, well, somehow it's not personal. But to take people like that . . . to see their faces and hear them . . .' She shook her head, refusing to let the tears flow.

Nena put an arm around Hajrija's shoulder but said nothing. In her mind's eye she could see her children being marched into the mosque in Zavik.

Behind them, Razor was wondering about himself and Hajrija, and about whether they would ever get the chance to be together. If they got out of this trip alive, then he would be going home to England and she . . . she might be going back to Sarajevo, or she might even want to stay in Zavik, if the town was still there. He could hardly send her love-letters at either address. And she could hardly come and visit him when the anti-sniper unit had their summer holidays.

What a fucking mess, he thought. And in any case, what did it say about him that he was worrying about his love-life after what they had just left behind? That he was an insensitive git? Or that he was more interested in life than death? Who the fuck knew?

A hundred yards ahead, the Dame gave Docherty the hand signal for halt before dropping to his knees and carefully advancing to the latest crest in the path. Reaching it, he lay flat in the snow and slowly scanned the valley below with his binoculars.

Docherty watched him, waiting for the thumbs-up to tell him that no enemy was in sight or suspected. Instead he saw

196

the Dame's shoulders slump momentarily, and then the Wearsider seemed to lie motionless for a minute or more, before placing his hand on his head to indicate he wanted Docherty to join him.

The PC wriggled forward, and found himself with a panoramic view of hills stretching away into the distance. A quarter of a mile away, the next village nestled in the valley below. He could see no sign of movement.

Docherty turned to the Dame, and saw tears running down his cheeks. With a sinking feeling he picked up his own binoculars and started scanning the village below. The first few houses seemed untouched, but then several came into view that had been burnt to the ground, and in the centre of the village, once more, there was the remains of what had probably been the mosque. He must have sealed his heart against this, Docherty thought, because he felt immune to grief.

And then he saw them, as the Dame had seen them, the crucified bodies on the side of the barn, and he felt the tears welling up in his own eyes.

They took down the corpses and, lacking the time to dig graves in the frozen earth, simply buried them beneath mounds of snow. Why, in any case, did these deserve graves when those bodies in the burnt-out mosque did not? They could not bury all the dead of this village, any more than all the dead of the last.

As before, a group of vultures hissed overhead, waiting for them to leave.

The road which ended here ran south down the valley, but they took the path to the east, which would lead them up over the last range of hills and down into Zavik's valley. It was almost noon now, and the sky was clouding over again, the wind whipping up fine sprays of snow and flinging them at the walkers.

The women were feeling the strain now. Unlike the four SAS men, neither had been forced to endure walks of nearly thirty miles across the Brecon Beacons, and both had developed blisters from wearing boots that were slightly too large for them. But they didn't complain, and they kept up with the pace.

The weather conditions continued to deteriorate. As Docherty halted to check the map against a world of snow and mist and pale, shadowy pines, one which seemed devoid of any reference points, Hajrija arrived at his shoulder to tell him where they were: only a hundred yards or so from the crest of the last ridge.

The view when they reached it was disappointing, merely one more white meadow below, and a hint of tree-covered slopes through the mist ahead.

'You can't see the town from here,' Hajrija said, 'but it's down there. This is where a lot of the townspeople come to ski on winter Saturdays,' she added. 'Or used to. There's a lodge down there, just above the trees. It was the only shelter up here.'

They moved slowly down the slope, waiting for the lodge to swim out of the murk. When it did so the binoculars revealed no sign of life. They advanced on it carefully nevertheless, watching for tell-tale tracks in the snow.

There was a musty smell inside, but no bodies. Cigarette ends and beer bottles littered the floor of the main room, and there were several cartridge cases arranged in a neat line along one of the window-ledges. Fighting men of some description had been here, but not for a while.

If the only shelter on the hills behind the town was unoccupied in this sort of weather, Docherty reasoned, then it seemed unlikely that there were any enemy units between them and the valley below. It was a comforting thought.

He put it to Hajrija, who agreed.

'In which case,' Docherty said, 'our first contact will probably be with Zavik's defensive perimeter. Assuming it has one. So where would it be.'

Hajrija shrugged. 'There is only one easy way down. It is a very – how you say?' – she drew hairpins in the air with her finger . . .

'Winding,' Docherty supplied.

'Yes, the Beatles. The long and winding road. But this is short and steep and winding.'

'There is no other way?'

'There's the Stair,' Nena said.

'Not in the winter,' Hajrija objected.

Nena shrugged. 'Maybe not. There is a long climb down past the waterfall,' she said to Docherty. 'We used to go up and down it when we were children, mostly because our parents said we should not. In winter it will be slippery and maybe impossible.'

'Which do you think will be safer?' Docherty asked the two women.

'The road,' Hajrija said flatly.

'Yes, I think so,' Nena agreed reluctantly. 'Though anyone below will be able to see us coming down the road long before we can explain who we are.'

They set off down the mountain, following the narrow road through a wide swathe of pines and out alongside another meadow. Then there were more trees and the road suddenly fell away. About two hundred yards below, the roofs of a town were dimly visible above the intervening trees, tucked inside a sharp bend of the pale-grey river. Docherty turned the binoculars on the road down, and found what looked like an ominous gap. He passed the binoculars to Hajrija.

'There is a bridge there before,' she said.

'Will there be a way across?'

'Not an easy one,' Nena said. 'The road crosses a stream there, almost like a waterfall. It is a long way down.'

'The Stair, then.'

'There is no other way.'

They left the road and hiked across the bottom of the meadow, and worked their way up across a tree-covered ridge and down into another cleft in the mountain face. This one was even steeper, and the depth of the snow varied wildly, making progress extremely slow. Docherty alternated between imagining how beautiful this would be in the summer and cursing the difficulty of their passage.

After an hour which seemed like three they arrived at the head of the Stair. The waterfall, no doubt deafening in spring, was barely audible above the wind, and with good reason. Only a trickle of water was actually falling – the rest was frozen in mid-flight, waiting for spring to set it free.

The Stair itself was easier than the SAS men had been led to expect. Flat rocks had been inset into the steeply sloping ground beside the waterfall, and though some were definitely slippery, and almost any slip potentially fatal, there was always a handhold to spare. Every twenty yards or so, there was a larger ledge to rest on.

Descending such a path with a fully laden bergen wasn't anyone's idea of fun, but after what they'd seen that day just being alive seemed like something to be thankful for. Hajrija was less than twenty feet from the bottom when they all heard the voice from below.

'Keep coming, and keep your hands away from your guns,' it said in Serbo-Croat.

Chris quickly translated the order, but in any case no one was going to risk opening fire on probable friends whom they couldn't even see.

'If it wasn't for the women you would be dead by now,' the voice said cheerfully.

It wasn't until they were all off the Stair that the three men stepped out from behind the overhanging rock. Each was carrying a Kalashnikov in firing position.

'Jusuf!' Hajrija said, recognizing the face of the oldest man. 'You can put down the guns.'

The man stared at her in bewilderment for a moment, and then recognition dawned. 'Hajrija Mejra? I did not see the girl inside the uniform. Where in God's name have you come from?'

'Sarajevo. And you know Nena.'

Jusuf's eyes grew even wider. 'Yes, yes, of course. Does the Commander know you are here?'

'My children,' Nena asked, heart in mouth, 'are they . . . are they well?'

'Yes, yes, I think so. My boy has the chickenpox, but . . .' The sense of relief took Nena's breath away.

'Where is Reeve?' Hajrija asked.

'At the HQ I think.'

'And where is that?' Hajrija asked patiently.

'First you must tell me who these men are,' he said obstinately.

'They are English. They are friends of Reeve.'

Jusuf's face lit up. 'That is wonderful news,' he said. 'Did he know you were all coming?'

'No, but if you take us to him . . .'

13

Nena Reeve strode purposefully across the town she had grown up in, towards the house on the hill where she had been born. The mist seemed to be thickening again as darkness began to fall, but from what she could tell the town seemed much the same as it had always been. There were no scars of war, and there were people on the streets, even a couple she recognized. She hurried past them, head down – the last thing she wanted to do now was stop and explain herself to mere acquaintances.

There were no lights showing in her parents' home, but the house itself looked the same as it always had. She pushed open the front door, and felt the warm air of life on her face. Voices sounded from the kitchen at the back, children's voices.

She stood a second by the parlour door, feeling almost limp, and then turned the old handle and walked across the threshold. By the light of the single kerosene lamp she could see the four faces turned towards the door – those of her father, mother, son and daughter. There was a moment of stunned silence, and then both children cried out in unison: 'Mama!'

* * *

On the other side of town John Reeve and two of his fellow-officers in the Zavik Militia were poring over a map in the back room of the Youth Hostel which served as their HQ.

'Hello, Reeve,' a familiar Scottish voice said from the doorway.

Reeve looked round, utter astonishment on his face. 'Jesus Christ,' he said, 'the fucking cavalry's arrived.'

Docherty grinned at him. Reeve wasn't wearing any sort of uniform, but he appeared fit and well. There were no weapons visible, but the looks of the other young men, the maps on the table and wall . . . the scene had all the makings of a military unit which knew what it was doing. And it was about as far removed from Brando's camp in *Apocalypse Now* as Docherty could imagine. He wasn't surprised, but he had been prepared to find the worst, and this wasn't it.

The two men shook hands, and Docherty introduced Razor, Chris and the Dame. Reeve in turn introduced the two Bosnians. The taller of the two, a serious-looking man with short, black hair and a pronounced Slavic face, was named Latinka Tijanic. The other man, also dark-haired, but with a rounder face and moustache, was Esad Cehajic.

'So what the fuck are you doing here?' Reeve asked.

'We've come to see you, but . . .'

At this moment Hajrija, who had been talking to their escort outside, appeared in the doorway.

'Hajrija?' Reeve said, staring at her with renewed astonishment. The last time he's seen her she'd been a student in jeans and T-shirt.

'*Zdravo*, Reeve.'

'How are you? How is Nena?'

'I was just about to tell you,' Docherty said. 'She came with us. She went straight on up to her folks' place. Are they OK? And the children?'

204

'They're fine. All of them.' Reeve seemed momentarily stunned. 'Jesus, Jamie, what's she doing here? How did you all get here?'

'It's a long story. Maybe . . .'

'I'd better get over there,' Reeve said suddenly. He grabbed his coat and looked around. 'Lads, make yourselves at home. Esad, look after them, will you? I'll be back.'

'How are you, Nena?' her father asked, when the children finally allowed him the opportunity. He looked older, Nena thought, whereas her mother looked much the same. He had been a schoolteacher by profession, but his life's vocation – from the years as a partisan in World War Two to his years as Mayor of Zavik – had been the Party and the idea of Yugoslavia. The collapse of everything he had fought and worked for must have been terrible for him, Nena realized. The erasure of a life.

'I'm fine,' she said. Two years before she might eventually have told her parents what had happened to her, but not now. There would be no point. 'But what has happened here, Papa?' she asked, partly to move the conversation away from herself.

'We have fought them, that is what has happened,' her father said. 'Your Reeve has been wonderful, Nena. Without him I dread to think how things would have gone.'

There must have been a trace of irony in her expression, because her father gave her an aggrieved look. 'This is a good man,' he insisted.

'I know,' she said.

'So why . . .'

She was saved by the good man's arrival. There was a rare look of uncertainty in his eyes, Nena thought, as she got up, fighting her own reluctance, to embrace him.

'How are you?' he asked.

'Fine. Tired. Happy to see these two,' she said, putting an arm around each child. They were looking wary, perhaps remembering the arguments which had been so frequent the last time their mother and father had been together.

'Are you sure you're OK?' he asked.

'I'm just exhausted. It was a hard journey.' Now that she knew everyone was safe all she wanted to do was sleep. In a proper bed, for a long time.

At the Youth Hostel Esad had made the visitors the best coffee they'd had since leaving England. They sipped at it gratefully, sitting in silence and resting their aching legs. Hajrija, meanwhile, was conducting an animated conversation in her native tongue with the serious-looking Tijanic, and Razor was torn between pleasure at her obvious happiness to be home and more than a slight stirring of jealousy. The darkness seemed to have gone from her eyes, he thought. She seemed so natural here, but it made him wonder whether the months in the anti-sniper unit had wrought changes inside her, hardened her in some way, or whether she had somehow managed to keep her real self at a distance from it all.

And that made him think about what the years in the Army had done to him. He knew men in the SAS who had been unable to cope with what they were required to do – some who had simply decided it wasn't for them and left, others who had turned themselves into machines – but he had never felt pushed in either of those directions. His defence had been not to take it too seriously; to stay loose and not get wound too tight by it all, the way the Dame seemed in danger of doing. When the feeling was there, you had to let yourself feel it, and then get on with the job in hand.

He was a survivor, he thought. And he had the feeling she was too. If only . . .

'There is a café,' she said suddenly in English. 'It is open, with food and drink. Not far. Not steaks and wine, you understand, but maybe music.'

'I could eat a horse,' Razor said.

'There'll probably be one on the menu,' Chris said.

They turned to Docherty. 'Go and eat,' the PC said. 'I'll wait here for Reeve to come back.'

Outside darkness had fallen, and the mist still clung to the valley floor, making it hard to see each other, let alone the direction they were supposed to be taking. Hajrija grabbed hold of Razor's hand. 'Make chain,' she said, and they did so, unable to think of a less embarrassing alternative. Chris found himself remembering a game they played at school, the chain of tagged kids reaching and twisting for one of the untagged to release them with a touch.

Hajrija led them unerringly down one street and then another, buildings occasionally looming through the patchy mist, until a hazy light announced their destination. The words René's Café on the glass door stood out against the yellow light within.

'What?!?' Razor exclaimed.

Inside, a large poster of the cast of *'Allo, 'Allo!* took pride of place behind the serving counter. The three Englishmen gazed at it open-mouthed.

'It is big hit on Yugoslav TV,' Hajrija explained. 'Like the Fools and Horses. Del-boys and lovely-jubbly,' she added gratuitously.

The café was empty when they arrived, but the menu surpassed expectations by containing both cheese and beer, and their own arrival seemed to trigger an avalanche of customers. The beer was strictly rationed to two bottles a customer, but this didn't seem to get in the way of the good feeling which encompassed everyone there. Men and women, old and young, talked in groups and pairs, sometimes reaching out to join in other conversations which caught their ear. Razor had grown up the only child of a single parent, but this was what he had always imagined a huge family gathering would be like. A sort of chaotic warmth.

'This is how it used to be,' Hajrija said, her breath brushing his cheek.

René stared down at him from the poster. 'I will only say this once,' Razor murmured to himself.

Reeve arrived back at the hostel looking more subdued than when he'd left. He didn't seem surprised to find only Docherty. 'Well, Jamie, this is a surprise,' he said, lighting a cigarette and blowing smoke at the ceiling.

'Aye, I expect it is,' Docherty agreed, thinking that Reeve seemed much the same as he'd ever been.

'I don't suppose it's a coincidence that you and Nena have turned up here together. You didn't just run into each other on Sarajevo Station, I suppose?'

Docherty smiled without much humour. 'She's had a bad time, Reeve. A really bad time.'

Reeve took a drag on the cigarette. 'Sarajevo used to be a lovely town,' he said mildly. 'She didn't tell me anything,' he added. 'So why are you all here?'

'To check you out,' Docherty said bluntly. 'Our beloved Government has been getting stick from all sides about this lunatic Brit in the Bosnian hills . . .'

'You're kidding. What's it matter to John Major, for Christ's sake? It's not as if any of those bastards *care* what's happening here.'

208

Docherty looked at him. 'You are still a serving soldier in their Army. They may not give a flying fuck about Bosnia but they have to care about that.'

Reeve grinned. 'Tell 'em I resign. Tell them I've taken out Bosnian citizenship and I'm as entitled to my piece of the war as any other Bosnian.'

'Have you?'

'You're joking. How the hell do you think I'd do that – by post? On the phone?'

'Aye, OK.'

'I mean, this is hard to believe,' Reeve went on. 'They actually sent you and three other guys into all this just to tell me to keep a low fucking profile? It's like infiltrating a patrol into Saddam Hussein's palace to steal his bog paper.'

'We weren't sent to tell you to keep a low profile,' Docherty said calmly. 'We were sent to find out what's been going on.'

Reeve stubbed out his cigarette, walked across to a cupboard and pulled out two glasses and a bottle. 'OK,' he said, unscrewing the top and pouring two respectable shots of plum brandy, 'I'll tell you.'

Docherty leaned back in his chair and sipped at the brandy. It was good.

'You know why I came back here?'

'To see the kids.'

'And you know about Nena and me splitting up?'

'Aye.'

'Well, when I came to see them she took the chance to go to Sarajevo, and then because of the war she couldn't get back here. Didn't want to either, from what I could tell. Doctoring's always been important to her, and she knew her parents were here to look after the kids if I left.'

'Why didn't you?'

209

'The Serbs came to call, like they did everywhere else around here. Only we stood up to the bastards – all the town, most of the local Serbs included – and kicked them back out again. We knew they'd try again, so we had to get ourselves organized properly, do some thinking about how to defend the place, and how to survive in a siege. And I was the only one with any real experience of anything like that. I couldn't leave.'

'You became "the Commander".'

'It's not like it sounds. No one else here could have handled it. Plus, I was English, so there didn't have to be any arguments about whether a Serb or a Croat or a Muslim should be top dog.' He smiled. 'I became sort of a mini-Tito,' he said. 'And I've done a good job.'

'I bet you have. Did you blow the bridge on the road behind the town?'

'Yeah, but only as a precaution. The Serbs can't get people in numbers up on this side of the valley. We blew the bridges over the river further down, and they can't get anything across. They could try from the back – I suppose that's the way you came in – but there are no roads and nowhere to shelter, and nothing much to build a shelter with. They couldn't get any heavy guns up there.'

'So what have they tried?'

'After the first visit they left us alone for a week, then tried surprising us in the middle of the night. We killed about twenty of them, and they left us alone for a couple of months after that. Except of course they blocked up the valley at both ends so nothing could come in or out. That was around August, and there was plenty of food in the town, but we had to start thinking about how we were going to survive the winter. We could cut down trees behind the town for fires, but the only generators we had needed oil, and there was hardly any left. So' – he opened his palms – 'we had to steal some.

'By this time I'd got a pretty good training programme going. I based it on what we taught the Dhofaris in Oman, remember? Once they were ready I took some of the lads on a recce, and we found the Serbs' local fuel depot in Sipovo. Nicking two tankers was easy enough – the depot wasn't even guarded – and we managed to bluff our way back through their roadblock. You can get a long way around here singing the right songs and sporting the right tattoos.' Reeve grinned reminiscently. 'Plus, of course, about a third of our men don't have to pretend – they really are Serbs.'

Docherty grinned back, relief spreading through him. Reeve hadn't been driven off the rails by the madness around him. In fact, as far as Docherty could tell, he seemed more insulated from it all than anyone they had met since leaving Split.

Reeve poured another two measures of plum brandy and lit another cigarette. 'The weaponry situation wasn't too good either,' he said. 'We had plenty of Kalashnikovs, and a couple of mortars we stole from the Serbs, but only a few SMGs and hardly any explosives. Luckily, we had an ex-Yugoslav Army officer in town – a Croat – who could lead us straight to an armoury outside Livno. The Croat Army was pissed off when we stole half their ordnance, but what the fuck?' He laughed. 'The main problem was carrying the goddam stuff back over the hills. We didn't think the Serbs would fall for the bluff twice, though God knows there's enough of them popping acid that they probably wouldn't have noticed. Probably just see pretty patterns as we went past.'

'How did you manage to piss off the Bosnian Government?' Docherty asked. 'And the UN?'

'Ah, that was a bit naughty,' Reeve admitted. 'We stole one of their supply shipments – mostly food.'

'You what!?'

'They had plenty to spare, Jamie. It was when they were still using the Kupres road to supply Vitez. The idiots left the key in the ignition when they stopped for a picnic lunch. They ran along behind us for about a quarter of a mile, shouting at us to bring it back.'

Docherty laughed. 'I talked to the commander at Vitez, and he didn't mention it,' he said.

'I'm not surprised,' Reeve said. 'It hardly adds lustre to the Cheshires' image, does it?'

'And the Bosnian Government?'

'We borrowed one of their armoured cars from Bugojno. It's not exactly state-of-the-art, I'm afraid – it was probably abandoned by the Red Army in 1945. But it works. We just drove it home through the Serb roadblock – and I mean through it – all hatches down. They didn't know what to make of it either, watching this armoured car blithely totalling one of their beloved Toyotas.' He took a gulp of the brandy. 'I've got to like this stuff. Where were we?'

'Stealing an armoured car.'

'Yeah, well. I don't see how the Bosnian Government can object to us doing their job for them. They should be holding us up as a shining example. Izetbegovic is fond of saying that Bosnia was overflowing with brotherly love and tolerance before the Serb shit hit the fan. I don't know how much of that is wishful thinking on his part, but Zavik is definitely Bosnia as it ought to be. We've got Serbs, Muslims, Croats, Jews, even a few Albanians, and yours truly, all getting along with each other. You take a walk through the town tomorrow morning – you'll find a mosque, an Orthodox church and a Catholic church, all in the same square, all open for business.'

'What about the Serbs outside the town?' Docherty wanted to know. 'Are they still keeping their distance?'

'No, they're hatching something. And they're more or less all around us now. Sooner or later they're going to drag some guns on to the hills opposite and start throwing shells at us. If they can be bothered. I hope they can't.' He took a last drag on the cigarette. 'And of course there's always a chance that peace will break out.'

'I wouldn't hold your breath,' Docherty said mildly. 'And I wouldn't be too optimistic about reconciliation,' he added. 'We've been in this country about a week, and I've seen things to trouble my sleep until I die.'

'Like what?'

Docherty told him about the villages in the hills, the hospital at Sarajevo, the women at Vogosca.

'What were you doing there?' Reeve asked.

Docherty cursed himself for the slip, but decided there was no going back. 'Rescuing Nena,' he said.

Reeve looked at him, sudden bleakness in his eyes. 'Oh Christ,' he said.

'She wasn't there long,' Docherty said, realizing as he did so how ludicrous it sounded.

Reeve was getting slowly to his feet. 'I should be with her,' he said. 'I . . .'

'Maybe you should let her come to you,' Docherty said gently, wondering if she would.

A quarter of a mile away, Nena lay in her old childhood bed in the house on the hill, curled up like a foetus, unable to sleep. Her mind was whirling around, and she seemed to lack the will to stop it. It was like a waking dream, a sort of seamless merging of scenes and people.

There was Docherty at their wedding, still treating Isabel as if she was an invalid, and there was Reeve on the day their son was born, looking like a boy himself, so young and proud, and there were the crucified bodies on the wall, the man and the woman and the two children, and there she was in the gymnasium at Vogosca with the waves of crying ebbing and flowing like a sea of sadness.

'Will you ever be the same again?' a voice asked, and she answered, angrily: 'No, of course not!' and then there was silence for a moment, a silence of snow and blue sky. Then the voice asked: 'Will you ever be happy again?' and she said: 'Yes, yes, I promise!' and she wondered if it was a promise she could keep.

They had been told to take their pick of the empty rooms at the youth hostel, and Hajrija picked out one on the first floor. 'Razor, can I talk with you,' she asked, beckoning him in.

'Sure,' he said, surprised but daring to hope.

She pushed the door shut behind him and stood there, not saying anything, just looking at him, waiting.

In the dark she looked so serious, he thought. So sad. He leaned forward and kissed her on the lips, and felt her arms reach around his neck, and her body press into his.

They kissed for what seemed like minutes, and then finally managed to shed their jackets and hats and belts before kissing for several more. They shed their boots and half tripped on to the narrow bed, slowly disentangling themselves from the top half of the Arctic gear, and lying there half-naked, oblivious to the cold. He kissed her breasts and raised his face to hers. In the darkness of the room all he could see

214

was a faint glow on either cheek and two excited eyes that shone deep and dark.

They made love as if they never would again, and then sank into an exhausted sleep.

Soon after dawn, as they were disentangling themselves for the third time, the window blew in, swiftly followed by the sound of an enormous explosion.

The first Serb shell had landed on Zavik.

They gingerly slid out from under the glass-strewn blanket. 'Are you OK?' Razor asked, holding her naked body against his own.

'Yes,' she answered. She was shivering, and not all from the cold.

'Some couples feel the earth move,' Razor murmured. 'We seem to hear the sound of breaking glass.'

14

The bombardment continued throughout the day. At first a shell would land every few minutes, but from mid-morning onwards the gaps became longer, as if the Serbs were either growing bored or intent on conserving ammunition. The previous day's mist had lifted, revealing a layer of clouds which grew more broken as the morning progressed. Whether this improvement in visibility was a good thing, Docherty was unable to decide. It presumably gave the Serbs more chance of hitting what they were aiming at, but since they were apparently content with landing their shells anywhere in the town, that didn't seem such an important consideration. For the townspeople, he suspected, a first taste of artillery bombardment in yesterday's mist would have been even more unnerving than what they were having to endure.

Most of the town's population – reckoned by Reeve at just over two thousand – were now sheltering in their own or a neighbour's basement or cellar, listening to each crack of man-made thunder and wondering where on their mental map of friends and acquaintances each particular blow had fallen.

One of the first shells had landed on the school. Two children had been crushed by a falling roof, and another

217

dozen injured, some of them seriously. About the same number of adults had been injured during the confusion of the first hour, and three men and two women had been killed, all in their beds, when their houses exploded around them.

Once the initial shock had subsided the more or less regular gaps between shells gave people a chance to move around in relative safety. It was Sarajevo without the snipers, Nena Reeve thought bitterly, as she hurried down the street towards the youth hostel. Optimistically, as it turned out. She arrived in the hostel's basement at the same time as one of Reeve's young soldiers, who had come with the news that a man had just been shot dead in the main square. Almost certainly by a sniper.

'What are you doing here?' Reeve asked, seeing her standing in the doorway.

'I assume you need doctors,' she said.

'Christ, yes. Hold on a minute.' He barked rapid-fire orders at two men, both of whom Nena suddenly recognized as the sons of an old friend. The last time she'd seen them they were about sixteen, and on their way to university in Belgrade.

Reeve stood up. 'We'll wait for the next shell and then I'll take you over to the hospital,' he said.

'Hospital?'

'We've cleared out one of the underground crypts in the old castle . . .' He raised a hand. 'I know it's not the ideal place, but it's safe from shelling. And it's the best I could think of at a moment's notice.'

She looked at him. 'You really are running this town, aren't you?' she said.

'Just about.'

'What about your career? The SAS?'

He shrugged. 'I couldn't leave the children at the beginning, and then I became kind of indispensable all round. I haven't had many choices, Nena . . .' He grinned suddenly. 'But in any case . . .'

There was the thud of an explosion, some distance away. 'Come on,' he said.

They went up the stairs, out into the street and turned uphill towards where the old ruined castle looked out over the town from its perch just beneath the clifftop. Away to the right the frozen waterfall was glistening in the sunlight.

'And some things are more important than the SAS,' he added, as if to himself. This was not the time to ask her about herself, he thought.

'You never used to think so,' she said. 'No, I'm sorry, that's not fair.'

'Maybe it is,' he said, as they reached the castle entrance. The booth where tourists had bought their entrance tickets was lying on its side in the snow like a badly made toboggan.

'How many other doctors are there in the town?' she asked.

'Two,' he said. 'Dr Muhmedalisa, remember him? He should be here. And then there's old Bosnic. He should have retired ages ago, but . . . His eyesight's more or less gone altogether, I'm afraid . . .'

They walked down steep stone steps and found themselves in a large, medieval-style chamber. Two oil stoves had been brought in to provide heat, and a man was busy trying to shut off the draughts. Mattresses had been arranged in two rows along either wall, and most were already occupied. The only doctor visible was patiently trying to undo a new bandage, holding it up to within an inch of his eyes. At the other end of the room a young girl was screaming in pain.

Nena went to look at her.

'Where's Muhmedalisa?' Reeve asked Bosnic.

'He was killed about two hours ago,' Bosnic said curtly.

'Oh shit.'

'That child needs morphine,' Nena said, hurrying up. 'Where are the drugs?'

'What we have are there,' Bosnic said, peering at her myopically. 'You're Nena Abdic, I remember your voice. You're a nurse.'

'A doctor now.' She was looking through the box. 'There's hardly anything here,' she said.

'It's all there is,' Reeve said.

'Won't Jamie and the others be carrying medical kits? And at least one of them should have medical training. That's the way it works, isn't it?'

'I'll go and find out,' Reeve said. 'Welcome home,' he added, as the girl started screaming again.

An hour later Chris and Razor were both helping out at the improvised hospital, and the SAS medical kits had been added to the town's supply. Docherty and the Dame were halfway up the mountain by this time, accompanying Reeve and Tijanic on a mission with two objectives. First they wanted to pinpoint the location of the Serbs' artillery piece, and second that of the sniper. In case they discovered the latter, the Dame had brought along the Accuracy International.

They hadn't needed to take the Stair; a couple of extended planks were available on the town side of the blown bridge. After they had walked across, another of Reeve's men had retracted the makeshift crossing and settled down to await their return.

It took them half an hour to reach the top of the toboggan meadow, and another to find a suitable place to sweep the far side of the valley with their binoculars. The gun wasn't immediately visible, but they had doubted whether it would be, even from the crest above them. The Serbs would have taken care to camouflage it at the very least, and probably to remove it completely from any possible enemy line of sight.

It was the Dame who found it, behind the crest of a hill away to the right of the town. He had the rifle's telescopic sight trained in just the right direction to catch a shimmering in the cold air as the Serb gun fired. As he patiently waited to confirm his suspicion, a head momentarily popped up above the horizon. A minute later the same shimmering accompanied the sound of the gun firing.

They marked a line in on Reeve's map and then moved a few hundred yards through the trees to the east. From there they were able to draw an intersecting line and plot the exact location of the gun.

Then they started scouring the whole far side of the valley, looking for the sniper. Two hours of lying in the snow later, they were beginning to despair of finding him when Reeve let out a quiet whoop of triumph. 'Start at the top of the minaret,' he said, 'and go straight up until you hit the track on the hill. Just to the right there's a group of trees. The one on the right-hand end just moved, and none of the others did.'

The Dame cradled the Accuracy International to his shoulder and stared through the sight. He thought he could detect a darker shadow inside the tree but he wasn't sure. 'Too far away,' he said. 'And in any case I can't get a clean shot from here. If I miss he'll just disappear into the trees.'

'How about from down in the town?' Docherty asked.

'No reason why not.'

Back in Zavik, Docherty and Reeve visited the hospital, where the situation, though far from good, had at least improved since the morning. 'There have only been a couple more wounded this afternoon,' Razor told them.

'Are any of these in danger?' Reeve asked, looking round.

'Quite a few.'

'We can't treat them here,' Nena said, coming over to join them. 'We don't have enough medicine, and I don't have the right kinds of skills.' She looked exhausted, Docherty thought, but something else as well. There was more than a trace of her old self present – having others to take care of had at least been good for her.

'There's nowhere else to take them,' Reeve was saying. 'You can give me a shopping list of medicines and I'll try and fill it, but we're talking about a minimum of several days. I can't risk the few men I've got on half-thought-out operations.'

'If you don't, then some of these children will be at risk.'

'OK, OK. But first we have to deal with the gun up there, or there'll be more and more wounded to deal with. Are you and your boys in on this, Jamie?'

Docherty gave him a wry smile. It was a question he'd been expecting since their location of the Serb gun. 'Probably,' he said. He looked at Reeve. 'But we're here in the first place because our bosses were pissed off at one Brit taking sides in this war. I think I'd better talk to the others before we add four more to the charge sheet.'

'Fair enough,' Reeve said equably.

'Are you two needed here?' Docherty asked Razor and Chris.

'Not at the moment,' Nena answered for them.

The three SAS men waited several minutes for the sound of a shell landing, then hurried back down to the hostel, taking care to make use of all the available cover.

'Where's the Dame?' Chris asked Docherty.

'Out hunting,' the PC said.

* * *

222

It had taken the Dame fifteen minutes to find what seemed a suitable location, in the upstairs room of an empty house on the western edge of the town. The tree in question was now only three hundred yards away, just within the limits of the Covert PM variant of the Accuracy International. He erected the built-in bipod support, put his eye to the Schmidt & Bender telescopic sight, and there was the Serbian sniper, or at least the edges of his body. The man was perched about ten feet up in the cedar tree, but mostly hidden behind the trunk, his rifle resting against a convenient branch. When he next went to use it, the Dame would have him.

The minutes went by. The Dame thought he could see cigarette smoke drifting out from behind the trunk, and had a mental picture of his dead father lighting one of the forty Players No. 6 he had smoked each day. Every time he had lit one up at home his mother had coughed, just the once, to register her disapproval. What with the all the new stuff about passive smoking, he supposed she'd been right.

There was movement in the tree, and the man's face came into view, a hand putting the cigarette to his mouth. The light was beginning to fade and there was a slight glow as he dragged on it. The man was an amateur, the Dame thought.

He watched as the Serb picked up his rifle – which looked suspiciously like a British Lee-Enfield – and slowly scanned the town across the river, looking for a target. An almost imperceptible tightening of the shoulders told the Dame he had found one.

The SAS man wriggled his shoulder to make sure the rifle's butt was comfortable, worked the bolt action, aligned the cross-hairs above the bridge of the Serb's nose, and squeezed the trigger. A black hole appeared where it was supposed to, and then the man was gone. The Dame shifted the telescopic

223

sight downwards, through the cloud of snow that was still falling from the disturbed branches, and found the dark shape lying motionless beneath the tree.

One more, he thought. One more.

He packed up the rifle and went back down through the empty house. At the doorway something strange made him pause. Then he realized: no shell had landed on the town for quite a while. Maybe the bastards had run out of them. Maybe they were having their tea break.

Back at the hostel he found the other three having one.

'Did you get him?' Docherty asked.

'Yep,' he said, looking round. 'Where's my cup of tea?'

Razor did the honours.

'OK,' Docherty said, when the requisite cup had been poured and sugared, 'we have some decisions to take.' He grunted. 'Like decide what the fuck we're doing here.'

'What are the choices, boss?' Chris asked seriously. 'This is not our war. I mean, I don't know who's in the right. Does anyone?'

'Ah, c'mon,' Razor said. 'You've just spent the day trying to patch up kids who've been hit by indiscriminate shell fire. You know that's not right.'

'Sure,' Chris said. 'And what happened to those women, I know. But what I don't know is whether we've just seen one side of all this. You were there when they threw the sniper out of the window. That wasn't right either.'

'He'd shot half a dozen kids!'

'I know. But my point is, I think the whole country's gone mad.'

'But . . .'

'Aye,' Docherty interjected, 'the whole country has gone mad, and it's not up to us to sort it out. Like Chris says, it's not our war. But . . . we're here, and I don't think we can just walk away from what we see with our own eyes. It may be only one side, but right here, right now, there's a town being destroyed for no other reason than that it wants to live in peace.'

'What are you saying we ought to do, boss?' Razor asked.

'I'm not. I don't know. And it's different for me – I don't have a future with the Regiment to worry about . . .'

'Fuck that for a game of soldiers,' Razor said.

'Yeah,' Chris agreed, 'that's not a problem.'

'Anyway, us three can say we were just following orders,' Razor said with a grin.

'Be my guest,' Docherty agreed. 'Problem is, I still haven't got any orders for you to follow.'

'OK,' Razor said. 'Try this. We're not hanging around to win the war for anyone, but we're not just making a run for good ol' Blighty. So we're going to do what we can and *then* head home. So what can we do?'

'Take out the Serb gun,' the Dame said.

'Aye. And maybe do something about those children. I have a feeling it's time I reported in. And I'm going to ask if someone can arrange choppers to take out the badly wounded and any other children whose parents want them to leave.'

'You think there's any chance they'll agree to that?' Chris asked doubtfully.

'Split's less than an hour away, and I can't see how anyone could see it as anything other than a humanitarian mission . . .' He shrugged. 'But I expect they'll say no. I can only find out by asking.'

'What are you going to say about Reeve?' Razor asked.

Docherty shrugged. 'I'll just tell them what's happened here. If they ask me, I shall say that in my opinion Sergeant Reeve has acted in the best interests of the people here and in the best traditions of the Regiment.'

'You're not going to mention the Cheshires' lorryload of frozen oven chips then, boss?' Razor asked.

The PC grunted. 'I don't think so,' he said, laughing. 'But I'd better talk to Reeve first, in any case. And I'll tell him we're on for tonight.' He paused. 'If any of you don't want to be involved in this, that's fine,' he said. 'If I wasn't a friend of Reeve's I'm not at all sure whether I'd be going.'

'We are, boss,' Razor said.

'I don't like people who can't even be bothered to aim their artillery,' Chris remarked.

Docherty found Reeve standing alone, smoking a cigarette, outside the entrance to the makeshift hospital.

'You're not running short on them, then?' he asked.

'These? No, we were lucky. There was a delivery lorry here a few days before the blockade was tightened. The driver was a Serb and wanted to risk it, but we dissuaded him.' Reeve smiled. 'He married one of the local girls a few weeks ago – a Croat. It's been an education, Jamie, this war. I wouldn't have missed it for the world.'

'I'm going to report in,' Docherty told him, 'tell them what the situation is here, and ask if they can arrange to fly out however many of those kids Nena thinks need to go.'

'OK,' Reeve said, after a moment's hesitation. 'And what's my report card going to say?'

'I'll just tell them what's happening. Tell them you've been looking after your kids, maybe offering some advice every now and then to the locals.'

'Thanks, Jamie.'

'Don't mention it. And you have four volunteers for tonight,' Docherty told him. 'And then I think we'll be on our way.'

'Missing Isabel?'

226

'You bet.'

'I've been missing Nena. More than I thought I would.' He grimaced. 'Have you talked to her? I haven't had a chance, yet. How is she, really?'

'I don't know, Reeve. But I don't think people bounce back from what she's been through. It'll take a lot of time.'

At the hostel, Docherty's departure left silence in its wake, as each of the other three men tried to make some sense of what he felt about the situation. For Razor there was the additional problem of what was going to happen between him and Hajrija. He hadn't seen her since their rude awakening that morning, and had no idea where she was. He hoped she wasn't regretting what had taken place the previous night.

He looked at the other two – the Dame sitting back with his eyes closed, Chris studying the map on the table – and wondered why there'd been no ribbing that morning. Maybe because they didn't think they knew him well enough, but he doubted it. Maybe because they knew he was serious about her.

Would she stay on in Zavik? It was her home town, after all. The thought of staying here with her crossed Razor's mind. He could certainly help out on the military and medical fronts – he wouldn't just be in the way. It would mean throwing career and pension out of the window, but that thought didn't deter him. If he'd been the type to care about things like that he wouldn't be in the fucking SAS, would he?

But he'd have to go with the others, at least as far as Split. They'd come in together and they'd go out the same way. He owed them that much.

'Assuming there's no reply from International Rescue,' he asked Chris and the Dame, 'how do you think we're going to get home?'

'The way we arrived, probably,' Chris said. 'A long walk out of here, and then . . .' He shrugged. 'We could walk to the coast in a few days. We've still got enough emergency rations.'

'We could,' Razor agreed, 'but I can't say as I fancy it. Unless you two are willing to carry me in a sedan chair.'

The Dame opened one disdainful eye, and closed it again.

'It was just a thought,' Razor said. He heard someone come in through the door upstairs and hoped it was Hajrija.

The boots which appeared on the stairs belonged to Docherty. 'You three could have a look at that map and come up with some suggestions for tonight,' he said, working the case containing the PRC 319 out of his bergen.

'I am, boss,' Chris said in an aggrieved tone.

Docherty grinned. 'Sorry.' He went back up the stairs with the radio, and out into the rapidly darkening street. Not far away he found a large enough expanse of open ground and set up the system, pointing the two tuning antennae up into the western sky and searching out the correct frequency. The PRC 319 was capable of carrying voice transmissions, but Docherty decided, mostly on instinct, to use the burst facility instead. He typed out 'Tito calling Churchill' and sent it. Almost instantaneously the words 'Churchill receiving' appeared on the tiny screen.

Docherty started typing with one finger. 'Tito group now in Zavik. Stop. No casualties. Stop. Our friend is here. Stop. Rumours unjustified. Stop. Town under artillery attack as of yesterday. Stop. Request helicopter extraction for seriously wounded children, numbering nine as of today. Stop. Will expect reply tomorrow 0700 GMT. Out.'

He packed up the set and squatted in the dark for an instant, looking up at the dark line of hills across the valley. Just one gun, he thought.

Better one less than one more.

15

They left the town shortly after nine o'clock, eleven men and one woman, walking in single file down the road which led up the valley to the west. Hajrija's presence was not appreciated by all – the acceptance she had won from her comrades in Sarajevo was only hearsay as far as Reeve and his men were concerned – and Docherty had felt more than a little reluctant when called as a witness to her competence. He suspected she was every bit as good a fighter as any in Reeve's unprofessional army, but the look on Razor's face was not a pretty sight.

The latter had already tried to dissuade her, and failed utterly. 'If you think I lie in bed all night waiting for you, you crazy,' Hajrija had told him. Now, walking along behind her, Razor was consoling himself with the thought that at least she was thinking about being in bed with him.

The twelve of them had a long way to go that night. The fact that Reeve and Chris had drawn up virtually identical plans of action might have reflected their common SAS training, but it also pointed to the paucity of options open to them. There were two ways up the three hundred-yard slopes opposite the town, one obvious, one not so obvious.

But any attacking force had first to cross the river, and here the options were more limited. With the road bridges already blown there was only one spot close to the town where a force could ford the icy waters with any ease, and if the Serbs had any sense at all they would surely have night glasses trained in that direction, particularly on the first night after beginning their bombardment.

So both the local ways up the slope were out. Instead, the two planners had recommended a four-mile walk up the valley to another crossing spot. From there they could climb up out of the valley, and then undertake a wide, flanking march around to the Serbs' rear. Such an approach might be exhausting, but, Reeve and Chris had both decided, offered the only reasonable chance of surprise.

And with any luck they would also come across the road the Serbs must have constructed to get the gun up to the top of the hill. It wouldn't do much good to take out one artillery piece if the enemy could just bring up another.

The walk was long but for the most part uneventful. The sky was full of broken cloud, and the quarter moon, when it rose, was bright enough to facilitate track-finding on their way out of the valley. Up on the rolling plateau it was almost too bright, combining with the snow to create a light that felt almost artificial. To Razor, walking at the rear, the column of black silhouettes against the moonlit white hills seemed like a scene caught by a camera's flash and then for ever frozen, locked in a denial of darkness.

It was almost three by the time they reached the Serbs' approach road. It had been a mere footpath on Reeve's local map, but the Serbs had widened and smoothed it, cutting down trees and inserting makeshift vehicle-width wooden bridges where dips or water made them necessary. Judging by the overlapping tracks in the snow they were making considerable use of it.

When the party reached the first bridge Reeve sent two of his men forward as advance scouts. The rest waited while a third man rigged the bridge with Czech-made Semtex – part of Reeve's Livno Armoury haul – and set up a time fuse. He did the same at the next, and the next, a formidable piece of construction that spanned a narrow ravine. Considering that Zavik had no apparent military value, Docherty thought, the Serbs were taking a lot of trouble over it. Someone had to be very angry – maybe Reeve had overdone it a little. But it was obviously too late to kiss and make up.

One of the two advance scouts returned with news of a sentry point a couple of hundred yards further up the mountain. The location had been chosen well, he said: the two men were on the far side of the next bridge, which crossed another long ravine. There was doubtless a way round it, but it would take time to find.

'Are they just standing there?' Reeve asked.

'No, they're sitting by one of those braziers warming their hands and chattering on about what a bastard their commander is.'

'Can we get a clean shot at them? Are they holding their guns?'

'Yes and yes,' the scout said.

Reeve turned to Docherty, who had been receiving a translation of all this from Chris. 'We need your silenced MP5s,' he said.

'What's the range?' Docherty asked the scout, Chris translating the question.

'From cover? About sixty yards.'

'Too far,' Docherty said, cursing the fact that they'd only brought one scope for the MP5s. 'Dame,' he said, 'do you

231

think you could take out two before the second man raises the alarm?'

'No reason why not,' the Wearsider said. Two more, he thought.

The scout led him up the widened path, which now ran diagonally across a forest-covered slope. A few minutes later they were joining the first scout, squatting down and staring out across a wide expanse of snow at the bridge and the two men by their brazier. It looked ridiculous, the Dame thought, just these two men on the side of a mountain sitting by a fire in the middle of the night.

He stood up, taking care to keep his body behind the trunk, and then inched himself slowly outwards, the MP5's retractable stock cradled against his shoulder, the telescopic sight to his right eye. It didn't feel as comfortable as the Accuracy International, but in this situation silence was everything. He examined the face of the Serb on the right, lit by the orange fire and big enough to fill the sight at this range.

He shifted the aim to the left and found the other face, which was laughing at something. He moved back swiftly to the first face, trying to accustom himself to the quick shift he would need. He was too close really: a hundred yards further back would have been better. Still, at that distance the gun would be reaching the limits of its effective range. And in any case he didn't fancy crawling back through the snow.

He felt easier moving from the right target to the left than vice versa. He aligned the cross-hairs on the side of the right-hand man's head, just above the ear. Aim by not aiming, he told himself, and let his grip slacken for a second.

Now. He squeezed the trigger once, smoothly slid his aim to the left, found the other target, squeezed again. He lowered the gun, and confirmed with his naked eye what his brain already knew. Both men were dead.

One of the two scouts was already scurrying back through the snow to collect the rest. The other was hurrying forward to check out his marksmanship. The Dame walked forward to join him, and they were both warming their hands on the brazier when the main party caught up with them.

Once the bridge had been rigged they resumed their climb, again through an expanse of forest. They were nearing the top now, but the scouts ranging fifty yards or so ahead found no more sentries. Instead they found a large clearing just below the ridge top. The gun which had done such damage sat to one side on its reinforced base, and the breakdown lorry which had presumably towed it up the mountain stood close by. On the other side of the clearing three transit vans were parked in a line, two of them in darkness, one showing a faint aura of light. Barely audible music seemed to be coming from the latter.

The snow had been mostly swept away from the clearing and the embers of a small fire were still glowing. Cooking utensils sat in a pile, and a pot had been filled with snow for whatever it was that Serb gunners drank for their breakfast.

'What now?' Docherty asked, as he and Reeve surveyed the scene from just inside the trees.

'We can't take prisoners,' Reeve said, looking at Docherty as if he was expecting an argument.

Docherty had none. These men were responsible for the children screaming in Zavik's makeshift hospital. And who knew what else, either in the past or the future. 'Let's do it quietly though,' he said. 'There may be more men on our route home, and I'd rather we surprised them than the other way round.'

'Semtex under each van, then,' Reeve said, as if he was decorating a stage. 'And one for the gun.'

'A fifteen-minute fuse for the vans, a couple more for the gun,' Docherty suggested.

Since both were demolition specialists, Reeve and the Dame supervised the laying of the charges. The latter approached the dimly lit van with appropriate caution, but the two men inside seemed fast asleep, oblivious to the Thin Lizzy tape playing on the van's stereo. Even outside the tightly shuttered van the smell of marijuana filled the cold air.

In ten minutes they were finished and the twelve-person patrol was on its way again, crossing the ridge top and starting down the slope on the quick route home. Once again two men were sent ahead to scout for the enemy.

The path wound steeply down through trees, and the going was easy enough to suggest it had been used with some regularity in recent days. After fourteen and a half minutes had passed on his watch Reeve halted the column, and they all waited in silence, hoping that nothing had gone wrong.

The first explosion was out by only two seconds, sending a yellow-white flash into the sky behind them. An image of the transit vans exploding in three simultaneous shafts of light came to Docherty's mind, and in his imagination he looked across the clearing to where the gun was still standing.

The second explosion was louder than the first, but not as spectacular. With grim smiles on their faces, and renewed caution, the twelve resumed their journey down the slope. About ten minutes later they emerged from a stand of trees to find the town spread out below them in the moonlight. Perhaps it was this which took the edge off their alertness, or maybe it was just that everything had gone too smoothly.

Either way, they were halfway past the Serb observation platform before they knew it was there.

It had been dug into the mountainside to give the Serbs a panoramic view of the town and valley below, and the radio link with the camp on the hilltop gave the gunners at least the option of directed fire. The explosions above had woken the two men who manned the platform, and the failure of their efforts to raise their superiors had made them jumpy. It might just be a lot of stoned fun going on up on the hill – maybe someone had fired a Croat from the gun or something – but it might be something dreamed up by the English lunatic in the town below.

They had been watching and waiting for several minutes, when the first shadows walked into their line of sight. Despite this, one Serb was surprised enough to shout rather than shoot. The other was either quicker of thought or more prone to violence, because he opened up immediately, killing one of Reeve's men, wounding another in the shoulder and giving Razor a second parting in his dark hair. The shock made the Londoner slip on the snow, and he went down flat on his back.

It seemed as if the whole party opened fire at the same moment, and in retrospect Docherty reckoned it a minor miracle that no one had been killed or wounded by friendly fire. The observation post, though, was riddled with enough bullets to kill ten, let alone two. And any chance of surprising any Serbs lower down the path had been shot just as comprehensively.

Razor's scalp hurt like hell, but there wasn't much blood, and he received some compensation from Hajrija's instant appearance at his side as he lay in the snow. Chris made quick examinations of both him and the man with the shoulder wound, and found nothing which would prevent them from walking. The party resumed its downward progress, with two men carrying the body of their dead friend. Reeve and Docherty spent the journey waiting for the scouts to report Serbs on the path ahead, but if any had been deployed there, they had apparently gone. An hour before dawn the troop forded the river below the broken bridge and re-entered the town.

The injured men were accompanied to the castle crypt, where Nena was found dozing fitfully on one of the few empty mattresses. After she and Chris had applied the necessary dressings, Docherty took her to one side, and told her he'd asked for nine of the children to be air-lifted out.

'Why nine?' she wanted to know.

'It seemed like a convincing number. I don't think they'll come anyway, but if they do, then we can ask them to take as many as you think should go.'

'Nine was a pretty good guess,' she said looking round.

Her eyes were bloodshot with exhaustion, Docherty noticed. He expected his own were too.

'If they don't come, most of those nine are going to die,' she said quietly.

It was getting lighter outside as Docherty walked back down to the hostel. Most of the townspeople were probably in their basements by now, waiting for the bombardment to resume. Well, they would be spared that, at least for the time it took the Serbs to repair their road, replace their personnel and find another gun. Weeks, he guessed. And then Reeve would go back up the mountain and destroy that one too.

The really different thing about this war, Docherty thought, was the lack of air power involved. It had to be the first war in Europe since World War One in which the aeroplane hadn't played a decisive role. Maybe that explained the medieval feel of the whole business.

It didn't explain crucifixions, though.

At the hostel he found all the others had disappeared to their beds, keen to grab back at least some of the sleeping hours they had lost. Docherty made himself some tea and sat in the basement room, thinking about his children, and wondering what they would think of their father's life when they were old enough to understand it. If they ever were, he thought wryly. When it came to the bigger picture he seemed to grow more confused as he got older, not less. A sign of growing wisdom, as Liam McCall would say. But not an excuse to stop looking.

At five to eight he collected the PRC 319 and went back up the hill to set it up for reception. At precisely 0800 Central European Time the words 'Churchill calling Tito' appeared on the tiny screen. 'Tito receiving' Docherty typed out, and waited, hoping against hope.

'Tito group return base soonest. Stop. Require Friend to accompany. Stop. No air assistance possible. Out.'

'Bastards,' Docherty murmured.

He packed up the radio and took it back to the hostel, then went up to the castle to tell Nena the bad news. She took it more stoically than he expected, but then he guessed she was used to such news after her months working in the Sarajevo hospital. Back at the hostel he set his alarm for noon, and sank into an exhausted sleep.

Almost instantly, it seemed, he was woken by the clock. The sun was shining full on his face, and outside he could hear people talking. From the window he could see two women walking away down the street, as if the previous day's bombardment had been just a bad dream.

He went to wake the others, but found their rooms empty. Chris and Razor were in the basement, drinking tea and waiting for him. Both looked pointedly at their watches as he came in.

Docherty poured himself a cup and sat down. 'I've got bad news,' he began.

'We know, boss,' Razor said. 'Nena told us. But Reeve has had an idea.'

'That sounds ominous,' Docherty murmured, just as Reeve himself appeared on the stairs, the Dame behind him.

'It seems to be OK,' the Wearsider said. 'Both cab windows are broken, so it's going to be a bit on the cold side . . .'

'What's OK?' Docherty asked.

'The cigarette lorry,' Reeve explained. 'The one you're taking the kids to Split in.'

Docherty looked at Razor, whose bandaged head gave him the look of a punk pirate.

'It's the only way, boss. If we can't fly the kids out, we have to drive them out, it's as simple as that.'

Docherty supposed it was.

'And we've got something else to show you,' Reeve said.

They all trooped up the stairs and out into the street. In front of the lorry stood an extremely basic-looking armoured car – one which looked old enough to have done service with Rommel in the desert. Its gun was obviously long gone, but it looked robust enough to shoot Niagara Falls. More surprisingly, given its age, the white vehicle bore the letters UN on its side.

'I told Reeve we had UN berets,' Razor explained.

'We'd already painted it white for winter camouflage,' Reeve added, 'but the logo is still wet.'

Docherty looked round at them. 'Let me get this straight. We're going to use this antique to escort a lorryload of children to Split, passing through at least one Serb blockade, and possibly several others, *en route*?'

'That's about it,' Reeve agreed.

Docherty shook his head and smiled. 'I like it.'

'We thought you would,' Razor said.

'I assume there's no problem with fuel?'

'Nope.'

'So who's coming on this jaunt?'

It was Reeve who answered. 'Eight children and two adults – they're a husband and wife, and they're in their seventies. Their basement ceiling collapsed on them yesterday. And Hajrija wants to come with you. She thinks it'll be easier to get back to Sarajevo from Split.'

'What about Nena?'

'She's staying here. She says there's nothing more she can do for the ones you're taking, and you have Chris and Razor. Zavik needs her more.'

And so do you and the kids, Docherty thought. He was glad they would at least have the chance to try again.

'When do we leave?' he asked.

'You're the boss,' Razor said.

Night or day, Docherty wondered. He was fed up with darkness. 'Dawn tomorrow,' he decided.

Later that evening Docherty visited Nena at her parents' home. She had managed to catch a few hours' sleep, and looked more like the woman he had known in years gone by, one with life in her eyes and a tendency to laugh. Not surprisingly, the children were still intent on monopolizing their mother, and there was not much opportunity for the two adults to share a serious conversation.

But there was one thing Docherty felt he had to say. 'If you ever decide to send the children out of here,' he said, 'but can't or don't want to leave yourself, then we'll be happy to look after them for you.'

239

'I can't imagine letting them go again,' she said, 'but thank you.'

'And as for Reeve,' Docherty said, 'you know him better than I do . . .'

'I think we know different sides.'

'Aye, maybe. But I know he's missed you, because he told me so. What that means . . .' He shrugged. 'Just thought I'd pass it on.'

She smiled ruefully at him. 'We'll see,' she said, just as her son imposed his head between theirs and began talking nineteen to the dozen.

An hour later Docherty and Reeve were drinking each other's health in René's Café. 'Didn't London even bother to mention me?' Reeve wanted to know.

'Oh aye, they bothered. "Require Friend to accompany." The friend is you.'

'What do they expect you to do – tie me up and throw me over your shoulder?'

'Christ knows. Who bloody cares?'

'What are you going to tell them?'

Docherty grunted. 'That you're more valuable here than they'll ever be anywhere. And that they can go fuck themselves.'

Reeve grinned. 'You know, I didn't think it was possible that you could grow more insubordinate with age, but you've managed it.' He raised his glass. 'Here's to the journey.'

16

The sun was still hidden behind the mountains, the town still far from awake, as the convoy began threading its way out through Zavik's narrow streets towards the road that ran west up the valley. A Renault Five containing Reeve and three of his men led the way, followed by Docherty and the Dame in the armoured car, with the lorry bringing up the rear. Razor was driving the lorry, while Chris and Hajrija served in the back as combination nurses and tail-gunners.

The number of passengers had dropped over the past twenty-four hours. The old woman had passed away in the night, and her husband's determination to live seemed to have died with her. It had taken all of Nena's persuasive powers to get him aboard the lorry.

One of the nine children had also died, and another two were withdrawn by parents unable to bear the thought of dispatching their only child into the void beyond the valley. Of the six that remained, four had been orphans since the first hour of the Serb bombardment forty-eight hours before, and the other two came from large families.

Half a mile outside the town the convoy passed through the inner ring of Zavik's defences, an apparently unmanned checkpoint where the road was hemmed in between a steep cliff and the river. The guards, Reeve had told them, were stationed out of sight above the road. With a flick of a detonator switch they could send half the cliff down on top of any hostile intruder.

They continued on up the winding valley, with all concerned keeping their eyes skinned for signs of an enemy presence. Reeve had sent scouts back up the mountain the day before, and they had found vultures hovering over the three burnt-out transit vans, but no sign that the Serbs below had discovered what had happened to their mountaintop unit.

It was this chronic lack of coordination between the various bands of irregulars which gave Docherty hope for the break-out attempt. As long as they could deal with the enemy piece-meal, they had a fighting chance of making the coast. But if one band managed to get word back to another, and give the other time to prepare a hot reception, then getting through might well prove impossible. There were simply too few of them, particularly since they also had six children to protect.

The convoy reached the checkpoint which marked the outer ring of Zavik's defences. Here the road was constrained between trees and the river, and two of the former had been cut down to block the road. The ropes and pulleys used to lift them aside were operated by men hidden deep in the trees – a technique which Docherty remembered Reeve using in a jungle exercise in Brunei twenty years before.

Sunlight was now slipping down the slopes across the river, and the only definite Serb checkpoint was not much more than a mile away. According to Reeve, it was usually manned by only three or four men, and then only out of habit. Why, after all, would anyone want to break out of Zavik into Serb territory?

The convoy came to a halt a quarter of a mile from the checkpoint, and the occupants of the Renault transferred to the armoured car. The vehicle was quite spacious inside, its Soviet makers having dispensed with luxuries like seats and equipment, but with six men aboard it was still something of a tight squeeze. Docherty was reminded of the stateroom scene from the Marx Brothers' *A Night at the Opera*, and hoped that they would burst out with as much alacrity, and rather more control, when the time came.

The armoured car rumbled down the road with its hatch down, the Dame peering forward through the open slit as he drove. Some way behind, Razor was edging the lorry slowly forward, letting the distance between the two vehicles lengthen.

As the leading one rounded a bend in the valley, the Dame saw the checkpoint up ahead. No attempt had been made to block the way, but two cars were parked between the road and a house set back from it. There were no people in sight.

The Dame picked up speed slightly, causing the armoured car to shudder violently for a second. The sound of its passage would be enough to wake the dead, he thought.

It woke the Serbs. One man half-clambered, half-fell out of one of the car doors, a rifle in his hand. He stood there for a moment, peering at the strange white object rumbling towards him, and then opened his mouth wide, presumably to shout. It was impossible to hear anything above the din of the armoured car.

As if by magic, three other figures emerged from the two cars at the exact same moment. Two were carrying Kalashnikovs, one an SMG. The Dame relayed this information to the men crowded in behind him. It was a pity the armoured car had no gun, the Dame thought, as he slowed the vehicle down.

The four Serbs had fanned out like Western gun-fighters, but the expressions on their faces were more amused than hostile. The Dame could almost hear the thought running through their minds: the fucking UN busybodies had gone and got themselves lost in the mountains.

The armoured car came to a full stop. 'They're ten yards away,' the Dame said, 'at ten o'clock, eleven o'clock, noon and two o'clock. The man at eleven o'clock has the SMG.'

'Ready?' Docherty asked. 'Steady. Go!'

In the same instant both side doors and the hatch swung open. Docherty was up through the latter like a jack-in-the-box, swinging the Browning toward the eleven o'clock position, fine-tuning his aim and firing before the man with the sub-machine-gun had time to raise it. He fell back, hitting the ground with the SMG still gripped in his lifeless hand.

Less than a second later the other three had joined him in death. Reeve and his three men had thrown themselves out through the side doors, and before the surprise had time to die on the faces of the Serbs, the attackers had rolled to a halt in the snow, guns already blazing.

The sound of the river re-emerged as the echoes of gunfire faded down the valley. Reeve and his men went to check out the house but, as expected, found no one there. Razor, meanwhile, was bringing the lorry forward on Docherty's signal.

'You know where you're going, then?' Reeve said. 'When you get to the crossroads go left, follow that road for about twelve miles and you'll reach the main road to the coast. Once you're on that I reckon your chances of getting hassled are less, especially with such a finely drawn UN logo. You could be in Split for lunch.'

244

Docherty offered Reeve his hand, wondering if they'd ever see each other again. 'Good luck, Reeve,' he said.

'Seconded,' Razor said from the lorry cab.

'You too. Now get going.'

Docherty climbed back aboard the armoured car and gave the Dame the nod. With a great whoosh of black smoke the vehicle started off, the lorry behind it. In the latter's side mirror Razor had a last glance of Reeve and his men walking back down the valley to where they had left the Renault. Behind them the bodies of the four Serbs lay sprawled and already forgotten in the snow.

The road continued up the ever-narrowing valley, until slopes seemed to rise up ahead of them as well as to either side. The crossroads finally appeared. The straight-ahead road was no more than a dirt track, the one across the river rendered unusable by the destruction of the bridge which had carried it. Their road climbed up through the trees in a succession of hairpin bends, emerging on to a snowswept plateau.

The armoured car, which had struggled up the steep incline, now found a new lease of life, and Docherty's worries about its staying power receded somewhat. He was riding with his balaclava-clad head out of the hatch, prepared to endure the stinging-cold wind if it meant having advance warning of any trouble on the road up ahead.

For the first few miles he might have been travelling in Antarctica. There were no signs of human habitation; the road itself offered the only proof that humans had ever passed that way. A polar bear sunning itself in a meadow wouldn't have seemed out of place.

They soon left the barren heights, winding their way down into another forested valley. The armoured car enjoyed descending even more than riding on the flat, and for the next few miles they made excellent speed. Docherty was just beginning to take Reeve's idea of lunch in Split seriously when disaster struck.

The two vehicles were nearing the bottom of a long, curving slope when the armoured car suffered a tremendous jolt, strong enough to almost launch Docherty out through the hatch. The PC was still thanking his lucky stars that no permanent damage had been done to the vehicle when the horn sounded behind them. The lorry was limping to a halt by the side of the road.

Docherty walked back to where Razor was examining the underside of the vehicle. The Londoner got back to his feet with a grim look on his face. 'The front axle's fucked,' he said. 'I'm sorry, boss, I didn't see the trench until it was too late.'

'Neither did the Dame,' Docherty said, looking around. The road ran uphill in both directions, and everything else was forested slope. The wind had got up, and it seemed to have grown appreciably colder since their departure from Zavik. He wondered what the fuck were they going to do now.

Chris emerged from the back of the lorry looking sombre. 'One of the kids got a knock on the head where he was already wounded,' he reported. 'Doesn't look good.'

Razor went to take a look, leaving the other three SAS men standing in the road.

'Any suggestions?' Docherty asked.

'Could we all get into the armoured car?' Chris asked.

'Not unless you're into breaking the number of people in an armoured car record. You might be able to get all the patients in, but not in the sort of comfort they'd need to survive a sixty-mile journey. And we'd be sitting ducks on top.'

'We could take the armoured car and go looking for another lorry,' the Dame suggested.

'How far are we from the main road?' Chris asked.

'About nine miles last time I looked,' Docherty said, taking the map out of his pocket and unfolding it. 'Yeah, I reckon we're about here,' he said, pointing with a finger. 'Between seven and nine miles.'

'Boss, I think someone's going to have to walk,' Chris said. 'The temperature's going down like a stone. I was already getting worried about how cold it was in the back of that lorry, and with this wind . . . I think the kids should be moved into the armoured car, where there's a heater.'

Docherty blew into the hands he was holding over his nose. 'OK,' he said eventually. 'I can't think of a better plan. Can either of you?' he asked Razor and Hajrija, who had just appeared beside them.

They couldn't, and for the next fifteen minutes Hajrija and the four SAS men ferried the wounded from one vehicle to the other, with Chris dividing up the small space between them, and keeping up a constant conversation with each child as he did so. The old man, once he realized how small the space was, adamantly refused to take up any of it. It took an almost superhuman effort on Hajrija's part to make him sit in the cab of the lorry, whose heater was fighting a losing battle with the broken windows.

'Say, three hours to get there, and, at best, twenty minutes to get back,' Docherty told those who were staying.

He and the Dame set off up the road, one ten yards behind the other, their MP5s cradled in their arms.

Once they were gone Razor and Hajrija took up stations about a hundred yards either side of the stranded vehicles. They had no idea what the chances of traffic were, but there had to be some, and anything which passed would inevitably see both lorry and armoured car. It might have been possible to get the latter off the road, but only at the expense of either lengthening the ferrying of the children or jolting them around inside.

Chris was left to look after them, which presented some difficulty. There was no room for him to get in with them, and he didn't think it would be wise to shut them up in the dark, no matter how warm they might then be. He compromised by keeping the hatch open, and talking to them through it.

It was mostly a one-sided conversation. Nearly all the children were in considerable pain, and their powers of concentration greatly diminished. What amazed Chris was their fortitude – though none was older than ten he heard no whining and saw very few tears. While telling a funny story he even had the feeling that some of the children were forcing themselves to smile out of sheer generosity.

As he looked down at their upturned faces, eyes bright in the gloom of the armoured car's belly, he had the feeling that here was a sight every soldier should see.

And it tore at his heart.

As the morning passed Docherty and the Dame ate up the miles. The road ran roughly south down the widening valley, keeping close to the river, and such houses as they saw in the distance were perched on the lower slopes. Several times the PC thought he saw far-off moving figures, but none appeared before them on the road, and no vehicles passed in either direction.

After an hour and a half's walking they found themselves looking down on a village which straddled the road, and which Docherty thought it prudent to bypass. The resulting trudge across forested slopes added an extra hour, and it was almost eleven o'clock before they came in sight of their destination. From a convenient hilltop they surveyed the cluster of buildings which marked the spot where their road met the main highway to Split.

One had been a garage, and one of the others probably a roadside restaurant. Maybe it still was, because two lorries were standing outside it. Through the binoculars Docherty could see that there was no one in either cab. Nor could he see any light or sign of life through the building's windows. That was the good news. The bad news was that any approach would involve a ten-minute walk across open country. The two men lay there in the snow, considering the situation. Another lorry came into view on the main road, a large articulated vehicle, and drove through the junction in the direction of the coast. A man appeared in the doorway of the supposed restaurant, looked out, and then disappeared back inside.

'We could wait for dark, boss,' the Dame said doubtfully, 'but the lorries might be gone by then.'

'And we can't leave the others stuck on an open road for the whole day,' Docherty said. 'I'm afraid we don't have many options where this one's concerned.'

The Dame smiled to himself, 'Then let's go, boss.'

'Aye, but by the road, I think. Let's just be two lonely soldiers trudging homewards in the snow.'

'Pity we don't know any of those Serb songs your mate Reeve was talking about.'

'I want us to look natural, not wake up the town.'

They worked their way back to the road and started off down the slight slope towards the junction. There were fields on either side, with a few bare trees by the banks of a meandering stream. A large, black bird suddenly detached itself from a branch, and whirled up into the sky, cawing loudly.

249

The sound of an approaching vehicle grew louder, and then came into view to the right. It was another large lorry, and like its predecessor, sped on through the junction. If there was no checkpoint here, Docherty thought, then there was no reason for there to be any soldiers.

They crossed the stream by a stone bridge and left the road, working their way along behind the buildings that faced the main highway. These were fairly new affairs, long and windowless. Agricultural storage sheds of some sort, Docherty guessed. He halted at the end of the second, dropped to his haunches, and inched an eye round the corner. As he expected, the restaurant was visible across the highway. No name or sign was visible, but a Coca-Cola sign hung drunkenly from a single fixing beside twin entrance doors. The two lorries were parked side by side and roughly parallel to the highway, their rear ends no more than five yards from the doorway.

He gave the Dame the hand signal for follow, and slipped across the gap. The next building looked like someone's house, but as was the case with so many of the Bosnian houses they had seen, no one seemed to be at home. They trudged their way through the untouched accumulation of winter snow, pushed aside an already rickety fence, and reached the next gap. Again Docherty edged his eye round the corner. This time part of a disused garage was in view – two old-fashioned petrol pumps wearing what looked like hats of snow.

They moved cautiously down the gap between the two houses, to where they could get a view up and down the highway. As Docherty had hoped, the doors and windows in the front of the restaurant were hidden from view by the two lorries.

The two SAS men jogged across the highway, Docherty keeping an open eye to the left, the Dame doing the same to the right. No one was in sight. Another ghost town, Docherty thought. Or at least he hoped it was.

They reached the space between the cabs of the two lorries. While the Dame kept guard Docherty hoisted himself up to see if there was a key in the ignition of the first lorry. There wasn't, but there was in the second. He took off his gloves and felt the bonnet. It seemed faintly warm.

'Check it out,' he whispered to the Dame, and moved down between the two vehicles towards their rears. He sank to his haunches so that he could see the bottom half of the restaurant's front door.

Behind him, the Dame climbed up into the cab and released the bonnet lock. It sprang loose with a sharp clunk. He sat there for a few seconds, ears straining for a sign that someone had heard, and then climbed back down. He leaned the MP5 up against a wheel and pushed up the bonnet. The engine was hot to the touch. He pushed the bonnet gently back down, just as the men emerged from the side door of the restaurant.

It all happened very quickly.

As one man shouted something in an indignant voice, the Dame considered and rejected the option of diving for the MP5. Maybe one of the Serbs was telepathic, because at that moment he saw the SMG, and pulled his AK47 into the firing position, screaming something as he did so. By this time the Dame's Browning was clearing the holster on his right thigh.

The two guns fired simultaneously, the Dame's 'double tap' piercing the man's upper trunk as his automatic burst stitched fire across the Dame's chest.

The Wearsider was already going down as the other Serbs opened up.

About five seconds had elapsed since the first shout, and Docherty had only moved a few yards down the corridor between the lorries. He saw the Dame fall, and sank to the ground himself. Six legs were visible beneath the lorry, and he opened up on them with the MP5.

Cries of pain told him he had hit at least some of them, but he was already rolling forward, under the lorry closest to the restaurant and out into the gap between the two. The Serbs leapt into view, two of them already down, one still on his feet. As the six eyes flashed towards him he opened up again with the silenced MP5, knocking the third man back across the other two.

He rolled again, into a small snowdrift at the foot of the restaurant wall, but no bullets came his way. As he got to his feet, he heard sounds through the wall behind him. He swung the MP5 round towards the front door just as it swung open, and a child stepped out. Somehow he didn't squeeze the trigger.

A voice shouted a question in a foreign language. A woman's voice.

Docherty strode across to the door, the small boy retreating before him, and edged his eye around the frame. A blonde woman was standing by a pile of chairs and table, frozen to the spot. She suddenly started screaming at him, though whether in anger or fear Docherty couldn't tell. He marched past her, and found the side door they had neglected to notice. Outside the dead Serbs lay twisted together. Like the stupid tattoo they were all wearing, Docherty thought. Solidarity hadn't saved these Serbs.

He glanced up and down the highway and saw nothing. The Dame was still breathing, but with difficulty and not, Docherty guessed, for long. Even if the heart had been spared the lungs seemed to have been shredded.

He lifted the Wearsider's body up into the cab, and propped him up in the driving seat with the aid of the safety belt. Then he took the MP5 and burst the other lorry's rear tyres.

As Docherty clambered back up into the cab the Dame's eyes seemed to flicker open briefly, and what could even have been a smile twitched at his lips. Then the eyes closed again. Docherty felt the carotid artery. The Dame was dead.

As he let in the clutch the door of the restaurant burst back open, and the child stumbled out. He had come to wave goodbye.

His mouth set in a grim line, Docherty hurled the lorry as fast as he could down the treacherous road. He knew there was nothing to be gained from blaming himself for the Dame's death, but he couldn't help doing so. How could he have missed the side door? How could either of them?

Just concentrate on the job, he told himself. He could wallow in guilt later.

There was no choice but to drive through the village they had avoided on the way down. He roared through faster than the road warranted, but no one stepped out with an upraised hand, and no bullets pursued him. The village was alive, though, and he saw several people watch the lorry go by, their bodies still and their expressions vacant, as if they feared doing something which would cause him to stop.

Less than twenty minutes had passed when he found himself driving down through the forest towards the armoured car and lorry. He flashed the headlights twice as he approached, and Razor materialized from behind a tree, a smile on his face.

'Hiya, boss,' he said, and then he saw the Dame. 'Oh shit,' he murmured, closing his eyes for a moment.

'Aye,' Docherty agreed. 'Come on, let's get out of this fucking country.'

With Razor on the running board, the lorry rolled on down the last hundred yards.

Chris leapt down from the armoured car and came across to meet it. 'The clock beat the Dame,' Razor said quietly, stepping to the ground.

Chris stopped in his tracks, opened his mouth to say something, and then saw his friend propped up in the seat. He walked round to the other side and looked at him. Docherty had closed the Dame's eyes and the Wearsider seemed strangely at peace, as if he'd finally come to terms with something.

'We'll mourn him later,' Docherty's voice said in his ear.

Chris nodded. 'Goodbye, mate,' he said to the dead man, and turned away.

'Razor, go and get Hajrija,' Docherty ordered. 'How are the children?' he asked Chris.

'As well as can be expected. Better, in fact.'

'Well, let's start shifting them.' As he walked round to the back of the lorry it occurred to him that he had no idea what was inside it. He swung one of the doors open to reveal wall-to-wall pinball machines.

'Christ almighty,' Docherty muttered. Of all the things he'd seen since landing in Split this took the biscuit. In the middle of a medieval war someone had been scouring the country – and presumably restaurants like the one he'd just returned from – and either buying up or stealing pinball machines.

A sudden rage filled him, and he leapt up into the lorry and began tearing the restraining ropes from the mute machines. The first one crashed down into the road, and the second followed. Soon there was a pile rising up beneath the tailgate, and he had to move the lorry forward to free it from their grasp.

He sat in the cab for a few seconds, letting the rage subside.

'You OK, boss?' Razor asked him through the open window.

'Aye,' Docherty said. He wanted to see Isabel, he thought. He wanted to see her that very moment.

It wasn't possible, so he got down from the cab and helped ferry the children from the armoured car to their new temporary home.

'What about the Dame?' Chris asked when they were finished.

'Wrap him in his sleeping bag, and put him in with the kids,' Docherty decided. He was wondering whether it was worth taking the armoured car any further. It really needed a crew of two – a navigator and a driver – and he wanted both Chris and Razor in the same vehicle as the children. Hajrija, when asked, said she was willing to try driving, but no, she had never actually driven anything, even a car . . .

There was also the chance of the ludicrous UN camouflage doing more harm than good. Anyone with half a brain wouldn't be fooled for more than a few seconds, and anyone in a real UN vehicle might decide the deception had hostile intent. Besides, driving along in the damn thing felt a bit like robbing orphans in a Mother Teresa mask.

He decided to abandon it, along with the mound of pinball machines. The old man too was left behind, in the cab of the broken lorry where he had fallen asleep and died.

With Razor at the wheel, Hajrija and Docherty beside him in the front seat, and Chris in the back, they set out once more. It was now the middle of the afternoon, and the wind had dropped again, leaving a slowly moving cloud mass to block out the sun.

They reached the junction within an hour of Docherty's last visit. Everyone had their guns at the ready as Razor turned on to the highway, but nothing moved in the cluster of buildings. The four dead men still lay in their tangled pile, and Docherty could see no sign of the woman or child.

The road soon started climbing up across a vast plateau, a thin strip between a sea of snow and the leaden sky. Two other lorries appeared, growing from dots in the distance to juggernauts thundering by, their drivers staring straight ahead, not risking eye contact.

After not much more than an hour the road was winding down towards Livno, and there they met their first checkpoint, manned by Croatian regular army forces. The officer in charge inspected their UN accreditations, no doubt took note of the pale-blue berets, and declined to make an issue of the fact that Hajrija was obviously only along for the ride. When he saw the children in the back, his face even softened, and they were waved on through.

'So far so good,' Razor said. 'And we're in Croat territory from now on, right?'

'Looks like it,' Docherty agreed. If it hadn't been for that one mistake, they would all have survived.

There was now only one more mountain range to cross, and the road ran steadily uphill, a huge lake below and to their left. The character of the country was changing too – even under the snow this land seemed more barren, with only a few twisted trees and sharp outcrops of dark rock jutting up out of the white overlay.

'This is Hercegovina,' Hajrija told them. 'There is nothing here,' she added. 'Even the water is in rocks, you understand?'

It was limestone country, Docherty realized. Where the rivers ran underground and people went potholing, for reasons that only they knew.

In the far distance he could see a large bird hovering in the air, and wondered idly what it was. Chris would know, he thought, and for a passing moment even wondered whether to stop the lorry and let the twitcher out of the back to identify it for him.

You're getting senile, he told himself. And that was yet another reason for this being the last mission of his soldiering career.

'Boss,' Razor said, interrupting the PC's reverie.

Docherty focused his attention on the two cars blocking their passage a couple of hundred yards ahead. The road was clinging to the side of a bare valley, and all around them precipitous slopes either rose to the sky or dropped to the depths. A wooden cabin had been erected in a rare piece of flat land adjoining the road, maybe as a hunting cabin, maybe a roadside café. From its roof fluttered the red-and-white checked flag of the Croats. Standing outside its doors was a transit van which had been plastered with metal sheets, apparently by a gang of deranged welders.

What the fuck was anyone doing up here? Docherty asked himself. Nothing good, was the likely answer.

He turned and rapped three times on the partition, giving Chris the signal for possible danger.

Razor sized up the two cars blocking the road as he slowed the lorry. They looked ripe for pushing aside, but to do so at speed might well kill one or more of the children.

'Stop twenty yards short,' Docherty told him, as the first figure emerged from the cabin. Like the men they'd seen in the Split restaurant he was dressed all in black, from the polished boots to the peaked leather cap. He was carrying an Uzi, as were the three identically dressed men who followed him out through the door.

Four again, Docherty thought. In this country the bastards did everything in fours. He loosened his anorak, checked the butt of the Browning in the cross-draw holster, and stepped down to the road.

'United Nations,' the leading Croat said, mouthing the two words as if he had just learnt them. He had short, dark

hair and a handsome, clean-shaven face. Only the yellow
teeth would have hindered a career in Nazi propaganda films.

Docherty passed over the UN and Croat accreditations
and examined the three men behind the leader. Between them
they had enough intelligence for a cabbage, he decided. One
was still listening to the Walkman clipped to his belt.

'I speak English,' the leader said, looking at Docherty.

'Good,' the PC replied. What do you want, he thought
– a diploma?

'What is in truck?' he asked.

'Sick children.'

'I see,' the leader said, and strode off up the road, only
missing half a step when he saw Hajrija in the cab. Razor
smiled down at him.

At the rear of the lorry Docherty called out a warning to
Chris, and slid the back door up. The Croat surveyed the
improvised ambulance.

'Where are children from?' he asked.

'Many places,' Docherty said. He signalled with his eyes
for Chris to join them in the road.

The Croat walked back down the other side of the lorry
and stared in at Hajrija. The other three men in black had
moved closer, but the Uzis were still loose in their hands.
'The woman is not United Nations,' he said.

'She is . . .'

'The children are Muslims,' the Croat said. 'But you can
go. Only leave the woman.' He smiled up at Razor, who smiled
back at him.

There were a few pregnant seconds of silence.

'I said, leave the woman behind, motherfucker!'

Razor took Docherty's signal, pulled the Browning up from
under the window and shot the man through the forehead.

258

Docherty and Chris were both drawing their Brownings at the same moment, the lessons of the Regiment's 'Killing House' training ground flashing through their minds, as they took out the three fumbling targets in front of them. Only one Uzi was fired, a short burst at the sky, as its holder fell backwards.

The man with the Walkman had got entangled in his earphone wires, and yanked the cassette player off his belt with the Uzi. The last sound to echo in the silence was of a spilt cassette tape landing in the middle of the road.

Docherty looked around. In the cab Razor had his arm around Hajrija. Chris had disappeared, probably to reassure the children. Another four men lay dead in front of him.

He walked across and began pulling the corpses out of the road. The tape caught his eye, and he picked it up. The writing was in English. The album was called *Cowboys from Hell*, by a group he'd never heard of called Pantera. One song was called 'Psycho Holiday', another 'Message in Blood'.

He looked at the four black-clad Croats, who had taken so much more trouble with their clothes than they had with their hearts or minds. If he looked inside the cabin, he'd probably find some sort of dope, some German beer or American Pepsi, a few hard-core porn magazines. All these men had needed for their perfect life was a woman toy, and they had just died trying to steal one.

Docherty looked up at the twisted rocks, the alien landscape. He had wanted to believe that this was a foreign war, a throwback, but somewhere deep inside himself he had always known otherwise. This was a war that came from the heart of what the world had become.

He climbed wearily back aboard the lorry, and nodded for Razor to resume their journey down to the sea.

Epilogue

They arrived in Split early in the evening, with the sun hanging low over the sea like a tourist postcard. The children were passed over to the care of the town's hospital, and hopes were high that all would recover. Where they would end up seemed to be anybody's guess. Once fit, Docherty guessed, they would just become one more group begging a home from a reluctant rest of Europe.

The SAS men were made to wait almost thirty-six hours, without explanation, for a flight home to the UK. After enduring an irritatingly lengthy stopover in Germany, they arrived at RAF Brize Norton shortly after nine in the morning. Rain was falling from a dull sky as they walked across the tarmac.

Barney Davies was there to meet them, along with an MoD man in civilian dress named Lavington. Before the tired returnees knew what was happening they found themselves being corralled into a small office. A tray had been set out with cups and a percolator full of coffee.

Docherty dropped his bergen on the floor. 'I'm going to ring my wife,' he said, and started back for the door.

'Can you do that afterwards, please?' the MoD man asked coldly.

Docherty stopped, turned and stared at him.

'She has already been informed that you're all right,' Lavington said.

'I want to hear her voice,' Docherty said quietly, and walked out of the office.

Lavington watched him go, a thoughtful look on his face, then turned his attention to Hajrija. Having apparently satisfied himself that she wasn't a member of the SAS, he asked the others who she was and what she was doing there.

'She wanted to see if England really was full of pricks like you,' Razor told him, at which point Barney Davies suggested they all have some coffee.

Out in the building's foyer Docherty was listening to the phone ring in Liam McCall's Glasgow house. 'Hello?' a voice answered in the familiar husky accent.

'Isabel,' he said.

'Jamie,' she said back, remembering how she'd felt when Barney Davies rang her two evenings before. Then she'd just uttered the two words '*dios gracias*' and almost collapsed with relief. 'Where are you?' she said now, her voice so happy it made him want to sing.

'Brize Norton. I'll be home tonight. Somehow or other.'

'I can't wait,' she said.

A few minutes later he was walking back to the office, wondering if it was worth even being polite. Probably, he thought. The others had careers to think about.

He found everyone drinking coffee in strained silence. After pouring himself a cup he sat down opposite Lavington. 'Let's get on with it, then,' he said.

'Very well,' the MoD man said stiffly. 'This is only a preliminary debriefing, of course. First, where is John Reeve? Your orders were clear – to bring him home.'

'He didn't want to come,' Docherty said. 'And there was no way we could have brought him against his will, even if I had thought that doing so was in anyone's best interests. Which I did not.'

Lavington pointed out that they were paid to obey the Crown, not formulate policy on their own. Docherty told him that in the SAS they tended to believe that the man on the spot was usually the man best placed to take decisions. 'John Reeve is looking after his children,' he added, 'as any father would.'

'If you could get out with a lorryload of children,' Lavington insisted, 'then so could he.'

'He also has a wife and her parents to worry about . . .'

'And a private army to lead.'

'He has no such thing,' Docherty lied. 'He may have given them some advice in the early days, but that's all. And I might add that we didn't all get out with the children. One of my men is still on the plane, in a coffin.'

Lavington looked at him. He could see they were all tired, he said. The debriefing would have to be postponed. After telling Barney Davies that he would call the next day the MoD man made his exit.

'Is that who sent us?' Razor asked disgustedly.

'No, I sent you,' Davies said. 'His masters sent the message you received in Zavik. I'm sorry about that, but the MoD and the politicians were adamant, and there was nothing I could do.' He gave them a wintry smile. 'I assumed you would ignore the part about Reeve, unless he really did need putting in a strait-jacket.'

'He's one of the sanest men in Bosnia,' Docherty said, 'though that's not saying very much.'

'And is he running an efficient private army?' Davies asked.

Docherty grinned at him. 'What do you think?'

Three days later Docherty was back in Hereford for Corporal Damien Robson's memorial service. Many of the men who had served with him were in attendance, including Chris and Razor. Joss Wynwood, who had led the patrol out of Colombia four years earlier, flew back from Hong Kong to be there.

An appreciable number of family members had also driven down from Sunderland, and after the service they were given a guided tour of the Stirling Lines barracks by Docherty and Barney Davies. Most walked around with a sort of wide-eyed wonder, as if they couldn't believe that their relation really had lived and worked there for the past seven years. From the conversations he had with several of them, Docherty got the impression that the Dame, though undoubtedly much loved, had been even more of a mystery to his family than he had been to his comrades in the SAS.

The day after the service Chris Martinson drove down through Hay-on-Wye and up into the Black Mountains. He had binoculars and book with him, but on this day his heart wasn't in it. Even the sudden appearance of a merlin only produced a brief burst of enthusiasm.

Over the last week he had been turning several important things over in his mind, trying to arrange them in some sort of pattern which made sense of his life, both now and in the future. The Dame's death had not shocked him – how could a soldier's death ever be surprising? – but some of the things they had seen in Bosnia continued to haunt him. The Sarajevo hospital for one, and the faces of the children they had brought out of Zavik and left to an uncertain future in Split.

He was over thirty now, and more than half convinced that it was time to consider a change of career. He already possessed sufficient medical skills to be useful in much of the Third World, and he had written off for more information about how to turn these skills into whatever qualifications he might need.

Chris didn't know how or why, but the time in Bosnia had tipped some balance in his mind. When it came down to it, he felt more comfortable helping children than he did killing evil men. He was not running away from the world as it was. He didn't just want out. If anything, he wanted in.

He looked up at the grey clouds scudding across the Welsh sky and wondered about the bird life in India. Or Africa. Or anywhere he could feel needed.

Razor was also aware that his life had reached a crossroads, and a happy one at that. He could still hardly believe that Hajrija had come to England with him, or how much they had enjoyed each other in the days that had followed.

He guessed he had the long wait at Split to thank. If she hadn't read all those English papers, and got so incensed at their reporting of the war in her native country, then she might not have come. 'Why don't you go back to journalism, then?' Docherty had suggested. 'Come back to England with us and start pestering them with the truth.'

Maybe she had just been waiting for the excuse, but she had come in any case, and they had enjoyed what felt like a four-day honeymoon in a Hereford hotel, emerging to eat and drink and ride round the wintry countryside, going back in to make love and talk and make love again.

Razor couldn't remember ever feeling happier, and the only shadow on this happiness was a slight but persistent sense of guilt. How could something so good, he asked himself, have come out of something so bad?

A week or so later David Owen and Cyrus Vance came up with their peace plan for Bosnia, which involved breaking the country into ten semi-autonomous and ethnically based cantons. The central government, although remaining in existence, would have little in the way of real power.

John and Nena Reeve heard the news as they sat round the kitchen table listening to the World Service. 'Maybe it means peace,' Reeve said.

Nena disagreed, but she didn't say so. Reeve had always had a child's naïvety when it came to politics.

They were both living in her parents' house, but despite parental disapproval were not sharing his bed. She had eventually told him the full story of what had happened to her, almost as much to hear herself tell it as for him to hear.

He had not disbelieved her, or accused her of not resisting; he had not behaved the way most of the Muslim women expected their men to behave. For that she supposed she was grateful, but she had expected nothing less, and rather hoped for more.

When it came down to it he didn't know how to react. He wanted to help, but he didn't know how to give himself, and that was all she wanted. He was still a child in more than politics, she reluctantly admitted to herself.

She looked across the table at him, and he grinned at her. This is the child who saved a town, she thought.

The trouble with being a soldier, Docherty thought to himself, was that you tended to see your comrades at their best and other people at their worst. Which, all in all, engendered a somewhat warped view of humanity.

He stared out at the islands and highlands silhouetted by the rising sun, and wondered whether humankind could claim any credit for its collective sense of what was beautiful.

The family was on its way back from a long weekend in Harris, where they had stayed with Docherty's friend, the retired priest Liam McCall. They had been lucky to hit one of those rare calms in the Hebrides' winter storm: the children had been able to run wild on the beach without being blown away to the mainland, and at night, while they slept the sort of sleep only fresh air exercise could induce, the three adults had been able to talk and work their way through a couple of bottles of malt whisky.

Docherty had so far been reluctant, without really knowing why, to tell his wife much of what had happened in Bosnia, but in Liam McCall's cottage, with the two people he cared for most in the world ready to listen, he found himself going through the whole story.

'The centre cannot hold . . . mere anarchy is loosed upon the world,' Liam had murmured, quoting his beloved Yeats.

'Aye,' Docherty had agreed. 'In Bosnia there was no sign of any centre that I could see.' He had stared into the whisky glass and said, surprising himself: 'And I think I've lost my own, at least for a while.'

'I lost mine a long time ago,' Isabel had said softly. 'But you can live without one. You can even love without one.'

For a second he had felt almost terrified, catching a dreadful glimpse of a world in which there was nothing to hang on to. And then his eyes had met Isabel's in a sharing that seemed infinitely sad.

Here now, on the deck of the ferry, with the sunlight dancing across the waves, the love of his life by his side, and their children running riot somewhere else on the ship, that world seemed far away.

But then the light was always brighter, coming out of the dark.